Henry James

Tales of Three Cities

Henry James

Tales of Three Cities

ISBN/EAN: 9783337023997

Printed in Europe, USA, Canada, Australia, Japan

Cover: Foto ©Andreas Hilbeck / pixelio.de

More available books at **www.hansebooks.com**

HENRY JAMES

TALES OF THREE CITIES

BOSTON

JAMES R. OSGOOD AND COMPANY

1884

𝔘𝔫𝔦𝔟𝔢𝔯𝔰𝔦𝔱𝔶 𝔓𝔯𝔢𝔰𝔰:
JOHN WILSON AND SON, CAMBRIDGE.

THE IMPRESSIONS OF A COUSIN.

IMPRESSIONS OF A COUSIN.

PART I.

NEW YORK, *April* 3, 1873. There are moments
when I feel that she has asked too much of me —
especially since our arrival in this country. These
three months have not done much toward making
me happy here. I don't know what the difference is
— or rather I do; and I say this only because it's less
trouble. It is no trouble, however, to say that I like
New York less than Rome: that, after all, *is* the difference. And then there's nothing to sketch! For ten
years I have been sketching, and I really believe I do
it very well. But how can I sketch Fifty-third Street?
There are times when I even say to myself, How can
I even endure Fifty-third Street? When I turn into
it from the Fifth Avenue the vista seems too hideous:
the narrow, impersonal houses, with the dry, hard tone
of their brown-stone, a surface as uninteresting as that
of sand-paper; their steep, stiff stoops, giving you
such a climb to the door; their lumpish balustrades,
porticoes, and cornices, turned out by the hundred and

adorned with heavy excrescences — such an eruption
of ornament and such a poverty of effect !   I suppose
my superior tone would seem very pretentious if any-
body were to read this shameless record of personal
emotion ; and I should be asked why an expensive up-
town residence is not as good as a slimy Italian palazzo.   My answer, of course, is that I can sketch the
palazzo and can do nothing with the up-town residence.   I can live in it, of course, and be very grateful for the shelter; but that does n't count.   Putting
aside that odious fashion of popping into the " parlors " as soon as you cross the threshold — no interval, no approach — these places are wonderfully
comfortable.   This one of Eunice's is perfectly arranged ; and we have so much space that she has
given me a sitting-room of my own — an immense
luxury.   Her kindness, her affection, are the most
charming, delicate, natural thing I ever conceived.
I don't know what can have put it into her head to
like me so much ; I suppose I should say into her
heart, only I don't like to write about Eunice's heart
— that tender, shrinking, shade-loving, and above all
fresh and youthful, organ.   There is a certain self-
complacency, perhaps, in my assuming that her generosity is mere affection ; for her conscience is so
inordinately developed that she attaches the idea of
duty to everything — even to her relations to a poor,
plain, unloved and unlovable third-cousin.   Whether
she is fond of me or not, she thinks it right to be
fond of me ; and the effort of her life is to do what

is right. In matters of duty, in short, she is a real little artist; and her masterpiece (in that way) is coming back here to live. She can't like it; her tastes are not here. If she did like it, I am sure she would never have invented such a phrase as the one of which she delivered herself the other day, — "I think one's life has more dignity in one's own country." That's a phrase made up after the fact. No one ever gave up living in Europe because there is a want of dignity in it. Poor Eunice talks of "one's own country" as if she kept the United States in the back-parlor. I have yet to perceive the dignity of living in Fifty-third Street. This, I suppose, is very treasonable; but a woman isn't obliged to be patriotic. I believe I should be a good patriot if I could sketch my native town. But I can't make a picture of the brown-stone stoops in the Fifth Avenue, or the platform of the elevated railway in the Sixth. Eunice has suggested to me that I might find some subjects in the Park, and I have been there to look for them. But somehow the blistered *sentiers* of asphalt, the rock-work caverns, the huge iron bridges spanning little muddy lakes, the whole crowded, cockneyfied place, making up so many faces to look pretty, don't appeal to me — have n't, from beginning to end, a discoverable "bit." Besides, it's too cold to sit on a campstool under this clean-swept sky, whose depths of blue air do very well, doubtless, for the floor of heaven, but are quite too far away for the ceiling of earth. The sky over here seems part of the world at large; in Europe it's part of the particular place. In summer, I dare say, it will be better; and it will go hard with me if I don't find somewhere some leafy lane, some cottage-roof, something in some degree mossy or mellow. Nature here, of course, is very fine, though I am afraid only in large pieces; and with my little yard-measure (it used to serve for the Roman Campagna!) I don't know what I shall be able to do. I must try to rise to the occasion.

The Hudson is beautiful; I remember that well enough; and Eunice tells me that when we are in *villeggiatura* we shall be close to the loveliest part of it. Her cottage or villa, or whatever they call it (Mrs. Ermine, by the way, always speaks of it as a "country-seat,") is more or less opposite to West Point, where it makes one of its grandest sweeps. Unfortunately, it has been let these three years that she has been abroad, and will not be vacant till the first of June. Mr. Caliph, her trustee, took upon himself to do that; very impertinently, I think, for certainly if I had Eunice's fortune I should n't let my houses — I mean, of course, those that are so personal. Least of all should I let my "country-seat." It's bad enough for people to appropriate one's sofas and tables, without appropriating one's flowers and trees and even one's views. There is nothing so personal as one's horizon, — the horizon that one commands, whatever it is, from one's window. Nobody else has just that one. Mr. Caliph, by the way, is apparently a person of the incalculable, irresponsible sort. It would have been natural to suppose that having the greater part of my cousin's property in his care, he would be in New York to receive her at the end of a long absence and a boisterous voyage. Common civility would have suggested that, especially as he was an old friend, or rather a young friend, of both her parents. It was an odd thing to make him sole trustee; but that was Cousin Letitia's doing: "she thought it would be so much easier for Eunice to see only one person." I believe she had found that effort the limit of her own energy; but she might have known that Eunice would have given her best attention, every day, to twenty men of business, if such a duty had been presented to her. I don't think poor Cousin Letitia knew very much; Eunice speaks of her much less than she speaks of her father, whose death would have been the greater sorrow if she dared to admit to herself that she preferred one of her parents to the other. The number of things that the poor girl doesn't dare to admit to herself! One of them, I am sure, is that Mr. Caliph is acting improperly in spending three months in Washington, just at the moment when it would be most convenient to her to see him. He has pressing business there, it seems (he is a good deal of a politician — not that I know what people do in Washington), and he writes to Eunice every week or two that he will "finish it up" in ten days more, and then will be completely at her service; but he never finishes it up, — never arrives. She has not seen him for three years; he certainly, I think, ought to have come out to her in Europe. She does n't know that, and I have n't cared to suggest it, for she wishes (very naturally) to think that he is a pearl of trustees. Fortunately he sends her all the money she needs; and the other day he sent her his brother, a rather agitated (though not in the least agitating) youth, who presented himself about lunch-time, — Mr. Caliph having (as he explained) told him that this was the best hour to call. What does Mr. Caliph know about it, by the way? It 's little enough he has tried! Mr. Adrian Frank had of course nothing to say about business; he only came to be agreeable, and to tell us that he had just seen his brother in Washington — as if that were any comfort! They are brothers only in the sense that they are children of the same mother; Mrs. Caliph having accepted consolations in her widowhood, and produced this blushing boy, who is ten years younger than the accomplished Caliph. (I say accomplished Caliph for the phrase. I have n't the least idea of his accomplishments. Somehow, a man with that name ought to have a good many.) Mr. Frank, the second husband, is dead as well as herself, and the young man has a very good fortune. He is shy and simple, colors immensely and becomes alarmed at his own silences; but is tall and straight and clear-eyed, and is, I imagine, a very estimable youth. Eunice says that he is as different as possible from his step-brother ; so that perhaps, though she does n't mean it in that way, his step-brother is not estimable.   I shall judge of that for myself, if he ever gives me a chance.

Young Frank, at any rate, is a gentleman, and in spite of his blushes has seen a great deal of the world. Perhaps that is what he is blushing for: there are so many things we have no reason to be proud of.   He stayed to lunch, and talked a little about the far East, — Babylon, Palmyra, Ispahan, and that sort of thing — from which he is lately returned.   He also is a sketcher, though evidently he does n't show.   He asked to see my things, however ; and I produced a few old water-colors, of other days and other climes, which I have luckily brought to America — produced them with my usual calm assurance.   It was clear he thought me very clever ; so I suspect that in not showing he himself is rather wise.   When I said there was nothing here to sketch, that rectangular towns won't do, etc., he asked me why I did n't try people.   What people ? the people in the Fifth Avenue ?   They are even less pictorial than their houses. I don't perceive that those in the Sixth are any better, or those in the Fourth and Third, or in the Seventh and Eighth.   Good heavens ! what a nomenclature !   The city of New York is like a tall sum in addition, and the streets are like columns of figures.   What a place for me to live, who hate arithmetic !   I have tried Mrs. Ermine, but that is only because she asked me to : Mrs. Ermine asks for whatever she wants. I don't think she cares for it much, for though it's bad, it's not bad enough to please her. I thought she would be rather easy to do, as her countenance is made up largely of negatives — no color, no form, no intelligence; I should simply have to leave a sort of brilliant blank. I found, however, there was difficulty in representing an expression which consisted so completely of the absence of that article. With her large, fair, featureless face, unillumined by a ray of meaning, she makes the most incoherent, the most unexpected, remarks. She asked Eunice, the other day, whether she should not bring a few gentlemen to see her — she seemed to know so few, to be so lonely. Then when Eunice thanked her, and said she need n't take that trouble: she was not lonely, and in any case did not desire her solitude to be peopled in that manner, — Mrs. Ermine declared blandly that it was all right, but that she supposed this was the great advantage of being an orphan, that you might have gentlemen brought to see you. "I don't like being an orphan, even for that," said Eunice; who indeed does not like it at all, though she will be twenty-one next month, and has had several years to get used to it. Mrs. Ermine is very vulgar, yet she thinks she has high distinction. I am very glad our cousinship is not on the same side. Except that she is an idiot and a bore, however, I think there is no harm in her. Her time is spent in contemplating the surface of things, — and for that I don't blame her, for I myself am very fond of the surface. But she does n't see what she looks at, and in short is very tiresome. That is one of the things poor Eunice won't admit to herself, — that Lizzie Ermine will end by boring us to death. Now that both her daughters are married, she has her time quite on her hands; for the sons-in-law, I am sure, can't encourage her visits. She may, however, contrive to be with them as well as here, for, as a poor young husband once said to me, a *belle-mère*, after marriage, is as inevitable as stickiness after eating honey. A fool can do plenty of harm without deep intentions. After all, intentions fail; and what you know an accident by is that it does n't. Mrs. Ermine does n't like me; she thinks she ought to be in my shoes — that when Eunice lost her old governess, who had remained with her as " companion," she ought, instead of picking me up in Rome, to have come home and thrown herself upon some form of kinship more cushiony. She is jealous of me, and vexed that I don't give her more opportunities; for I know she has made up her mind that I ought to be a Bohemian : in that case she could persuade Eunice that I am a very unfit sort of person. I am single, not young, not pretty, not well off, and not very desirous to please; I carry a palette on my thumb, and very often have stains on my apron — though except for those stains I pretend to be immaculately neat. What right have I *not* to be a Bohemian, and not to teach Eunice to make cigarettes? I am convinced Mrs. Ermine is disappointed that I don't smoke. Perhaps, after all, she is right,

and that I am too much a creature of habits, of rules.
A few people have been good enough to call me an
artist; but I am not. I am only, in a small way, a
worker. I walk too straight; it's ten years since any
one asked me to dance ! I wish I could oblige you,
Mrs. Ermine, by dipping into Bohemia once in a
while. But one can't have the defects of the qualities
one does n't possess. I am not an artist, I am too
much of a critic. I suppose a she-critic is a kind of
monster; women should only be criticised. That's
why I keep it all to myself — myself being this little
book. I grew tired of myself some months ago, and
locked myself up in a desk. It was a kind of pun-
ishment, but it was also a great rest, to stop judging,
to stop caring, for a while. Now that I have come
out, I suppose I ought to take a vow not to be ill-
natured.

As I read over what I have written here, I wonder
whether it was worth while to have reopened my
journal.   Still, why not have the benefit of being
thought disagreeable, —the luxury of recorded observation ? If one is poor, plain, proud — and in this
very private place I may add, clever — there are certain necessary revenges !

April 10.   Adrian Frank has been here again,
and we rather like him. (That will do for the first
note of a more genial tone.) His eyes are very blue,
and his teeth very white — two things that always
please me. He became rather more communicative,
and almost promised to show me his sketches — in

spite of the fact that he is evidently as much as ever struck with my own ability. Perhaps he has discovered that I am trying to be genial! He wishes to take us to drive—that is, to take Eunice; for of course I shall go only for propriety. She does n't go with young men alone; that element was not included in her education. She said to me yesterday, "The only man I shall drive alone with will be the one I marry." She talks so little about marrying, that this made an impression on me. That subject is supposed to be a girl's inevitable topic; but no young women could occupy themselves with it less than she and I do. I think I may say that we never mention it at all. I suppose that if a man were to read this, he would be greatly surprised and not particularly edified. As there is no danger of any man's reading it, I may add that I always take tacitly for granted that Eunice will marry. She does n't in the least pretend that she won't; and if I am not mistaken, she is capable of conjugal affection. The longer I live with her, the more I see that she is a dear girl. Now that I know her better, I perceive that she is perfectly natural. I used to think that she tried too much — that she watched herself, perhaps, with a little secret admiration. But that was because I could n't conceive of a girl's motives being so simple. She only wants not to suffer — she is immensely afraid of that. Therefore, she wishes to be universally tender — to mitigate the general sum of suffering, in the hope that she herself may come off easily. Poor thing! she does n't know that we can diminish the amount of suffering for others only by taking to ourselves a part of their share. The amount of that commodity in the world is always the same; it is only the distribution that varies. We all try to dodge our portion; and some of us succeed. I find the best way is not to think about it, and to make little water-colors. Eunice thinks that the best way is to be very generous, to condemn no one unheard.

A great many things happen that I don't mention here; incidents of social life, I believe they call them. People come to see us, and sometimes they invite us to dinner. We go to certain concerts, many of which are very good. We take a walk every day; and I read to Eunice, and she plays to me. Mrs. Ermine makes her appearance several times a week, and gives us the news of the town — a great deal more of it than we have any use for. She thinks we live in a hole; and she has more than once expressed her conviction that I can do nothing socially for Eunice. As to that, she is perfectly right; I am aware of my social insignificance. But I am equally aware that my cousin has no need of being pushed. I know little of the people and things of this place; but I know enough to see that whatever they are, the best of them are at her service. Mrs. Ermine thinks it a great pity that Eunice should have come too late in the season to "go out" with her; for after this, there are few entertainments at which my protecting presence is not sufficient. Besides, Eunice is n't eager; I often wonder at her indifference. She never thinks of the dances she has missed, nor asks about those at which she still may figure. She is n't sad, and it does n't amount to melancholy; but she certainly is rather detached. She likes to read, to talk with me, to make music, and to dine out when she supposes there will be "real conversation." She is extremely fond of real conversation; and we flatter ourselves that a good deal of it takes place between us. We talk about life and religion and art and George Eliot; all that, I hope, is sufficiently real. Eunice understands everything, and has a great many opinions; she is quite the modern young woman, though she has n't modern manners. But all this does n't explain to me why, as Mrs. Ermine says, she should wish to be so dreadfully quiet. That lady's suspicion to the contrary notwithstanding, it is not I who make her so. I would go with her to a party every night if she should wish it, and send out cards to proclaim that we "receive." But her ambitions are not those of the usual girl; or at any rate, if she is waiting for what the usual girl waits for, she is waiting very patiently. As I say, I can't quite make out the secret of her patience. However, it is not necessary I should; it was no part of the bargain on which I came to her that we were to conceal nothing from each other. I conceal a great deal from Eunice; at least I hope I do: for instance, how fearfully I am bored. I think I am as patient as she; but then I have certain things to help me— my age, my resignation, my ability, and, I suppose I may add, my conceit. Mrs. Ermine does n't bring the young men, but she talks about them, and calls them Harry and Freddy. She wants Eunice to marry, though I don't see what she is to gain by it. It is apparently a disinterested love of matrimony, — or rather, I should say, a love of weddings. She lives in a world of " engagements," and announces a new one every time she comes in. I never heard of so much marrying in all my life before. Mrs. Ermine is dying to be able to tell people that Eunice is engaged : that distinction should not be wanting to a cousin of hers. Whoever marries her, by the way, will come into a very good fortune. Almost for the first time, three days ago, she told me about her affairs.

She knows less about them than she believes,—I could see that; but she knows the great matter; which is that in the course of her twenty-first year, by the terms of her mother's will, she becomes mistress of her property, of which for the last seven years Mr. Caliph has been sole trustee. On that day Mr. Caliph is to make over to her three hundred thousand dollars, which he has been nursing and keeping safe. So much on every occasion seems to be expected of this wonderful man! I call him so because I think it was wonderful of him to have been appointed sole depositary of the property of an orphan by a very anxious, scrupulous, affectionate mother, whose one desire, when she made her will, was to prepare for her child a fruitful majority, and whose acquaintance with him had not been of many years, though her esteem for him was great. He had been a friend — a very good friend — of her husband, who, as he neared his end, asked him to look after his widow. Eunice's father did n't however make him trustee of his little estate; he put that into other hands, and Eunice has a very good account of it. It amounts, unfortunately, but to some fifty thousand dollars. Her mother's proceedings with regard to Mr. Caliph were very feminine — so I may express myself in the privacy of these pages. But I believe all women are very feminine in their relations with Mr. Caliph. " Haroun-al-Raschid " I call him to Eunice; and I suppose he expects to find us in a state of Oriental prostration. She says, however, that he is not the least of a Turk, and that nothing could be kinder or more considerate than he was three years ago, before she went to Europe. He was constantly with her at that time, for many mouths; and his attentions have evidently made a great impression on her. That sort of thing naturally would, on a girl of seventeen; and I have told her she must be prepared to think him much less brilliant a personage to-day. I don't know what he will think of some of her plans of expenditure, — laying out an Italian garden at the house on the river, founding a cot at the children's hospital, erecting a music-room in the rear of this house. Next winter Eunice proposes to receive; but she wishes to have an originality, in the shape of really good music. She will evidently be rather extravagant, at least at first. Mr. Caliph of course will have no more authority; still, he may advise her as a friend.

April 23. This afternoon, while Eunice was out, Mr. Frank made his appearance, having had the civility, as I afterwards learned, to ask for me, in spite of the absence of the *padronina*. I told him she was at Mrs. Ermine's, and that Mrs. Ermine was her cousin.

"Then I can say what I should not be able to say if she were here," he said, smiling that singular smile which has the effect of showing his teeth and drawing the lids of his eyes together. If he were a young countryman, one would call it a grin. It is not exactly a grin, but it is very simple.

"And what may that be?" I asked, with encouragement.

He hesitated a little, while I admired his teeth, which I am sure he has no wish to exhibit; and I expected something wonderful. "Considering that she is fair, she is really very pretty," he said at last.

I was rather disappointed, and I went so far as to say to him that he might have made that remark in her presence.

This time his blue eyes remained wide open: "So you really think so?"

"'Considering that she's fair,' that part of it, perhaps, might have been omitted; but the rest surely would have pleased her."

"Do you really think so?"

"Well, 'really very pretty' is, perhaps, not quite

right; it seems to imply a kind of surprise. You might have omitted the 'really.'"

" You want me to omit everything," he said, laughing, as if he thought me wonderfully amusing.

"The gist of the thing would remain, 'You are very pretty;' that would have been unexpected and agreeable."

"I think you are laughing at me!" cried poor Mr. Frank, without bitterness. "I have no right to say that till I know she likes me."

"She does like you; I see no harm in telling you so." He seemed to me so modest, so natural, that I felt as free to say this to him as I would have been to a good child : more, indeed, than to a good child, for a child to whom one would say that would be rather a prig; and Adrian Frank is not a prig. I could see that by the way he answered; it was rather odd.

"It will please my brother to know that !"

"Does he take such an interest in the impressions you make ?"

"Oh, yes; he wants me to appear well." This was said with the most touching innocence; it was a complete confession of inferiority. It was, perhaps, the tone that made it so; at any rate, Adrian Frank has renounced the hope of ever appearing as well as his brother. I wonder if a man must be really inferior, to be in such a state of mind as that. He must at all events be very fond of his brother, and even, I think, have sacrificed himself a good deal.

This young man asked me ever so many questions about my cousin; frankly, simply, as if when one wanted to know, it was perfectly natural to ask. So it is, I suppose; but why should he want to know? Some of his questions were certainly idle. What can it matter to him whether she has one little dog or three, or whether she is an admirer of the music of the future? "Does she go out much, or does she like a quiet evening at home?" "Does she like living in Europe, and what part of Europe does she prefer?" "Has she many relatives in New York, and does she see a great deal of them?" On all these points I was obliged to give Mr. Frank a certain satisfaction; and after that, I thought I had a right to ask why he wanted to know. He was evidently surprised at being challenged, blushed a good deal, and made me feel for a moment as if I had asked a vulgar question. I saw he had no particular reason; he only wanted to be civil, and that is the way best known to him of expressing an interest. He was confused; but he was not so confused that he took his departure. He sat half an hour longer, and let me make up to him by talking very agreeably for the shock I had administered. I may mention here — for I like to see it in black and white — that I *can* talk very agreeably. He listened with the most flattering attention, showing me his blue eyes and his white teeth in alternation, and laughing largely, as if I had a command of the comical, — I am not conscious of that. At last, after I had paused a little, he said to me, apropos

of nothing: "Do you think the realistic school are
— a — to be admired ?"   Then I saw that he had
already forgotten my earlier check, — such was the
effect of my geniality, — and that he would ask me as
many questions about myself as I would let him.   I
answered him freely, but I answered him as I chose.
There are certain things about myself I never shall
tell, and the simplest way not to tell is to say the
contrary.   If people are indiscreet, they must take
the consequences.   I declared that I held the realistic
school in horror; that I found New York the most
interesting, the most sympathetic of cities; and that
I thought the American girl the finest result of civilization.   I am sure I convinced him that I am a
most remarkable woman.   He went away before
Eunice returned.   He is a charming creature — a
kind of Yankee Donatello.   If I could only be his
Miriam, the situation would be almost complete,
for Eunice is an excellent Hilda.

April 26.   Mrs. Ermine was in great force to-day;
she described all the fine things Eunice can do when
she gets her money into her own hands.   A set of
Mechlin lace, a *rivière* of diamonds which she saw the
other day at Tiffany's, a set of Russian sables that she
knows of somewhere else, a little English phaeton with
a pair of ponies and a tiger, a family of pugs to waddle
about in the drawing-room — all these luxuries Mrs.
Ermine declares indispensable.   "I should like to
know that you have them — it would do me real
good," she said to Eunice.   "I like to see people with

handsome things. It would give me more pleasure to know you have that set of Mechlin than to have it myself. I can't help that — it's the way I am made. If other people have handsome things I see them more; and then I do want the good of others — I don't care if you think me vain for saying so. I shan't be happy till I see you in an English phaeton. The groom ought n't to be more than three foot six. I think you ought to show for what you are."

"How do you mean, for what I am?" Eunice asked.

"Well, for a charming girl, with a very handsome fortune."

"I shall never show any more than I do now."

"I will tell you what you do — you show Miss Condit." And Mrs. Ermine presented me her large, foolish face. "If you don't look out, she'll do you up in Morris papers, and then all the Mechlin lace in the world won't matter!"

"I don't follow you at all — I never follow you," I said, wishing I could have sketched her just as she sat there. She was quite grotesque.

"I would rather go without you," she repeated.

"I think that after I come into my property I shall do just as I do now," said Eunice. "After all, where will the difference be? I have to-day everything I shall ever have. It's more than enough."

"You won't have to ask Mr. Caliph for everything."

"I ask him for nothing now."

"Well, my dear," said Mrs. Ermine, "you don't deserve to be rich."

"I am not rich," Eunice remarked.

"Ah, well, if you want a million!"

"I don't want anything," said Eunice.

That's not exactly true. She does want something, but I don't know what it is.

May 2. Mr. Caliph is really very delightful. He made his appearance to-day and carried everything before him. When I say he carried everything, I mean he carried me; for Eunice had not my prejudices to get over. When I said to her after he had gone, "Your trustee is a very clever man," she only smiled a little, and turned away in silence. I suppose she was amused with the air of importance with which I announced this discovery. Eunice had made it several years ago, and could not be excited about it. I had an idea that some allusion would be made to the way he has neglected her — some apology at least for his long absence. But he did something better than this. He made no definite apology; he only expressed, in his manner, his look, his voice, a tenderness, a kind of charming benevolence, which included and exceeded all apologies. He looks rather tired and preoccupied; he evidently has a great many irons of his own in the fire, and has been thinking these last weeks of larger questions than the susceptibilities. of a little girl in New York who happened several years ago to have an exuberant mother. He is thoroughly genial, and is

the best talker I have seen since my return. A
totally different type from the young Adrian. He is
not in the least handsome — is, indeed, rather ugly;
but with a fine, expressive, pictorial ugliness. He is
forty years old, large and stout, may even be pro-
nounced fat; and there is something about him that
I don't know how to describe except by calling it a
certain richness. I have seen Italians who have it
but this is the first American. He talks with his
eyes, as well as with his lips, and his features are
wonderfully mobile. His smile is quick and delightful; his hands are well-shaped, but distinctly fat;
he has a pale complexion and a magnificent brown
beard — the beard of Haroun-al-Raschid. I suppose
I must write it very small; but I have an intimate
conviction that he is a Jew, or of Jewish origin. I
see that in his plump, white face, of which the tone
would please a painter, and which suggests fatigue
but is nevertheless all alive; in his remarkable eye,
which is full of old expressions — expressions which
linger there from the past, even when they are not
active to-day; in his profile, in his anointed beard, in
the very rings on his large pointed fingers. There is
not a touch of all this in his step-brother; so I suppose the Jewish blood is inherited from his father.
I don't think he looks like a gentleman; he is something apart from all that. If he is not a gentleman,
he is not in the least a bourgeois — neither is he of
the artist type. In short, as I say, he is a Jew; and
Jews of the upper class have a style of their own. He

is very clever, and I think genuinely kind. Nothing could be more charming than his way of talking to Eunice — a certain paternal interest mingled with an air of respectful gallantry (he gives her good advice, and at the same time pays her compliments); the whole thing being not in the least overdone. I think he found her changed — "more of a person," as Mrs. Ermine says; I even think he was a little surprised. She seems slightly afraid of him, which rather surprised me — she was, from her own account, so familiar with him of old. He is decidedly florid, and was very polite to me — that was a part of the floridity. He asked if we had seen his step-brother; begged us to be kind to him and to let him come and see us often. He does n't know many people in New York, and at that age it is everything (I quote Mr. Caliph) for a young fellow to be at his ease with one or two charming women. "Adrian takes a great deal of knowing; is horribly shy; but is most intelligent, and has one of the sweetest natures ! I 'm very fond of him — he 's all I 've got. Unfortunately the poor boy is cursed with a competence. In this country there is nothing for such a young fellow to do; he hates business, and has absolutely no talent for it. I shall send him back here the next time I see him." Eunice made no answer to this, and, in fact, had little answer to make to most of Mr. Caliph's remarks, only sitting looking at the floor with a smile. I thought it proper therefore to reply that we had found Mr. Frank very pleasant, and hoped he would soon come

again. Then I mentioned that the other day I had
had a long visit from him alone; we had talked for
an hour, and become excellent friends. Mr. Caliph,
as I said this, was leaning forward with his elbow
on his knee and his hand uplifted, grasping his
thick beard. The other hand, with the elbow out,
rested on the other knee; his head was turned toward me, askance. He looked at me a moment with
his deep bright eye — the eye of a much older man
than he; he might have been posing for a water-
color. If I had painted him, it would have been in
a high-peaked cap, and an amber-colored robe, with a
wide girdle of pink silk wound many times round
his waist, stuck full of knives with jewelled handles.
Our eyes met, and we sat there exchanging a glance.
I don't know whether he's vain, but I think he must
see I appreciate him; I am sure he understands
everything.

"I like you when you say that," he remarked at
the end of a minute.   .

"I'm glad to hear you like me!" This sounds
horrid and pert as I relate it.

"I don't like every one," said Mr. Caliph.

"Neither do Eunice and I; do we, Eunice?"

"I am afraid we only try to," she answered, smiling her most beautiful smile.

"Try to? Heaven forbid! I protest against that,"
I cried. I said to Mr. Caliph that Eunice was too good.

"She comes honestly by that. Your mother was
an angel, my child," he said to her.

Cousin Letitia was not an angel, but I have mentioned that Mr. Caliph is florid. "You used to be very good to her," Eunice murmured, raising her eyes to him.

He had got up; he was standing there. He bent his head, smiling like an Italian. "You must be the same, my child."

"What can I do?" Eunice asked.

"You can believe in me — you can trust me."

"I do, Mr. Caliph. Try me and see!"

This was unexpectedly gushing, and I instinctively turned away. Behind my back, I don't know what he did to her — I think it possible he kissed her. When you call a girl "my child," I suppose you may kiss her; but that may be only my bold imagination. When I turned round he had taken up his hat and stick, to say nothing of buttoning a very tightly-fitting coat round a very spacious person, and was ready to offer me his hand in farewell.

"I am so glad you are with her. I am so glad she has a companion so accomplished — so capable."

"So capable of what?" I said, laughing; for the speech was absurd, as he knows nothing about my accomplishments.

There is nothing solemn about Mr. Caliph; but he gave me a look which made it appear to me that my levity was in bad taste. Yes, humiliating as it is to write it here, I found myself rebuked by a Jew with fat hands! "Capable of advising her well!" he said, softly.

" Ah, don't talk about advice," Eunice exclaimed. "Advice always gives an idea of trouble; and I am very much afraid of trouble."

" You ought to get married," he said, with his smile coming back to him.

Eunice colored and turned away, and I observed — to say something — that this was just what Mrs. Ermine said.

" Mrs. Ermine ? ah, I hear she 's a charming woman !" And shortly after that he went away.

That was almost the only weak thing he said — the only thing for mere form, for of course no one can really think her charming; least of all a clever man like that. I don't like Americans to resemble Italians, or Italians to resemble Americans; but putting that aside, Mr. Caliph is very prepossessing. He is wonderfully good company; he will spoil us for other people. He made no allusion to business, and no appointment with Eunice for talking over certain matters that are pending; but I thought of this only half an hour after he had gone. I said nothing to Eunice about it, for she would have noticed the omission herself, and that was enough. The only other point in Mr. Caliph that was open to criticism is his asking Eunice to believe in him — to trust him. Why shouldn't she, pray ? If that speech was curious — and, strange to say, it almost appeared so — it was incredibly naïf. But this quality is insupposable of Mr. Caliph; who ever heard of a naïf Jew ? After he had gone I was on the point of saying to Eunice,

"By the way, why did you never mention that he is a Hebrew? That's an important detail." But an impulse that I am not able to define stopped me, and now I am glad I did n't speak. I don't believe Eunice ever made the discovery, and I don't think she would like it if she did make it. That I should have done so on the instant only proves that I am in the habit of studying the human profile!

May 9. Mrs. Ermine must have discovered that Mr. Caliph has heard she is charming, for she is perpetually coming in here with the hope of meeting him. She appears to think that he comes every day; for when she misses him, which she has done three times (that is, she arrives just after he goes), she says that if she does n't catch him on the morrow she will go and call upon him. She is capable of that, I think; and it makes no difference that he is the busiest of men and she the idlest of women. He has been here four times since his first call, and has the air of wishing to make up for the neglect that preceded it. His manner to Eunice is perfect; he continues to call her "my child," but in a superficial, impersonal way, as a Catholic priest might do it. He tells us stories of Washington, describes the people there, and makes us wonder whether we should care for K Street and $14\frac{1}{2}$ Street. As yet, to the best of my knowledge, not a word about Eunice's affairs; he behaves as if he had simply forgotten them. It was, after all, not out of place the other day to ask her to "believe in him;" the faith would n't come as a matter of course. On the other hand he is so pleasant that one would believe in him just to oblige him. He has a great deal of trust-business, and a great deal of law-business of every kind. So at least he says; we really know very little about him but what he tells us. When I say "we," of course I speak mainly for myself, as I am perpetually forgetting that he is not so new to Eunice as he is to me. She knows what she knows, but I only know what I see. I have been wondering a good deal what is thought of Mr. Caliph "down-town," as they say here, but without much result, for naturally I can't go down-town and see. The appearance of the thing prevents my asking questions about him; it would be very compromising to Eunice, and make people think that she complains of him — which is so far from being the case. She likes him just as he is, and is apparently quite satisfied. I gather, moreover, that he is thought very brilliant, though a little peculiar, and that he has made a great deal of money. He has a way of his own of doing things, and carries imagination and humor, and a sense of the beautiful, into Wall Street and the Stock Exchange. Mrs. Ermine announced the other day that he is "considered the most fascinating man in New York;" but that is the romantic up-town view of him, and not what I want. His brother has gone out of town for a few days, but he continues to recommend the young Adrian to our hospitality. There is something really touching in his relation to that rather limited young man.

May 11. Mrs. Ermine is in high spirits; she has met Mr. Caliph — I don't know where — and she quite confirms the up-town view. She thinks him the most fascinating man she has ever seen, and she wonders that we should have said so little about him. He is so handsome, so high-bred; his manners are so perfect; he's a regular old dear. I think, of course ill-naturedly, several degrees less well of him since I have heard Mrs. Ermine's impressions. He is not handsome, he is not high-bred, and his manners are not perfect. They are original, and they are expressive; and if one likes him there is an interest in looking for what he will do and say. But if one should happen to dislike him, one would detest his manners and think them familiar and vulgar. As for breeding, he has about him, indeed, the marks of antiquity of race; yet I don't think Mrs. Ermine would have liked me to say, "Oh, yes, all Jews have blood!" Besides, I could n't before Eunice. Perhaps I consider Eunice too much; perhaps I am betrayed by my old habit of trying to see through mill-stones; perhaps I interpret things too richly — just as (I know) when I try to paint an old wall I attempt to put in too much "character;" character being in old walls, after all, a finite quantity. At any rate she seems to me rather nervous about Mr. Caliph: that appeared after a little when Mrs. Ermine came back to the subject. She had a great deal to say about the oddity of her never having seen him before, of old, "for after all," as she remarked,

"we move in the same society — he moves in the
very best."   She used to hear Eunice talk about her
trustee, but she supposed a trustee must be some
horrid old man with a lot of papers in his hand, sitting all day in an office.   She never supposed he was
a prince in disguise.   "We've got a trustee somewhere, only I never see him; my husband does all
the business.   No wonder he keeps him out of the
way if he resembles Mr. Caliph."   And then suddenly
she said to Eunice, "My dear, why don't you marry
him?   I should think you would want to."   Mrs.
Ermine does n't look through mill-stones; she con-
tents herself with giving them a poke with her
parasol.   Eunice colored, and said she had n't been
asked; she was evidently not pleased with Mrs.
Ermine's joke, which was of course as flat as you
like.   Then she added in a moment — "I should be
very sorry to marry Mr. Caliph, even if he were to
ask me.   I like him, but I don't like him enough for
that."

"I should think he would be quite in your style,
— he's so literary.   They say he writes," Mrs. Ermine
went on.

"Well, I don't write," Eunice answered, laughing.

"You could if you would try.   I 'm sure you could
make a lovely book."   Mrs. Ermine's amiability is
immense.

"It's safe for you to say that — you never read."

"I have no time," said Mrs. Ermine, "but I like

literary conversation. It saves time, when it comes in that way. Mr. Caliph has ever so much."

"He keeps it for you. With us he is very frivolous," I ventured to observe.

"Well, what you call frivolous! I believe you think the prayer-book frivolous."

"Mr. Caliph will never marry any one," Eunice said, after a moment. "That I am very sure of."

Mrs. Ermine stared; there never is so little expression in her face as when she is surprised. But she soon recovered herself. "Don't you believe that! He will take some quiet little woman, after you have all given him up."

Eunice was sitting at the piano, but had wheeled round on the stool when her cousin came in. She turned back to it and struck a few vague chords, as if she were feeling for something. "Please don't speak that way; I don't like it," she said, as she went on playing.

"I will speak any way you like!" Mrs. Ermine cried, with her vacant laugh.

"I think it very low." For Eunice this was severe. "Girls are not always thinking about marriage. They are not always thinking of people like Mr. Caliph —that way."

"They must have changed then, since my time! Was n't it so in yours, Miss Condit?" She's so stupid that I don't think she meant to make a point.

"I had no 'time,' Mrs. Ermine. I was born an old maid."

"Well, the old maids are the worst. I don't see why it's low to talk about marriage. It's thought very respectable to marry. You have only to look round you."

"I don't want to look round me; it's not always so beautiful, what you see," Eunice said, with a small laugh and a good deal of perversity, for a young woman so reasonable.

"I guess you read too much," said Mrs. Ermine, getting up and setting her bonnet-ribbons at the mirror.

"I should think he would hate them!" Eunice exclaimed, striking her chords.

"Hate who?" her cousin asked.

"Oh, all the silly girls."

"Who is 'he,' pray?" This ingenious inquiry was mine.

"Oh, the Grand Turk!" said Eunice, with her voice covered by the sound of her piano. Her piano is a great resource.

May 12. This afternoon, while we were having our tea, the Grand Turk was ushered in, carrying the most wonderful bouquet of Boston roses that seraglio ever produced. (That image, by the way, is rather mixed; but as I write for myself alone, it may stand.) At the end of ten minutes he asked Eunice if he might see her alone—"on a little matter of business." I instantly rose to leave them, but Eunice said that she would rather talk with him in the library; so she led him off to that apartment. I remained in the drawing-room, saying to myself that I had at last discovered the *fin mot* of Mr. Caliph's peculiarities, which is so very simple that I am a great goose not to have perceived it before. He is a man with a system; and his system is simply to keep business and entertainment perfectly distinct. There may be pleasure for him in his figures, but there are no figures in his pleasure — which has hitherto been to call upon Eunice as a man of the world. To-day he was to be the trustee; I could see it in spite of his bouquet, as soon as he came in. The Boston roses did n't contradict that, for the excellent reason that as soon as he had shaken hands with Eunice, who looked at the flowers and not at him, he presented them to Catherine Condit. Eunice then looked at this lady; and as I took the roses I met her eyes, which had a charming light of pleasure. It would be base in me, even in this strictly private record, to suggest that she might possibly have been displeased; but if I cannot say that the expression of her face was lovely without appearing in some degree to point to an ignoble alternative, it is the fault of human nature. Why Mr. Caliph should suddenly think it necessary to offer flowers to Catherine Condit — that is a line of inquiry by itself. As I said some time back, it 's a part of his floridity. Besides, any presentation of flowers seems sudden; I don't know why, but it 's always rather a *çoup de théatre*. I am writing late at night; they stand on my table, and their fragrance is in the air. I don't say it for the flowers, but

no one has ever treated poor Miss Condit with such
consistent consideration as Mr. Caliph. Perhaps she
is morbid: this is probably the Diary of a Morbid
Woman; but in such a matter as that she admires
consistency.   That little glance of Eunice comes
back to me as I write; she is a pure, enchanting
soul. Mrs. Ermine came in while she was in the
library with Mr. Caliph, and immediately noticed the
Boston roses, which effaced all the other flowers in
the room.

"Were they sent from her seat?" she asked. Then,
before I could answer, "I am going to have some
people to dinner to-day; they would look very well
in the middle."

"If you wish me to offer them to you, I really
can't; I prize them too much."

"Oh, are they yours?   Of course you prize them!
I don't suppose you have many."

"These are the first I have ever received — from
Mr. Caliph."

"From Mr. Caliph?   Did he give them to *you?*"
Mrs. Ermine's intonations are not delicate.   That
"*you*" should be in enormous capitals.

"With his own hand — a quarter of an hour ago."
This sounds triumphant, as I write it; but it was no
great sensation to triumph over Mrs. Ermine.

She laid down the bouquet, looking almost thought-
ful. "He *does* want to marry Eunice," she declared
in a moment. This is the region in which, after a
flight of fancy, she usually alights. I am sick of the

irrepressible verb; just at that moment, however, it was unexpected, and I answered that I did n't understand.

"That 's why he gives you flowers," she explained. But the explanation made the matter darker still, and Mrs. Ermine went on: "Is n't there some French proverb about paying one's court to the mother in order to gain the daughter? Eunice is the daughter, and you are the mother."

"And you are the grandmother, I suppose! Do you mean that he wishes me to intercede?"

"I can't imagine why else!" and smiling, with her wide lips, she stared at the flowers.

"At that rate you too will get your bouquet," I said.

"Oh, I have no influence! You ought to do something in return — to offer to paint his portrait."

"I don't offer that, you know; people ask me. Besides, you have spoiled me for common models!"

It strikes me, as I write this, that we had gone rather far — farther than it seemed at the time. We might have gone farther yet, however, if at this moment Eunice had not come back with Mr. Caliph, who appeared to have settled his little matter of business briskly enough. He remained the man of business to the end, and, to Mrs. Ermine's evident disappointment, declined to sit down again. He was in a hurry; he had an engagement.

"Are you going up or down? I have a carriage at the door," she broke in.

"At Fifty-third Street one is usually going down;" and he gave his peculiar smile, which always seems so much beyond the scope of the words it accompanies. "If you will give me a lift I shall be very grateful."

He went off with her, she being much divided between the prospect of driving with him and her loss of the chance to find out what he had been saying to Eunice. She probably believed he had been proposing to her, and I hope he mystified her well in the carriage.

He had not been proposing to Eunice; he had given her a cheque, and made her sign some papers. The cheque was for a thousand dollars, but I have no knowledge of the papers. When I took up my abode with her, I made up my mind that the only way to preserve an appearance of disinterestedness was to know nothing whatever of the details of her pecuniary affairs. She has a very good little head of her own, and if she should n't understand them herself it would be quite out of my power to help her. I don't know why I should care about *appearing* disinterested, when I have in quite sufficient measure the consciousness of being so; but in point of fact I do, and I value that purity as much as any other. Besides, Mr. Caliph is her supreme adviser and of course makes everything clear to her. At least I hope he does. I could n't help saying as much as this to Eunice.

"My dear child, I suppose you understand what

you sign. Mr. Caliph ought to be — what shall I call it ? — crystalline."

She looked at me with the smile that had come into her face when she saw him give me the flowers. "Oh, yes, I think so. If I did n't, it 's my own fault. He explains everything so beautifully that it 's a pleasure to listen. I always read what I sign."

" Je l'espère bien ! " I said, laughing.

She looked a little grave. " The closing up a trust is very complicated."

" Yours is not closed yet ? It strikes me as very slow."

" Everything can't be done at once. Besides, he has asked for a little delay. Part of my affairs, indeed, are now in my own hands; otherwise I should n't have to sign."

" Is that a usual request — for delay ? "

" Oh, yes, perfectly. Besides, I don't want everything in my own control. That is, I want it some day, because I think I ought to accept the responsibilities, as I accept all the pleasures ; but I am not in a hurry. This way is so comfortable, and Mr. Caliph takes so much trouble for me."

" I suppose he has a handsome commission," I said, rather crudely.

" He has no commission at all; he would never take one."

" In your place, I would much rather he should take one."

"I have asked him to, but he won't!" Eunice said, looking now extremely grave.

Her gravity indeed was so great that it made me smile. "He is wonderfully generous!"

"He is indeed."

"And is it to be indefinitely delayed — the termination of his trust?"

"Oh, no; only a few months, 'till he gets things into shape,' as he says."

"He has had several years for that, has n't he?"

Eunice turned away; evidently our talk was painful to her. But there was something that vaguely alarmed me in her taking, or at least accepting, the sentimental view of Mr. Caliph's services. "I don't think you are kind, Catherine; you seem to suspect him," she remarked, after a little.

"Suspect him of what?"

"Of not wishing to give up the property."

"My dear Eunice, you put things into terrible words! Seriously, I should never think of suspecting him of anything so silly. What could his wishes count for? Is not the thing regulated by law — by the terms of your mother's will? The trust expires of itself at a certain period, does n't it? Mr. Caliph, surely, has only to act accordingly."

"It is just what he is doing. But there are more papers necessary, and they will not be ready for a few weeks more."

"Don't have too many papers; they are as bad as too few. And take advice of some one else — say of your cousin Ermine, who is so much more sensible than his wife."

"I want no advice," said Eunice, in a tone which showed me that I had said enough. And presently she went on, "I thought you liked Mr. Caliph."

"So I do, immensely. He gives beautiful flowers."

"Ah, you are horrid!" she murmured.

"Of course I am horrid. That's my business — to be horrid." And I took the liberty of being so again, half an hour later, when she remarked that she must take good care of the cheque Mr. Caliph had brought her, as it would be a good while before she should have another. "Why should it be longer than usual?" I asked. "Is he going to keep your income for himself?"

"I am not to have any till the end of the year — any from the trust, at least. Mr. Caliph has been converting some old houses into shops, so that they will bring more rent. But the alterations have to be paid for — and he takes part of my income to do it."

"And pray what are you to live on meanwhile?"

"I have enough without that; and I have savings."

"It strikes me as a cool proceeding, all the same."

"He wrote to me about it before we came home, and I thought that way was best."

"I don't think he ought to have asked you," I said. "As your trustee, he acts in his discretion."

"You are hard to please," Eunice answered.

That is perfectly true; but I rejoined that I could n't make out whether he consulted her too much or too little.   And I don't know that my failure to make it out in the least matters!

May 13.   Mrs. Ermine turned up to-day at an earlier hour than usual, and I saw as soon as she got into the room that she had something to announce. This time it was not an engagement.   "He sent me a bouquet — Boston roses — quite as many as yours! They arrived this morning, before I had finished breakfast."   This speech was addressed to me, and Mrs. Ermine looked almost brilliant.   Eunice scarcely followed her.

"She is talking about Mr. Caliph," I explained.

Eunice stared a moment; then her face melted into a deep little smile.   "He seems to give flowers to every one but to me."   I could see that this reflection gave her remarkable pleasure.

"Well, when he gives them, he's thinking of you," said Mrs. Ermine.   "He wants to get us on his side."

"On his side?"

"Oh, yes; some day he will have need of us!"   And Mrs. Ermine tried to look sprightly and insinuating. But she is too utterly *fade,* and I think it is not worth while to talk any more to Eunice just now about her trustee.   So, to anticipate Mrs. Ermine, I said to her quickly, but very quietly —

"He sent you flowers simply because you had taken him into your carriage last night.   It was an acknowledgment of your great kindness."

She hesitated a moment.   "Possibly.   We had a charming drive — ever so far down-town."   Then, turning to Eunice, she exclaimed, "My dear, you don't know that man till you have had a drive with him!" When does one know Mrs. Ermine? Every day she is a surprise!

May 19. Adrian Frank has come back to New York, and has been three times at this house — once to dinner, and twice at tea-time. After his brother's strong expression of the hope that we would take an interest in him, Eunice appears to have thought that the least she could do was to ask him to dine. She appears never to have offered this privilege to Mr. Caliph, by the way; I think her view of his cleverness is such that she imagines she knows no one sufficiently brilliant to be invited to meet him. She thought Mrs. Ermine good enough to meet Mr. Frank, and she had also young Woodley — Willie Woodley, as they call him — and Mr. Latrobe. It was not very amusing. Mrs. Ermine made love to Mr. Woodley, who took it serenely; and the dark Latrobe talked to me about the Seventh Regiment — an impossible subject. Mr. Frank made an occasional remark to Eunice, next whom he was placed; but he seemed constrained and frightened, as if he knew that his step-brother had recommended him highly and felt it was impossible to come up to the mark. He is really very modest; it is impossible not to like him. Every now and then he looked at me, with his clear blue eye conscious and expanded, as if to beg me to help him on with Eunice; and then, when I threw in a word, to give their conversa-

tion a push, he looked at her in the same way, as if
to express the hope that she would not abandon him.
There was no danger of this, she only wished to be
agreeable to him ; but she was nervous and preoccupied, as she always is when she has people to dinner
— she is so afraid they may be bored — and I think
that half the time she did n't understand what he
said. She told me afterwards that she liked him
more even than she liked him at first ; that he has, in
her opinion, better manners, in spite of his shyness,
than any of the young men ; and that he must have a
nice nature to have such a charming face ; — all this
she told me, and she added that, notwithstanding all
this, there is something in Mr. Adrian Frank that
makes her uncomfortable. It is perhaps rather heart-
less, but after this, when he called two days ago, I
went out of the room and left them alone together.
The truth is, there is something in this tall, fair,
vague, inconsequent youth, who would look like a
Prussian lieutenant if Prussian lieutenants ever hesitated, and who is such a singular mixture of confusion and candor — there is something about him that
is not altogether to my own taste, and that is why
I took the liberty of leaving him. Oddly enough,
I don't in the least know what it is ; I usually know
why I dislike people. I don't dislike the blushing
Adrian, however — that is, after all, the oddest part.
No, the oddest part of it is that I think I have a feeling of pity for him ; that is probably why (if it were
not my duty sometimes to remain) I should always

depart when he comes. I don't like to see the people
I pity; to be pitied by me is too low a depth. Why
I should lavish my compassion on Mr. Frank of
course passes my comprehension. He is young, intelligent, in perfect health, master of a handsome
fortune, and favorite brother of Haroun-al-Raschid.
Such are the consequences of being a woman of imagination. When, at dinner, I asked Eunice if he
had been as interesting as usual, she said she would
leave it to me to judge; he had talked altogether
about Miss Condit! He thinks her very attractive!
Poor fellow, when it is necessary he does n't hesitate,
though I can't imagine why it should be necessary.
I think that *au fond* he bores Eunice a little; like
many girls of the delicate, sensitive kind, she likes
older, more confident men.

May 24. He has just made me a remarkable
communication! This morning I went into the Park
in quest of a " bit," with some colors and brushes in
a small box, and that wonderfully compressible campstool which I can carry in my pocket. I wandered
vaguely enough, for half an hour, through the care-
fully-arranged scenery, the idea of which appears to
be to represent the earth's surface *en raccourci*, and
at last discovered a small clump of birches which,
with their white stems and their little raw green
bristles, were not altogether uninspiring. The place
was quiet — there were no nurse-maids nor bicycles;
so I took up a position and enjoyed an hour's successful work. At last I heard some one say behind

me, "I think I ought to tell you I'm looking!" It was Adrian Frank, who had recognized me at a distance, and, without my hearing him, had walked across the grass to where I sat. This time I could n't leave him, for I had n't finished my sketch. He sat down near me, on an artistically-preserved rock, and we ended by having a good deal of talk — in which, however, I did the listening, for I can't express myself in two ways at once. What I listened to was this — that Mr. Caliph wishes his step-brother to "make up" to Eunice, and that the candid Adrian wishes to know what I think of his chances.

"Are you in love with her?" I asked.

"Oh dear, no! If I were in love with her I should go straight in, without — without this sort of thing."

"You mean without asking people's opinion?"

"Well, yes. Without asking even yours."

I told him that he need n't say "even" mine; for mine would not be worth much. His announcement rather startled me at first, but after I had thought of it a little, I found in it a good deal to admire. I have seen so many "arranged" marriages that have been happy, and so many "sympathetic" unions that have been wretched, that the political element does n't altogether shock me. Of course I can't imagine Eunice making a political marriage, and I said to Mr. Frank, very promptly, that she might consent if she could be induced to love him, but would never be governed in her choice by his advantages. I said "advantages" in order to be polite; the singular number would have served all the purpose.   His only advantage is his fortune; for he has neither looks, talents, nor position that would dazzle a girl who is herself clever and rich.   This, then, is what Mr. Caliph has had in his head all this while — this is what has made him so anxious that we should like his step-brother.   I have an idea that I ought to be rather scandalized, but I feel my pulse and find that I am almost pleased.   I don't mean at the idea of her marrying poor Mr. Frank; I mean at such an indication that Mr. Caliph takes an interest in her.   I don't know whether it is one of the regular duties of a trustee to provide the trustful with a husband; perhaps in that case his merit may be less.   I suppose he has said to himself, that if she marries his step-brother she won't marry a worse man.   Of course it is possible that he may not have thought of Eunice at all, and may simply have wished the guileless Adrian to do a good thing without regard to Eunice's point of view.   I am afraid that even this idea does n't shock me.   Trying to make people marry is, under any circumstances, an unscrupulous game; but the offence is minimized when it is a question of an honest man marrying an angel.   Eunice is the angel, and the young Adrian has all the air of being honest. It would, naturally, not be the union of her secret dreams, for the hero of those pure visions would have to be clever and distinguished.   Mr. Frank is neither of these things, but I believe he is perfectly good.   Of course he is weak — to come and take a wife simply because his brother has told him to — or is he doing it simply for form, believing that she will never have him, that he consequeutly does n't expose himself, and that he will therefore have on easy terms, since he seems to value it, the credit of having obeyed Mr. Caliph? Why he should value it is a matter between themselves, which I am not obliged to know. I don't think I care at all for the relations of men between themselves. Their relations with women are bad enough, but when there is no woman to save it a little —*merci!* I should n't think that the young Adrian would care to subject himself to a simple refusal, for it is not gratifying to receive the cold shoulder, even from a woman you don't want to marry. After all, he may want to marry her; there are all sorts of reasons in things. I told him I would n't undertake to do anything, and the more I think of it the less I am willing. It would be a weight off my mind to see her comfortably settled in life, beyond the possibility of marrying some highly varnished brute — a fate in certain circumstances quite open to her. She is perfectly capable — with her folded angel's wings — of bestowing herself upon the baker, upon the fishmonger, if she was to take a fancy to him. The clever man of her dreams might beat her or get tired of her; but I am sure that Mr. Frank, if he should pronounce his marriage-vows, would keep them to the letter. From that to pushing her into his arms, however, is a long way. I went so far as to tell him that he had my good wishes ; but I made him understand that I can give him no help. He sat for some time poking a hole in the earth with his stick and watching the operation. Then he said, with his wide, exaggerated smile — the one thing in his face that recalls his brother, though it is so different — " I think I should like to try." I felt rather sorry for him, and made him talk of something else; and we separated without his alluding to Eunice, though at the last he looked at me for a moment intently, with something on his lips which was probably a return to his idea. I stopped him; I told him I always required solitude for my finishing-touches. He thinks me *brusque* and queer, but he went away. I don't know what he means to do; I am curious to see whether he will begin his siege. It can scarcely be said, as yet, to have begun — Eunice, at any rate, is all unconscious.

June 6. Her unconsciousness is being rapidly dispelled; Mr. Frank has been here every day since I last wrote. He is a singular youth, and I don't make him out; I think there is more in him than I supposed at first. He does n't bore us, and he has become, to a certain extent, one of the family. I like him very much, and he excites my curiosity. I don't quite see where he expects to come out. I mentioned some time back that Eunice had told me he made her uncomfortable; and now, if that continues, she appears to have resigned herself. He has asked her repeatedly to drive with him, and twice

she has consented; he has a very pretty pair of
horses, and a vehicle that holds but two persons. I
told him I could give him no positive help, but I do
leave them together.   Of course Eunice has noticed
this — it is the only intimation I have given her that
I am aware of his intentions.   I have constantly expected her to say something, but she has said nothing,
and it is possible that Mr. Frank is making an impression.   He makes love very reasonably; evidently
his idea is to be intensely gradual.   Of course it
is n't gradual to come every day; but he does very
little on any one occasion.   That, at least, is my impression; for when I talk of his making love I don't
mean that I see it.   When the three of us are together he talks to me quite as much as to her, and
there is no difference in his manner from one of us
to the other.   His shyness is wearing off, and he
blushes so much less that I have discovered his natural hue.   It has several shades less of crimson than
I supposed.   I have taken care that he should not
see me alone, for I don't wish him to talk to me of
what he is doing — I wish to have nothing to say
about it.   He has looked at me several times in the
same way in which he looked just before we parted,
that day he found me sketching in the park; that is,
as if he wished to have some special understanding
with me.   But I don't want a special understanding,
and I pretend not to see his looks.   I don't exactly
see why Eunice does n't speak to me, and why she
expresses no surprise at Mr. Frank's sudden devotion.

Perhaps Mr. Caliph has notified her, and she is prepared for everything — prepared even to accept the
young Adrian. I have an idea he will be rather
taken in if she does. Perhaps the day will come
soon when I shall think it well to say: "Take care,
take care; you *may* succeed!" He improves on acquaintance; he knows a great many things, and he is
a gentleman to his finger-tips. We talk very often
about Rome; he has made out every inscription for
himself, and has got them all written down in a little
book. He brought it the other afternoon and read
some of them out to us, and it was more amusing
than it may sound. I listen to such things because I
can listen to anything about Rome; and Eunice listens
possibly because Mr. Caliph has told her to. She
appears ready to do anything he tells her; he has been
sending her some more papers to sign. He has not
been here since the day he gave me the flowers; he
went back to Washington shortly after that. She has
received several letters from him, accompanying docu-
ments that look very legal. She has said nothing
to me about them, and since I uttered those words of
warning which I noted here at the time, I have
asked no questions and offered no criticism. Sometimes I wonder whether I myself had not better
speak to Mr. Ermine; it is only the fear of being
idiotic and meddlesome that restrains me. It seems
to me so odd there should be no one else; Mr. Caliph
appears to have everything in his own hands. We
are to go down to our "seat," as Mrs. Ermine says,

next week.   That brilliant woman has left town herself, like many other people, and is staying with
one of her daughters.   Then she is going to the
other, and then she is coming to Eunice, at Cornerville.

PART II.

June 8.   Late this afternoon — about an hour before dinner — Mr. Frank arrived with what Mrs. Ermine calls his equipage, and asked her to take a short drive with him.   At first she declined — said it was too hot, too late, she was too tired; but he seemed very much in earnest, and begged her to think better of it. She consented at last, and when she had left the room to arrange herself, he turned to me with a little grin of elation.   I saw he was going to say something about his prospects, and I determined, this time, to give him a chance.   Besides, I was curious to know how he believed himself to be getting on.   To my surprise, he disappointed my curiosity; he only said, with his timid brightness, " I am always so glad when I carry my point."

" Your point ?   Oh, yes.   I think I know what you mean."

" It's what I told you that day."   He seemed slightly surprised that I should be in doubt as to whether he had really presented himself as a lover.

" Do you mean to ask her to marry you ? "

He stared a little, looking graver.   " Do you mean to-day ? "

"Well, yes, to-day, for instance; you have urged her so to drive."

"I don't think I will do it to-day; it's too soon."

His gravity was natural enough, I suppose; but it had suddenly become so intense that the effect was comical, and I could not help laughing. "Very good; whenever you please."

"Don't you think it's too soon?" he asked.

"Ah, I know nothing about it."

"I have seen her alone only four or five times."

"You must go on as you think best," I said.

"It's hard to tell. My position is very difficult." And then he began to smile again. He is certainly very odd.

It is my fault, I suppose, that I am too impatient of what I don't understand; and I don't understand this odd mixture of the perfunctory and the passionate, or the singular alternation of Mr. Frank's confessions and reserves. "I can't enter into your position," I said; "I can't advise you or help you in any way." Even to myself my voice sounded a little hard as I spoke, and he was evidently discomposed by it.

He blushed as usual, and fell to putting on his gloves. "I think a great deal of your opinion, and for several days I have wanted to ask you."

"Yes, I have seen that."

"How have you seen it?"

"By the way you have looked at me."

He hesitated a moment. "Yes, I have looked at

you — I know that. There is a great deal in your face to see."

This remark, under the circumstances, struck me as absurd; I began to laugh again. "You speak of it as if it were a collection of curiosities." He looked away now, he would n't meet my eye, and I saw that I had made him feel thoroughly uncomfortable. To lead the conversation back into the commonplace, I asked him where he intended to drive.

"It does n't matter much where we go — it 's so pretty everywhere now." He was evidently not thinking of his drive, and suddenly he broke out, "I want to know whether you think she likes me."

"I have n't the least idea. She has n't told me."

"Do you think she knows that I mean to propose to her ?"

"You ought to be able to judge of that better than I."

"I am afraid of taking too much for granted; also of taking her by surprise."

"So that — in her agitation — she might accept you ? Is that what you are afraid of ?"

"I don't know what makes you say that. I wish her to accept me."

"Are you very sure ?"

"Perfectly sure. Why not? She is a charming creature."

"So much the better, then ; perhaps she will."

"You don't believe it," he exclaimed, as if it were very clever of him to have discovered that.

"You think too much of what I believe. That has nothing to do with the matter."

"No, I suppose not," said Mr. Frank, apparently wishing very much to agree with me.

"You had better find out as soon as possible from Eunice herself," I added.

"I have n't expected to know — for some time."

"Do you mean for a year or two ? She will be ready to tell you before that."

"Oh no — not a year or two ; but a few weeks."

"You know you come to the house every day. You ought to explain to her."

"Perhaps I had better not come so often."

"Perhaps not !"

"I like it very much," he said, smiling.

I looked at him a moment; I don't know what he has got in his eyes. "Don't change ! You are such a good young man that I don't know what we should do without you." And I left him to wait alone for Eunice.

From my window, above, I saw them leave the door; they make a fair, bright young couple as they sit together. They had not been gone a quarter of an hour when Mr. Caliph's name was brought up to me. He had asked for me — me alone ; he begged that I would do him the favor to see him for ten minutes. I don't know why this announcement should have made me nervous ; but it did. My heart beat at the prospect of entering into direct relations with Mr. Caliph. He is very clever, much thought of, and talked of; and yet I had vaguely suspected him — of I don't know what! I became conscious of that, and felt the responsibility of it; though I did n't foresee, and indeed don't think I foresee yet, any danger of a collision between us. It is to be noted, moreover, that even a woman who is both plain and conceited must feel a certain agitation at entering the presence of Haroun-al-Raschid. I had begun to dress for dinner, and I kept him waiting till I had taken my usual time to finish. I always take some such revenge as that upon men who make me nervous. He is the sort of man who feels immediately whether a woman is well-dressed or not; but I don't think this reflection really had much to do with my putting on the freshest of my three little French gowns.

He sat there, watch in hand; at least he slipped it into his pocket as I came into the room. He was not pleased at having had to wait, and when I apologized, hypocritically, for having kept him, he answered, with a certain dryness, that he had come to transact an important piece of business in a very short space of time. I wondered what his business could be, and whether he had come to confess to me that he had spent Eunice's money for his own purposes. Did he wish me to use my influence with her not to make a scandal? He did n't look like a man who has come to ask a favor of that kind; but I am sure that if he ever does ask it he will not look at all as he might be expected to look. He was clad in white garments, from head to foot, in recognition of the hot weather,.and he had half a dozen roses in his button-hole. This time his flowers were for himself. His white clothes made him look as big as Henry VIII.; but don't tell me he is not a Jew! He's a Jew of the artistic, not of the commercial, type; and as I stood there I thought him a very strange person to have as one's trustee. It seemed to me that he would carry such an office into transcendental regions, out of all common jurisdictions; and it was a comfort to me to remember that I have no property to be taken care of. Mr. Caliph kept a pocket-handkerchief, with an enormous monogram, in his large tapering hand, and every other moment he touched his face with it. He evidently suffers from the heat. With all that, *il est bien beau.* His business was not what had at first occurred to me; but I don't know that it was much less strange.

"I knew I should find you alone, because Adrian told me this morning that he meant to come and ask our young friend to drive. I was glad of that; I have been wishing to see you alone, and I did n't know how to manage it."

"You see it 's very simple. Did n't you send your brother?" I asked. In another place, to another person, this might have sounded impertinent; but evidently, addressed to Mr. Caliph, things have a special measure, and this I instinctively felt. He will take a great deal, and he will give a great deal.

He looked at me a moment, as if he were trying to

measure what I would take. "I see you are going to be a very satisfactory person to talk with," he answered. "That's exactly what I counted on. I want you to help me."

"I thought there was some reason why Mr. Frank should urge Eunice so to go," I went on; refreshed a little, I admit, by these words of commendation. "At first she was unwilling."

"Is she usually unwilling — and does he usually have to be urgent?" he asked, like a man pleased to come straight to the point.

"What does it matter, so long as she consents in the end?" I responded, with a smile that made him smile. There is a singular stimulus, even a sort of excitement, in talking with him; he makes one wish to venture. And this not as women usually venture, because they have a sense of impunity, but, on the contrary, because one has a prevision of penalties — those penalties which give a kind of dignity to sarcasm. He must be a dangerous man to irritate.

"Do you think she will consent, in the end?" he inquired; and though I had now foreseen what he was coming to, I felt that, even with various precautions which he had plainly decided not to take, there would still have been a certain crudity in it when, a moment later, he put his errand into words. "I want my little brother to marry her, and I want you to help me bring it about." Then he told me that he knew his brother had already spoken to me, but that he believed I had not promised him much countenance. He wished me to think well of the plan; it would be a delightful marriage.

"Delightful for your brother, yes. That's what strikes me most."

"Delightful for him, certainly; but also very pleasant for Eunice, as things go here. Adrian is the best fellow in the world; he's a gentleman; he has n't a vice or a fault; he is very well educated; and he has twenty thousand a year. A lovely property."

"Not in trust?" I said, looking into Mr. Caliph's extraordinary eyes.

"Oh, no; he has full control of it. But he is wonderfully careful."

"He does n't trouble you with it?"

"Oh, dear, no; why should he? Thank God, I have n't got that on my back. His property comes to him from his father, who had nothing to do with me; did n't even like me, I think. He has capital advisers — presidents of banks, overseers of hospitals, and all that sort of thing. They have put him in the way of some excellent investments."

As I write this, I am surprised at my audacity; but, somehow, it did n't seem so great at the time, and he gave absolutely no sign of seeing more in what I said than appeared. He evidently desires the marriage immensely, and he was thinking only of putting it before me so that I too should think well of it; for evidently, like his brother, he has the most exaggerated opinion of my influence with Eunice. On Mr. Frank's part this does n't surprise me so much; but I confess it seems to me odd that a man of Mr. Caliph's acuteness should make the mistake of taking me for one of those persons who covet influence and like to pull the wires of other people's actions. I have a horror of influence, and should never have consented to come and live with Eunice if I had not seen that she is at bottom much stronger than I, who am not at all strong, in spite of my grand airs. Mr. Caliph, I suppose, cannot conceive of a woman in my dependent position being indifferent to opportunities for working in the dark; but he ought to leave those vulgar imputations to Mrs. Ermine. He ought, with his intelligence, to see one as one is; or do I possibly exaggerate that intelligence? "Do you know I feel as if you were asking me to take part in a conspiracy?" I made that announcement with as little delay as possible.

He stared a moment, and then he said that he did n't in the least repudiate that view of his proposal. He admitted that he was a conspirator — in an excellent cause. All match-making was conspiracy. It was impossible that as a superior woman I should enter into his ideas, and he was sure that I had seen too much of the world to say anything so *banal* as that the young people were not in love with each other. That was only a basis for marriage when better things were lacking. It was decent, it was fitting, that Eunice should be settled in life; his conscience would not be at rest about her until he should see that well arranged. He was not in the least afraid of that word "arrangement;" a marriage was an eminently practical matter, and it could not be too much arranged. He confessed that he took the European view. He thought that a young girl's elders ought to see that she marries in a way in which certain definite proprieties are observed. He was sure of his brother; he knew how faultless Adrian was. He talked for some time, and said a great deal that I had said to myself the other day, after Mr. Frank spoke to me; said, in particular, very much what I had thought, about the beauty of arrangements — that there are far too few among Americans who marry; that we are the people in the world who divorce and separate most; that there would be much less of that sort of thing if young people were helped to choose, if marriages were, as one might say, presented to them. I listened to Mr. Caliph with my best attention, thinking it was odd that, on his lips, certain things which I had phrased to myself in very much the same way should sound so differently. They ought to have sounded better, uttered as they were with the energy, the authority, the lucidity, of a man accustomed to making arguments; but somehow they did n't. I am afraid I am very perverse. I answered — I hardly remember what; but there was a taint of that perversity in it. As he rejoined, I felt that he was growing urgent — very urgent; he has an immense desire that something may be done. I remember saying at last, "What I don't understand is why your brother should wish to marry my cousin. He has told me he is not in love with her. Has your presentation of the idea, as you call it — has that been enough ? Is he acting simply at your request ?"

I saw that his reply was not perfectly ready, and for a moment those strange eyes of his emitted a ray that I had not seen before. They seemed to say, "Are you really taking liberties with me ? Be on your guard ; I may be dangerous." But he always smiles. Yes, I think he is dangerous, though I don't know exactly what he could do to me. I believe he would smile at the hangman, if he were condemned to meet him. He is very angry with his brother for having admitted to me that the sentiment he entertains for Eunice is not a passion ; as if it would have been possible for him, under my eyes, to pretend that he is in love ! I don't think I am afraid of Mr. Caliph ; I don't desire to take liberties with him (as his eyes seemed to call it) or with any one ; but, decidedly, I am not afraid of him. If it came to protecting Eunice, for instance ; to demanding justice — But what extravagances am I writing ? He answered, in a moment, with a good deal of dignity, and even a good deal of reason, that his brother has the greatest admiration for my cousin, that he agrees fully and cordially with everything he (Mr. Caliph) has said to him about its being an excellent match, that he wants very much to marry, and wants to marry as a gentleman should. If he is not in love with Eunice, moreover, he is not in love with any one else.

"I hope not!" I said, with a laugh; whereupon Mr. Caliph got up, looking, for him, rather grave.

"I can't imagine why you should suppose that Adrian is not acting freely. I don't know what you imagine my means of coercion to be."

"I don't imagine anything. I think I only wish he had thought of it himself."

"He would never think of anything that is for his good. He is not in the least interested."

"Well, I don't know that it matters, because I don't think Eunice will see it — as we see it."

"Thank you for saying 'we.' Is she in love with some one else?"

"Not that I know of; but she may expect to be, some day. And better than that, she may expect — very justly — some one to be in love with her."

"Oh, in love with her! How you women talk! You all of you want the moon. If she is not content to be thought of as Adrian thinks of her, she is a very silly girl. What will she have more than tenderness? That boy is all tenderness."

"Perhaps he is too tender," I suggested. "I think he is afraid to ask her."

"Yes, I know he is nervous — at the idea of a refusal. But I should like her to refuse him once."

"It is not of that he is afraid — it is of her accepting him."

Mr. Caliph smiled, as if he thought this very ingenious. "You don't understand him. I'm so sorry! I had an idea that — with your knowledge of human nature, your powers of observation — you would have perceived how he is made. In fact, I rather counted on that." He said this with a little tone of injury which might have made me feel terribly inadequate if it had not been accompanied with a glance that seemed to say that, after all, he was generous and he forgave me. "Adrian's is one of those natures that are inflamed by not succeeding. He does n't give up; he thrives on opposition. If she refuses him three or four times he will adore her!"

"She is sure then to be adored — though I am not sure it will make a difference with her. I have n't yet seen a sign that she cares for him."

"Why then does she go out to drive with him ?" There was nothing brutal in the elation with which Mr. Caliph made this point; still, he looked a little as if he pitied me for exposing myself to a refutation so prompt.

"That proves nothing, I think. I would go to drive with Mr. Frank, if he should ask me, and I should be very much surprised if it were regarded as an intimation that I am ready to marry him."

Mr. Caliph had his hands resting on his thighs, and in this position, bending forward a little, with his smile he said, "Ah, but he does n't want to marry *you* !"

That was a little brutal, I think; but I should have appeared ridiculous if I had attempted to resent it. I simply answered that I had as yet seen no sign even that Eunice is conscious of Mr. Frank's inten-

tions. I think she is, but I don't think so from anything she has said or done. Mr. Caliph maintains
that she is capable of going for six months without
betraying herself, all the while quietly considering
and making up her mind. It is possible he is right —
he has known her longer than I. He is far from
wishing to wait for six months, however; and the part
I must play is to bring matters to a crisis. I told
him that I did n't see why he did not speak to her directly — why he should operate in this roundabout
way. Why should n't he say to her all that he had
said to me — tell her that she would make him very
happy by marrying his little brother ? He answered
that this is impossible, that the nearness of the relationship would make it unbecoming ; it would look
like a kind of nepotism. The thing must appear to
come to pass of itself — and I, somehow, must be the
author of that appearance ! I was too much a woman
of the world, too acquainted with life, not to see the
force of all this. He had a great deal to say about my
being a woman of the world; in one sense it is not all
complimentary ; one would think me some battered
old dowager who had married off fifteen daughters.
I feel that I am far from all that when Mr. Caliph
leaves me so mystified. He has some other reason
for wishing these nuptials than love of the two young
people, but I am unable to put my hand on it.
Like the children at hide-and-seek, however, I think
I "burn." I don't like him, I mistrust him ; but he is
a very charming man. His geniality, his richness, his

magnetism, I suppose I should say, are extraordinary ; he fascinates me, in spite of my suspicions. The truth is, that in his way he is an artist, and in my little way I am also one; and the artist in me recognizes the artist in him, and cannot quite resist the temptation to foregather. What is more than this, the artist in him has recognized the artist in me — it is very good of him — and would like to establish a certain freemasonry. "Let us take together the artistic view of life;" that is simply the meaning of his talking so much about my being a woman of the world. That is all very well; but it seems to me there would be a certain baseness in our being artists together at the expense of poor little Eunice. I should like to know some of Mr. Caliph's secrets, but I don't wish to give him any of mine in return for them. Yet I gave him something before he departed : I hardly know what, and hardly know how he extracted it from me. It was a sort of promise that I would after all speak to Eunice, — "as I should like to have you, you know." He remained there for a quarter of an hour after he got up to go; walking about the room with his hands on his hips; talking, arguing, laughing, holding me with his eyes, his admirable face — as natural, as dramatic, and at the same time as diplomatic, as an Italian. I am pretty sure he was trying to produce a certain effect, to entangle, to magnetize me. Strange to say, Mr. Caliph compromises himself, but he does n't compromise his brother. He has a private reason, but his brother has nothing to do with his privacies. That was my last word to him.

"The moment I feel sure that I may do something for your brother's happiness — your brother's alone — by pleading his cause with Eunice — that moment I will speak to her. But I can do nothing for yours."

In answer to this, Mr. Caliph said something very unexpected. "I wish I had known you five years ago!"

There are many meanings to that; perhaps he would have liked to put me out of the way. But I could take only the polite meaning. "Our acquaintance could never have begun too soon."

"Yes, I should have liked to know you," he went on, "in spite of the fact that you are not kind, that you are not just. Have I asked you to do anything for my happiness? My happiness is nothing. I have nothing to do with happiness. I don't deserve it. It is only for my little brother — and for your charming cousin."

I was obliged to admit that he was right; that he had asked nothing for himself. "But I don't want to do anything for you even by accident!" I said — laughing, of course.

This time he was grave. He stood looking at me a moment, then put out his hand. "Yes, I wish I had known you!"

There was something so expressive in his voice, so handsome in his face, so tender and respectful in his manner, as he said this, that for an instant I was really moved, and I was on the point of saying with feeling, "I wish indeed you had!" But that instinct of which I have already spoken checked me — the sense that somehow, as things stand, there can be no *rapprochement* between Mr. Caliph and me that will not involve a certain sacrifice of Eunice. So I only replied, "You seem to me strange, Mr. Caliph. I must tell you that I don't understand you."

He kept my hand, still looking at me, and went on as if he had not heard me. "I am not happy — I am not wise nor good." Then suddenly, in quite a different tone, "For God's sake, let her marry my brother!"

There was a quick passion in these words which made me say, "If it is so urgent as that, you certainly ought to speak to her. Perhaps she'll do it to oblige you!"

We had walked into the hall together, and the last I saw of him he stood in the open doorway, looking back at me with his smile. "Hang the nepotism! I *will* speak to her!"

Comerville, July 6. A whole month has passed since I have made an entry; but I have a good excuse for this dreadful gap. Since we have been in the country I have found subjects enough and to spare, and I have been painting so hard that my hand, of an evening, has been glad to rest. This place is very lovely, and the Hudson is as beautiful as the Rhine. There are the words, in black and white, over my signature; I can't do more than that. I have said it a dozen times, in answer to as many challenges, and now I record the opinion with all the solemnity I can give it. May it serve for the rest of the summer! This is an excellent old house, of the style that was thought impressive, in this country, forty years ago. It is painted a cheerful slate-color, save for a multitude of pilasters and facings which are picked out in the cleanest and freshest white. It has a kind of clumsy gable or apex, on top; a sort of roofed terrace, below, from which you may descend to a lawn dotted with delightful old trees; and between the two, in the second story, a deep verandah, let into the body of the building, and ornamented with white balustrades, considerably carved, and big blue stone jars. Add to this a multitude of green shutters and striped awnings, and a mass of Virginia creepers and wisterias, and fling over it the lavish light of the American summer, and you have a notion of some of the conditions of our *villeggiatura.* The great condition, of course, is the splendid river lying beneath our rounded headland in vast silvery stretches, and growing almost vague on the opposite shore. It is a country of views; you are always peeping down an avenue, or ascending a mound, or going round a corner, to look at one. They are rather too shining, too high-pitched, for my little purposes; all nature seems glazed with light and varnished with freshness. But I manage to scrape something off. Mrs. Ermine is here, as brilliant as her setting; and so, strange to say, is Adrian Frank. Strange for this reason, that the night before we left town I went into Eunice's room and asked her whether she knew, or rather whether she suspected, what was going on. A sudden impulse came to me ; it seemed to me unnatural that in such a situation I should keep anything from her. I don't want to interfere, but I think I want even less to carry too far my aversion to interference, and without pretending to advise Eunice, it was revealed to me that she ought to know that Mr. Caliph had come to see me on purpose to induce me to work upon her. It was not till after he was gone that it occurred to me he had sent his brother in advance, on purpose to get Eunice out of the way, and that this was the reason the young Adrian would take no refusal. He was really in excellent training. It was a very hot night. Eunice was alone in her room, without a lamp ; the windows were wide open, and the dusk was clarified by the light of the street. She sat there, among things vaguely visible, in a white wrapper, with her fair hair on her shoulders, and I could see her eyes move toward me when I asked her whether she knew that Mr. Frank wished to marry her. I could see her smile, too, as she answered that she knew he thought he did, but also knew he didn't.

"Of course I have only his word for it," I said.

"Has he told you ? "

"Oh, yes, and his brother, too."

"His brother ? " And Eunice slowly got up.

"It 's an idea of Mr. Caliph's as well. Indeed Mr.

Caliph may have been the first. He came here to-day, while you were out, to tell me how much he should like to see it come to pass. He has set his heart upon it, and he wished me to engage to do all in my power to bring it about. Of course I can't do anything, can I ?"

She had sunk into her chair again as I went on; she sat there looking before her, in the dark. Before she answered me she gathered up her thick hair with her hands, twisted it together, and holding it in place, on top of her head, with one hand, tried to fasten a comb into it with the other. I passed behind her to help her; I could see she was agitated. "Oh, no, you can't do anything," she said, after a moment, with a laugh that was not like her usual laughter. "I know all about it; they have told me, of course." Her tone was forced, and I could see that she had not really known all about it — had not known that Mr. Caliph is pushing his brother. I went to the window and looked out a little into the hot, empty street, where the gas-lamps showed me, up and down, the hundred high stoops, exactly alike and as ugly as a bad dream. While I stood there a thought suddenly dropped into my mind, which has lain ever since where it fell. But I don't wish to move it, even to write it here. I stayed with Eunice for ten minutes; I told her everything that Mr. Caliph had said to me. She listened in perfect silence — I could see that she was glad to listen. When I related that he did n't wish to speak to her himself on behalf of his brother, because that would seem indelicate, she broke in, with a certain eagerness, " Yes, that is very natural!"

"And now you can marry Mr. Frank without my help!" I said, when I had done.

She shook her head sadly, though she was smiling again. "It's too late for your help. He has asked me to marry him, and I have told him he can hope for it—never!"

I was surprised to hear he had spoken, and she said nothing about the time or place. It must have been that afternoon, during their drive. I said that I was rather sorry for our poor young friend, he was such a very nice fellow. She agreed that he was remarkably nice, but added that this was not a sufficient reason for her marrying him; and when I said that he would try again, that I had Mr. Caliph's assurance that he would not be easy to get rid of and that a refusal would only make him persist, she answered that he might try as often as he liked, he was so little disagreeable to her that she would take even that from him. And now, to give him a chance to try again, she has asked him down here to stay, thinking apparently that Mrs. Ermine's presence puts us *en règle* with the proprieties. I should add that she assured me there was no real danger of his trying again; he had told her he meant to, but he had said it only for form. Why should he, since he was not in love with her? It was all an idea of his brother's, and she was much obliged to Mr. Caliph, who took his duties much too seriously and was not in the least

bound to provide her with a husband. Mr. Frank
and she had agreed to remain friends, as if nothing
had happened; and I think she then said something
about her intending to ask him to this place. A few
days after we got here, at all events, she told me that
she had written to him, proposing his coming; whereupon I intimated that I thought it a singular overture
to make to a rejected lover whom one did n't wish to
encourage.   He would take it as encouragement, or
at all events Mr. Caliph would. She answered that
she did n't care what Mr. Caliph thinks, and that she
knew Mr. Frank better than I, and knew therefore
that he had absolutely no hope. But she had a
particular reason for wishing him to be here. That
sounded mysterious, and she could n't tell me more;
but in a month or two I would guess her reason. As
she said this she looked at me with a brighter smile
than she has had for weeks; for I protest that she
is troubled — Eunice is greatly troubled. Nearly a
month has elapsed, and I have n't guessed that reason.
Here is Adrian Frank, at any rate, as I say; and I
can't make out whether he persists or renounces.
His manner to Eunice is just the same; he is always
polite and always shy, never inattentive and never unmistakable. He has not said a word more to me about
his suit. Apart from this he is very sympathetic, and
we sit about sketching together in the most frater-
nal manner. He made to me a day or two since a
very pretty remark; viz., that he would rather copy a
sketch of mine than try, himself, to do the place from

nature. This perhaps does not look so *galant* as I repeat it here; but with the tone and glance with which he said it, it really almost touched me. I was glad, by the way, to hear from Eunice the night before we left town that she does n't care what Mr. Caliph thinks; only, I should be gladder still if I believed it. I don't, unfortunately; among other reasons because it does n't at all agree with that idea which descended upon me with a single jump — from heaven knows where — while I looked out of her window at the stoops. I observe with pleasure, however, that he does n't send her any more papers to sign. These days pass softly, quickly, but with a curious, an unnatural, stillness. It is as if there were something in the air — a sort of listening hush. That sounds very fantastic, and I suppose such remarks are only to be justified by my having the artistic temperament — that is, if I have it! If I have n't, there is no excuse; unless it be that Eunice is distinctly uneasy, and that it takes the form of a voluntary, exaggerated calm, of which I feel the contact, the tension. She is as quiet as a mouse and yet as restless as a flame. She is neither well nor happy; she does n't sleep. It is true that I asked Mr. Frank the other day what impression she made on him, and he replied, with a little start, and a smile of alacrity, "Oh, delightful, as usual!" — so that I saw he did n't know what he was talking about. He is tremendously sunburnt, and as red as a tomato. I wish he would look a little less at my daubs and a little more at the woman he wishes to marry. In summer I always suffice to myself, and I am so much interested in my work that if I hope, devoutly, as I do, that nothing is going to happen to Eunice, it is probably quite as much from selfish motives as from others. If anything were to happen to her I should be immensely interrupted. Mrs. Ermine is bored, *par exemple!* She is dying to have a garden-party, at which she can drag a long train over the lawn; but day follows day and this entertainment does not take place. Eunice has promised it, however, for another week, and I believe means to send out invitations immediately. Mrs. Ermine has offered to write them all; she has, after all, *du bon.* But the fatuity of her misunderstandings of everything that surrounds her passes belief. She sees nothing that really occurs, and gazes complacently into the void. Her theory is always that Mr. Caliph is in love with Eunice, — she opened up to me on the subject only yesterday, because with no one else to talk to but the young Adrian, who dodges her, she does n't in the least mind that she hates me, and that I think her a goose — that Mr. Caliph is in love with Eunice, but that Eunice, who is queer enough for anything, does n't like him, so that he has sent down his step-brother to tell stories about the good things he has done, and to win over her mind to a more favorable view. Mrs. Ermine believes in these good things, and appears to think such action on Mr. Caliph's part both politic and dramatic. She has not the smallest suspicion of the real little drama that has been going on under her nose. I wish I had that absence of vision; it would be a great rest. Heaven knows I see more than I want — for instance when I see that my poor little cousin is pinched with pain and yet that I can't relieve her, can't even advise her. I could n't do the former even if I would, and she would n't let me do the latter even if I could. It seems too pitiful, too incredible, that there should be no one to turn to. Surely, if I go up to town for a day next week, as seems probable, I may call upon William Ermine. Whether I *may* or not, I will.

July 11. She has been getting letters, and they have made her worse. Last night I spoke to her — I asked her to come into my room. I told her that I saw she was in distress; that it was terrible to me to see it; that I was sure that she has some miserable secret. Who was making her suffer this way? No one had the right — not even Mr. Caliph, if Mr. Caliph it was, to whom she appeared to have conceded every right. She broke down completely, burst into tears, confessed that she is troubled about money. Mr. Caliph has again requested a delay as to his handing in his accounts, and has told her that she will have no income for another year. She thinks it strange; she is afraid that everything is n't right. She is not afraid of being poor; she holds that it 's vile to concern one's self so much about money. But there is something that breaks her heart in thinking that Mr. Caliph should be in fault. She had always admired him, she had always believed in him, she had always — What it was, in the third place, that she had always done I did n't learn, for at this point she buried her head still deeper in my lap and sobbed for half an hour. Her grief was melting. I was never more troubled, and this in spite of the fact that I was furious at her strange air of acceptance of a probable calamity. She is afraid that everything is n't right, forsooth! I should think it was not, and should think it had n't been for heaven knows how long. This is what has been in the air; this is what was hanging over us. But Eunice is simply amazing. She declines to see a lawyer; declines to hold Mr. Caliph accountable, declines to complain, to inquire, to investigate in any way. I am sick, I am terribly perplexed — I don't know what to do. Her tears dried up in an instant as soon as I made the very obvious remark that the beautiful, the mysterious, the captivating Caliph is no better than a common swindler; and she gave me a look which might have frozen me if when I am angry I were freezable. She took it *de bien haut ;* she intimated to me that if I should ever speak in that way again of Mr. Caliph we must part company forever. She was distressed ; she admitted that she felt injured. I had seen for myself how far that went. But she did n't pretend to judge him. He had been in trouble, — he had told her that ; and his trouble was worse than hers, inasmuch as his honor was at stake, and it had to be saved.

"It 's charming to hear you speak of his honor,"

I cried, quite regardless of the threat she had just uttered. "Where was his honor when he violated the most sacred of trusts ? Where was his honor when he went off with your fortune ? Those are questions, my dear, that the courts will make him answer. He shall make up to you every penny that he has stolen, or my name is not Catherine Condit !"

Eunice gave me another look, which seemed meant to let me know that I had suddenly become in her eyes the most indecent of women; and then she swept out of the room. I immediately sat down and wrote to Mr. Ermine, in order to have my note ready to send up to town at the earliest hour the next morning. I told him that Eunice was in dreadful trouble about her money-matters, and that I believed he would render her a great service, though she herself had no wish to ask it, by coming down to see her at his first convenience. I reflected, of course, as I wrote, that he could do her no good if she should refuse to see him ; but I made up for this by saying to myself that I at least should see him, and that he would do me good. I added in my note that Eunice had been despoiled by those who had charge of her property ; but I did n't mention Mr. Caliph's name. I was just closing my letter when Eunice came into my room again. I saw in a moment that she was different from anything she had ever been before — or at least had ever seemed. Her excitement, her passion, had gone down ; even the traces of her tears had vanished. She was perfectly quiet, but all her softness

had left her. She was as solemn and impersonal as
the priestess of a cult. As soon as her eyes fell upon
my letter, she asked me to be so good as to inform
her to whom I had been writing. I instantly satisfied her, telling her what I had written; and she
asked me to give her the document. "I must let
you know that I shall immediately burn it up," she
added; and she went on to say that if I should send
it to Mr. Ermine she herself would write to him by
the same post that he was to heed nothing I had said.
I tore up my letter, but I announced to Eunice that
I would go up to town and see the person to whom I
had addressed it. "That brings us precisely to what
I came in to say," she answered; and she proceeded
to demand of me a solemn vow that I would never
speak to a living soul of what I had learned in regard
to her affairs. They were her affairs exclusively, and
no business of mine or of any other human being;
and she had a perfect right to ask and to expect this
promise. She has, indeed — more's the pity; but it
was impossible to me to admit just then — indignant
and excited as I was — that I recognized the right.
I did so at last, however, and I made the promise.
It seems strange to me to write it here; but I am
pledged by a tremendous vow, taken in this "intimate" spot, in the small hours of the morning, never
to lift a finger, never to speak a word, to redress any
wrong that Eunice may have received at the hands
of her treacherous trustee, to bring it to the knowledge of others, or to invoke justice, compensation, or

pity. How she extorted this promise from me is more than I can say : she did so by the force of her will, which, as I have already had occasion to note, is far stronger than mine ; and by the vividness of her passion, which is none the less intense because it burns inward and makes her heart glow while her face remains as clear as an angel's. She seated herself with folded hands, and declared she would n't leave the room until I had satisfied her. She is in a state of extraordinary exaltation, and from her own point of view she was eloquent enough. She returned again and again to the fact that she did not judge Mr. Caliph ; that what he may have done is between herself and him alone ; and that if she had not been betrayed to speaking of it to me in the first shock of finding that certain allowances would have to be made for him, no one need ever have suspected it. She was now perfectly ready to make those allowances. She was unspeakably sorry for Mr. Caliph. He had been in urgent need of money, and he had used hers : pray, whose else would I have wished him to use ? Her money had been an insupportable bore to him from the day it was thrust into his hands. To make him her trustee had been in the worst possible taste ; he was not the sort of person to make a convenience of, and it had been odious to take advantage of his good nature. She had always been ashamed of owing him so much. He had been perfect in all his relations with her, though he must have hated her and her wretched little investments

from the first. If she had lost money, it was not his fault; he had lost a great deal more for himself than he had lost for her. He was the kindest, the most delightful, the most interesting of men. Eunice brought out all this with pure defiance; she had never treated herself before to the luxury of saying it, and it was singular to think that she found her first pretext, her first boldness, in the fact that he had ruined her. All this looks almost grotesque as I write it here; but she imposed it upon me last night with all the authority of her passionate little person. I agreed, as I say, that the matter was none of my business; that is now definite enough. Two other things are equally so. One is that she is to be plucked like a chicken; the other is that she is in love with the precious Caliph, and has been so for years! I did n't dare to write that the other night, after the beautiful idea had suddenly flowered in my mind; but I don't care what I write now. I am so horribly tongue-tied that I must at least relieve myself here. Of course I wonder now that I never guessed her secret before; especially as I was perpetually hovering on the edge of it. It explains many things, and it is very terrible. In love with a pick-pocket! *Merci!* I am glad fate has n't played me that trick.

July 14. I can't get over the idea that he is to go scot-free. I grind my teeth over it as I sit at work, and I find myself using the most livid, the most brilliant colors. I have had another talk with

Eunice, but I don't in the least know what she is to live on. She says she has always her father's property, and that this will be abundant; but that of course she cannot pretend to live as she has lived hitherto. She will have to go abroad again and economize; and she will probably have to sell this place — that is, if she can. "If she can" of course means, if there is anything to sell; if it isn't devoured with mortgages. What I want to know is, whether Justice, in such a case as this, will not step in, notwithstanding the silence of the victim. If I could only give her a hint — the angel of the scales and sword — in spite of my detestable promise! I can't find out about Mr. Caliph's impunity, as it is impossible for me to allude to the matter to any one who would be able to tell me. Yes, the more I think of it the more reason I see to rejoice that fate has n't played me that trick of making me fall in love with a pickpocket! Suffering keener than my poor little cousin's I cannot possibly imagine, or a power of self-sacrifice more awful. Fancy the situation, when the only thing one can do for the man one loves, is to forgive him for thieving! What a delicate attention, what a touching proof of tenderness! This Eunice can do; she has waited all these years to do something. I hope she is pleased with her opportunity. And yet when I say she has forgiven him for thieving, I lose myself in the mystery of her exquisite spirit. Who knows what it is she has forgiven — does she even know herself? She consents to being injured, despoiled,

have invited a thousand people.   I can't imagine who
they all are.   It is an extraordinary time for Eunice
to be giving a party — the day after she discovers
that she is penniless ; but of course it is n't Eunice,
it 's Mrs. Ermine.   I said to her yesterday that if she
was to change her mode of life — simple enough
already, poor thing — she had better begin at once;
and that her garden-party under Mrs. Ermine's
direction would cost her a thousand dollars.   She
answered that she must go on, since it had already
been talked about; she wished no one to know anything — to suspect anything.   This would be her
last extravagance, her farewell to society.   If such
resources were open to us poor heretics, I should
suppose she meant to go into a convent.   She exasperates me too — every one exasperates me.   It is
some satisfaction, however, to feel that my exaspera-
tion clears up my mind.   It is Caliph who is "sold,"
after all.   He would not have invented this alliance
for his brother if he had known — if he had faintly
suspected — that Eunice was in love with him, inasmuch as in this case he had assured impunity.
Fancy his not knowing it — the idiot!

July 10. They are still directing cards, and Mrs.
Ermine has taken the whole thing on her shoulders.   She has invited people that Eunice has never
heard of — a pretty rabble she will have made of it!
She has ordered a band of music from New York,
and a new dress for the occasion — something in the
last degree *champêtre.*   Eunice is perfectly indifferent

to what she does; I have discovered that she is thinking only of one thing. Mr. Caliph is coming, and the
bliss of that idea fills her mind. The more people
the better; she will not have the air of making petty
economies to afflict him with the sight of what he
has reduced her to!

"This is the way Eunice ought to live," Mrs. Ermine said to me this afternoon, rubbing her hands,
after the last invitation had departed. When I say
the last, I mean the last till she had remembered
another that was highly important, and had floated
back into the library to scribble it off. She writes a
regular invitation-hand — a vague, sloping, silly hand,
that looks as if it had done nothing all its days but
write, " Mr. and Mrs. Ermine request the pleasure ; "
or, " Mr. and Mrs. Ermine are delighted to accept."
She told me that she knew Eunice far better than
Eunice knew herself, and that her line in life was
evidently to " receive." No one better than she would
stand in a doorway and put out her hand with a smile ;
no one would be a more gracious and affable hostess,
or make a more generous use of an ample fortune.
She is really very trying, Mrs. Ermine, with her ample
fortune ; she is like a clock striking impossible hours.
I think she must have engaged a special train for her
guests — a train to pick up people up and down the
river. Adrian Frank went to town to-day; he comes
back on the 23d, and the festival takes place the next
day. The festival, — Heaven help us! Eunice is evidently going to be ill; it 's as much as I can do to

keep from adding that it serves her right ! It 's a
great relief to me that Mr. Frank has gone; this has
ceased to be a place for him.   It is ever so long since
he has said anything to me about his " prospects."
They are charming, his prospects !

July 26.   The garden-party has taken place, and
a great deal more besides.   I have been too agitated,
too fatigued and bewildered, to write anything here;
but I can't sleep to-night — I 'm too nervous — and
it is better to sit and scribble than to toss about.
I may as well say at once that the party was very
pretty — Mrs. Ermine may have that credit.   The
day was lovely; the lawn was in capital order; the
music was good, and the *buffet* apparently inexhaust-
ible.   There was an immense number of people;
some of them had come even from Albany — many
of them strangers to Eunice, and protegés only of
Mrs. Ermine; but they dispersed themselves on the
grounds, and I have not heard as yet that they stole
the spoons or plucked up the plants.   Mrs. Ermine,
who was exceedingly *champêtre* — white muslin and
corn-flowers — told me that Eunice was " receiving
adorably;" was in her native element.   She evidently inspired great curiosity; that was why every
one had come.   I don't mean because every one sus-
pects her situation, but because as yet, since her return, she has been little seen and known, and is
supposed to be a distinguished figure — clever, beautiful, rich, and a *parti*.   I think she satisfied every
one; she was voted most interesting, and except that

she was deadly pale, she was prettier than any one
else. Adrian Frank did not come back on the 23d,
and did not arrive for the festival. So much I note
without as yet understanding it. His absence from
the garden-party, after all his exertions under the
orders of Mrs. Ermine, is in need of an explanation.
Mr. Caliph could give none, for Mr. Caliph was there.
He professed surprise at not finding his brother; said
he had not seen him in town, that he had no idea
what had become of him. This is probably perfectly
false. I am bound to believe that everything he says
and does is false; and I have no doubt that they met
in New York, and that Adrian told him his reason —
whatever it was — for not coming back. I don't
know how to relate what took place between Mr.
Caliph and me; we had an extraordinary scene, — a
scene that gave my nerves the shaking from which
they have not recovered. He is truly a most amazing personage. He is altogether beyond me; I don't
pretend to fathom him. To say that he has no moral
sense is nothing. I have seen other people who have
had no moral sense; but I have seen no one with
that impudence, that cynicism, that remorseless cruelty. We had a tremendous encounter; I thank
heaven that strength was given me! When I found
myself face to face with him, and it came over me
that, blooming there in his diabolical assurance, it
was he — he with his smiles, his bows, his gorgeous
bontonnière, the wonderful air he has of being anointed
and gilded — he that had ruined my poor Eunice,

who grew whiter than ever as he approached: when I felt all this my blood began to tingle, and if I were only a handsome woman I might believe that my eyes shone like those of an avenging angel. He was as fresh as a day in June, enormous, and more than ever like Haroun-al-Raschid. I asked him to take a walk with me; and just for an instant, before accepting, he looked at me, as the French say, in the white of the eyes. But he pretended to be delighted, and we strolled away together to the path that leads down to the river. It was difficult to get away from the people — they were all over the place; but I made him go so far that at the end of ten minutes we were virtually alone together. It was delicious to see how he hated it. It was then that I asked him what had become of his step-brother, and that he professed, as I have said, the utmost ignorance of Adrian's whereabouts. I hated him; it was odious to me to be so close to him; yet I could have endured this for hours in order to make him feel that I despised him. To make him feel it without saying it — there was an inspiration in that idea; but it is very possible that it made me look more like a demon than like the angel I just mentioned. I told him in a moment, abruptly, that his step-brother would do well to remain away altogether in future; it was a farce his pretending to make my cousin reconsider her answer.

"Why, then, did she ask him to come down here?" He launched this inquiry with confidence.

"Because she thought it would be pleasant to have a man in the house; and Mr. Frank is such a harmless, discreet, accommodating one."

"Why, then, do you object to his coming back?"

He had made me contradict myself a little, and of course he enjoyed that. I was confused — confused by my agitation; and I made the matter worse. I was furious that Eunice had made me promise not to speak, and my anger blinded me, as great anger always does, save in organizations as fine as Mr. Caliph's.

"Because Eunice is in no condition to have company. She is very ill; you can see for yourself."

"Very ill? with a garden-party and a band of music! Why, then, did she invite us all?"

"Because she is a little crazy, I think."

"You are very consistent!" he cried with a laugh. "I know people who think every one crazy but themselves. I have had occasion to talk business with her several times of late, and I find her mind as clear as a bell."

"I wonder if you will allow me to say that you talk business too much? Let me give you a word of advice: wind up her affairs at once without any more procrastination, and place them in her own hands. She is very nervous; she knows this ought to have been done already. I recommend you strongly to make an end of the matter."

I had no idea I could be so insolent, even in conversation with a swindler. I confess I did n't do it so well as I might, for my voice trembled perceptibly in the midst of my efforts to be calm. He had picked up two or three stones and was tossing them into the river, making them skim the surface for a long distance. He held one poised a moment, turning his eye askance on me; then he let it fly, and it danced for a hundred yards. I wondered whether in what I had just said I broke my vow to Eunice; and it seemed to me that I did n't, inasmuch as I appeared to assume that no irreparable wrong had been done her.

"Do you wish yourself to get control of her property?" Mr. Caliph inquired, after he had made his stone skim. It was magnificently said, far better than anything I could do; and I think I answered it — though it made my heart beat fast — almost with a smile of applause.

"Are n't you afraid?" I asked in a moment, very gently.

"Afraid of what, — of you?"

"Afraid of justice — of Eunice's friends?"

"That means you, of course. Yes, I am very much afraid. When was a man not, in the presence of a clever woman?"

"I am clever; but I am not clever enough. If I were, you should have no doubt of it."

He folded his arms as he stood there before me, looking at me in that way I have mentioned more than once — like a genial Mephistopheles. "I must repeat what I have already told you, that I wish I had known you ten years ago!"

" How you must hate me to say that ! " I exclaimed. "That's some comfort, just a little — your hating me."

" I can't tell you how it makes me feel to see you so indiscreet," he went on, as if he had not heard me. "Ah, my dear lady, don't meddle — a woman like you !   Think of the bad taste of it."

" It's bad if you like ; but yours is far worse."

" Mine !   What do you know about mine ?   What do you know about me ?   See how superficial it makes you."   He paused a moment, smiling almost compassionately ; and then he said, with an abrupt change of tone and manner, as if our conversation wearied him and he wished to sum up and return to the house, " See that she marries Adrian ; that's all you have to do ! "

" That's a beautiful idea of yours !   You know you don't believe in it yourself ! " . These words broke from me as he turned away, and we ascended the hill together.

" It's the only thing I believe in," he answered, very gravely.

" What a pity for you that your brother does n't !   For he does n't — I persist in that ! "   I said this because it seemed to me just then to be the thing I could think of that would exasperate him most.   The event proved I was right.

He stopped short in the path — gave me a very bad look.   " Do you want him for yourself ?   Have *you* been making love to him ? "

"Ah, Mr. Caliph, for a man who talks about taste ! " I answered.

" Taste be damned ! " cried Mr. Caliph, as we went on again.

" That's quite my idea ! " He broke into an unexpected laugh, as if I had said something very amusing, and we proceeded in silence to the top of the hill. Then I suddenly said to him, as we emerged upon the lawn, " Are n't you really a little afraid ? "

He stopped again, looking toward the house and at the brilliant groups with which the lawn was covered. We had lost the music, but we began to hear it again. "Afraid ? of course I am ! I 'm immensely afraid. It comes over me in such a scene as this. But I don't see what good it does you to know."

" It makes me rather happy." That was a fib ; for it did n't, somehow, when he looked and talked in that way. He has an absolutely bottomless power of mockery ; and really, absurd as it appears, for that instant I had a feeling that it was quite magnanimous of him not to let me know what he thought of my idiotic attempt to frighten him. He feels strong and safe somehow, somewhere ; but I can't discover why he should, inasmuch as he certainly does n't know Eunice's secret, and it is only her state of mind that gives him impunity. He believes her to be merely credulous ; convinced by his specious arguments that everything will be right in a few months ; a little nervous, possibly — to justify my account of her — but for the present, at least, completely at his mercy. The present, of course, is only what now concerns him; for the future he has invented Adrian Frank. How he clings to this invention was proved by the last words he said to me before we separated on the lawn; they almost indicate that he has a conscience, and this is so extraordinary —

"She must marry Adrian! She must marry Adrian!"

With this he turned away and went to talk to various people whom he knew. He talked to every one; diffused his genial influence all over the place, and contributed greatly to the brilliancy of the occasion. I had n't therefore the comfort of feeling that Mrs. Ermine was more of a waterspout than usual, when she said to me afterwards that Mr. Caliph was a man to adore, and that the party would have been quite "ordinary" without him. " I mean in comparison, you know." And then she said to me suddenly, with her blank impertinence: "Why don't you set your cap at him? I should think you would!"

"Is it possible you have not observed my frantic efforts to captivate him?" I answered. "Did n't you notice how I drew him away and made him walk with me by the river? It's too soon to say, but I really think I am gaining ground." For so mild a pleasure it really pays to mystify Mrs. Ermine! I kept away from Eunice till almost every one had gone. I knew that she would look at me in a certain way, and I did n't wish to meet her eyes. I have a bad conscience, for turn it as I would I *had* broken my vow. Mr. Caliph went away without my meeting him again; but I saw that half an hour before he left he strolled to a distance with Eunice. I instantly guessed what his business was; he had made up his mind to present to her directly, and in person, the question of her marrying his step-brother. What a happy inspiration, and what a well-selected occasion! When she came back I saw that she had been crying, though I imagine no one else did. I know the signs of her tears, even when she has checked them as quickly as she must have done to-day. Whatever it was that had passed between them, it diverted her from looking at me, when we were alone together, in that way I was afraid of. Mrs. Ermine is prolific; there is no end to the images that succeed each other in her mind. Late in the evening, after the last carriage had rolled away, we went up the staircase together, and at the top she detained me a moment.

"I have been thinking it over, and I am afraid that there is no chance for you. I have reason to believe that he proposed to-day to Eunice!"

August 19. Eunice is very ill, as I was sure she would be, after the effort of her horrible festival. She kept going for three days more; then she broke down completely, and for a week now she has been in bed. I have had no time to write, for I have been constantly with her in alternation with Mrs. Ermine. Mrs. Ermine was about to leave us after the garden-party, but when Eunice gave up she announced that she would stay and take care of her. Eunice tells me that she is a good nurse, except that she talks too much, and of course she gives me a chance to rest. Eunice's condition is strange ; she has no fever, but her life seems to have ebbed away. She lies with her eyes shut, perfectly conscious, answering when she is spoken to, but immersed in absolute rest. It is as if she had had some terrible strain or fatigue, and wished to steep herself in oblivion. I am not anxious about her — am much less frightened than Mrs. Ermine or the doctor, to whom she is apparently dying of weakness. I tell the doctor I understand her condition — I have seen her so before. It will last probably a month, and then she will slowly pull herself together. The poor man accepts this theory for want of a better, and evidently depends upon me to see her through, as he says. Mrs. Ermine wishes to send for one of the great men from New York, but I have opposed this idea, and shall continue to oppose it. There is (to my mind) a kind of cruelty in exhibiting the poor girl to more people than are absolutely necessary. The dullest of them would see that she is in love. The seat of her illness is in her mind, in her soul, and no rude hands must touch her there. She herself has protested — she has murmured a prayer that she may be forced to see no one else. " I only want to be left alone — to be left alone." So we leave her alone — that is, we simply watch and wait. She will recover — people don't die of these things ; she will live to suffer —

to suffer always. I am tired to-night, but Mrs. Ermine is with her, and I shall not be wanted till morning; therefore, before I lie down, I will repair in these remarkable pages a serious omission. I scarcely know why I should have written all this, except that the history of things interests me, and I find that it is even a greater pleasure to write it than to read it. If what I have committed to this little book hitherto has not been profitless, I must make a note of an incident which I think more curious than any of the scenes I have described.

Adrian Frank reappeared the day after the garden-party — late in the afternoon, while I sat in the verandah and watched the sunset, and Eunice strolled down to the river with Mrs. Ermine. I had heard no sound of wheels, and there was no evidence of a vehicle or of luggage. He had not come through the house, but walked round it from the front, having apparently been told by one of the servants that we were in the grounds. On seeing me he stopped, hesitated a moment, then came up to the steps, shook hands in silence, seated himself near me and looked at me through the dusk. This was all tolerably mysterious, and it was even more so after he had explained a little. I told him that he was a " day after the fair ; " that he had been considerably missed, and even that he was slightly wanting in respect to Eunice. Since he had absented himself from her party, it was not quite delicate to assume that she was ready to receive him at his own time. I don't know what made me so truculent — as if there were any danger of his having really not considered us, or his lacking a good reason. It was simply, I think, that my talk with Mr. Caliph the evening before had made me so much bad blood, and left me in a savage mood. Mr. Frank answered that he had not stayed away by accident — he had stayed away on purpose; he had been for several days at Saratoga, and on returning to Cornerville had taken quarters at the inn in the village. He had no intention of presuming further on Eunice's hospitality, and had walked over from the hotel simply to bid us good-evening and give an account of himself.

"My dear Mr. Frank, your account is not clear!" I said, laughing. "What in the world were you doing at Saratoga?" I must add that his humility had completely disarmed me; I was ashamed of the brutality with which I had received him, and convinced afresh that he was the best fellow in the world.

"What was I doing at Saratoga? I was trying hard to forget you!"

This was Mr. Frank's rejoinder; and I give it exactly as he uttered it; or rather not exactly, inasmuch as I cannot give the tone — the quick, startling tremor of his voice. But those are the words with which he answered my superficially-intended question. I saw in a moment that he meant a great deal by them — I became aware that we were suddenly in deep waters; that *he* was, at least, and that he was trying to draw me into the stream. My surprise was immense, complete ; I had absolutely not suspected what he went on to say to me. He said many things — but I need n't write them here. It is not in detail that I see the propriety of narrating this incident ; I suppose a woman may be trusted to remember the form of such assurances. Let me simply say that the poor dear young man has an idea that he wants to marry me. For a moment, —just a moment — I thought he was jesting ; then I saw, in the twilight, that he was pale with seriousness. He is perfectly sincere. It is strange, but it is real, and, moreover, it is his own affair. For myself, when I have said I was amazed, I have said everything ; *en tête-à-tête* with myself I need n't blush and protest. I was not in the least annoyed or alarmed ; I was filled with kindness and consideration, and I was extremely interested. He talked to me for a quarter of an hour ; it seemed a very long time. I asked him to go away; not to wait till Eunice and Mrs. Ermine should come back. Of course I refused him, by the way.

It was the last thing I was expecting at this time of day, and it gave me a great deal to think of. I lay awake that night; I found I was more agitated than I supposed, and all sorts of visions came and went in my head. I shall not marry the young Adrian : I am bound to say that vision was not one of them ; but as I thought over what he had said to me it became more clear, more conceivable. I began now to be a little surprised at my surprise. It appears that I have had the honor to please him from the first; when he began to come to see us it was not for Eunice, it was for me. He made a general confession on this subject. He was afraid of me; he thought me proud, sarcastic, cold, a hundred horrid things; it did n't seem to him possible that we should ever be on a footing of familiarity which would enable him to propose to me. He regarded me, in short, as unattainable, out of the question, and made up his mind to admire me forever in silence. (In plain English, I suppose, he thought I was too old, and he has simply got used to the difference in our years.) But he wished to be near me, to see me, and hear me (I am really writing more details than seem worth while); so that when his step-brother recommended him to try and marry Eunice, he jumped at the opportunity to make good his place. This situation reconciled everything. He could oblige his brother, he could pay a high compliment to my cousin, and he could see me every day or two. He was convinced from the first that he was in no danger; he was morally sure that Eunice would never smile upon his suit. He did n't know why, and he does n't know why yet; it was only an instinct. That suit was avowedly perfunctory; still the young Adrian has been a great comedian. He assured me that if he had proved to be wrong, and Eunice had suddenly accepted him, he would have gone with her to the altar and made her an excellent husband; for he would have acquired in this manner the certainty of seeing for the rest of his life a great deal of me ! To think of one's possessing, all unexpected, this miraculous influence ! When he came down here, after Eunice had refused him, it was simply for the pleasure of living in the house with me ; from that moment there was no comedy — everything was clear and comfortable betwixt him and Eunice. I asked him if he meant by this that she knew of the sentiments he entertained for her companion, and he answered that he had never breathed a word on this subject, and flattered himself that he had kept the thing dark. He had no reason to believe that she guessed his motives, and I may add that I have none either ; they are altogether too extraordinary ! As I have said, it was simply time, and the privilege of seeing more of me, that had dispelled his hesitation. I did n't reason with him, and though once I was fairly enlightened I gave him the most respectful attention, I did n't appear to consider his request too seriously. But I *did* touch upon the fact that I am five or six years older than he : I suppose I need n't mention that it was not in a spirit of coquetry. His rejoinder was very gallant; but it belongs to the class of details. He is really in love, — heaven forgive him ! but I shall not marry him. How strange are the passions of men !

I saw Mr. Frank the next day; I had given him leave to come back at noon. He joined me in the grounds, where as usual I had set up my easel. I left it to his discretion to call first at the house and explain both his absence and his presence to Eunice and Mrs. Ermine — the latter especially — ignorant as yet of his visit the night before, of which I had not spoken to them. He sat down beside me on a garden-chair and watched me as I went on with my work. For half an hour very few words passed between us; I felt that he was happy to sit there, to be near me, to see me — strange as it seems! and for myself there was a certain sweetness in knowing it, though it was the sweetness of charity, not of elation or triumph. He must have seen I was only pretending to paint — if he followed my brush, which I suppose he did n't. My mind was full of a determination I had arrived at after many waverings in the hours of the night. It had come to me toward morning as a kind of inspiration. I could never marry him, but was there not some way in which I could utilize his devotion? At the present moment, only forty-eight hours later, it seems strange, unreal, almost grotesque; but for ten minutes I thought I saw the light. As we sat there under the great trees, in the stillness of the noon, I suddenly turned and said to him —

"I thank you for everything you have told me; it gives me very nearly all the pleasure you could wish. I believe in you; I accept every assurance of your devotion. I think that devotion is capable of going very far; and I am going to put it to a tremendous test, one of the greatest, probably, to which a man was ever subjected."

He stared, leaning forward, with his hands on his knees. "Any test — any test — " he murmured.

"Don't give up Eunice, then; make another trial; I wish her to marry you!"

My words may have sounded like an atrocious joke, but they represented for me a great deal of hope and cheer. They brought a deep blush into Adrian Frank's face; he winced a little, as if he had been struck by a hand whose blow he could not return, and the tears suddenly started to his eyes. "Oh, Miss Condit!" he exclaimed.

What I saw before me was bright and definite; his distress seemed to me no obstacle, and I went on with a serenity of which I longed to make him perceive the underlying support. " Of course what I say seems to you like a deliberate insult; but nothing would induce me to give you pain if it were possible to spare you. But it is n't possible, my dear friend; it is n't possible. There is pain for you in the best thing I can say to you; there are situations in life in which we can only accept our pain. I can never marry you; I shall never marry any one. I am an old maid, and how can an old maid have a husband? I will be your friend, your sister, your brother, your mother, but I will never be your wife. I should like immensely to be your brother; for I don't like the brother you have got, and I think you deserve a better one. I believe, as I tell you, in everything you have said to me — in your affection, your tenderness, your honesty, the full consideration you have given

to the whole matter. I am happier and richer for
knowing it all ; and I can assure you that it gives
something to life which life did n't have before.   We
shall be good friends, dear friends, always, whatever
happens.   But I can't be your wife — I want you
for some one else.   You will say I have changed —
that I ought to have spoken in this way three months
ago.   But I have n't changed — it is circumstances
that have changed.   I see reasons for your marrying
my cousin that I did n't see then.   I can't say that
she will listen to you now, any more than she did
then ; I don't speak of her ; I speak only of you and of
myself.   I wish you to make another attempt ; and I
wish you to make it, this time, with my full confidence and support.   Moreover, I attach a condition to
it, — a condition I will tell you presently.   Do you
think me slightly demented, malignantly perverse,
atrociously cruel ?   If you could see the bottom of my
heart you would find something there which, I think,
would almost give you joy.   To ask you to do something you don't want to do as a substitute for something you desire, and to attach to the hard achieve-
ment a condition which will require a good deal of
thinking of and will certainly make it harder — you
may well believe I have some extraordinary reason
for taking such a line as this.   For remember, to
begin with, that I can never marry you."

"Never — never — never ? "

"Never, never, never."

"And what is your extraordinary reason ? "

"Simply that I wish Eunice to have your protection, your kindness, your fortune."

" My fortune ? "

" She has lost her own.   She will be poor."

" Pray, how has she lost it ? " the poor fellow asked, beginning to frown, and more and more bewildered.

" I can't tell you that, and you must never ask. But the fact is certain.   The greater part of her property has gone ; she has known it for some little time."

" For some little time ? Why, she never showed any change."

" You never saw it, that was all ! You were thinking of me," and I believe I accompanied this remark with a smile — a smile which was most inconsiderate, for it could only mystify him more.

I think at first he scarcely believed me.   " What a singular time to choose to give a large party ! " he exclaimed, looking at me with eyes quite unlike his old — or rather his young — ones; eyes that, instead of overlooking half the things before them (which was their former habit), tried to see a great deal more in my face, in my words, than was visible on the surface. I don't know what poor Adrian Frank saw — I shall never know all that he saw.

" I agree with you that it was a very singular time," I said.   " You don't understand me — you can't — I don't expect you to ; " I went on.   " That is what I mean by devotion, and that is the kind of appeal I make to you : to take me on trust, to act in the dark, to do something simply because I wish it."

He looked at me as if he would fathom the depths of my soul, and my soul had never seemed to myself so deep. " To marry your cousin, — that 's all ? " he said, with a strange little laugh.

" Oh, no, it 's not all : to be very kind to her as well."

" To give her plenty of money, above all ? "

" You make me feel very ridiculous ; but I should not make this request of you if you had not a fortune."

" She can have my money without marrying me."

" That 's absurd.   How could she take your money ? "

" How, then, can she take me ? "

" That 's exactly what I wish to see.   I told you with my own lips, weeks ago, that she would only marry a man she should love ; and I may seem to contradict myself in taking up now a supposition so different.   But, as I tell you, everything has changed."

" You think her capable, in other words, of marrying for money."

" For money ?   Is your money all there is of you ? Is there a better fellow than you — is there a more perfect gentleman ? "

He turned away his face at this, leaned it in his hands, and groaned.   I pitied him, but I wonder now that I should n't have pitied him more ; that my pity should not have checked me.   But I was too full of my idea. "It 's like a fate," he murmured ; "first my brother, and then you. I can't understand."

"Yes, I know your brother wants it—wants it now more than ever. But I don't care what your brother wants; and my idea is entirely independent of his. I have not the least conviction that you will succeed at first any better than you have done already. But it may be only a question of time, if you will wait and watch, and let me help you. You know you asked me to help you before, and then I would n't. But I repeat it again and again, at present everything is changed. Let me wait with you, let me watch with you. If you succeed, you will be very dear to me ; if you fail, you will be still more so. You see it 's an act of devotion, if there ever was one. I am quite aware that I ask of you something unprecedented and extraordinary. Oh, it may easily be too much for you. I can only put it before you — that 's all ; and as I say, I can help you. You will both be my children — I shall be near you always. If you can't marry me, perhaps you will make up your mind that this is the next best thing. You know you said that last night, yourself."

He had begun to listen to me a little, as if he were being persuaded. "Of course, I should let her know that I love you."

"She is capable of saying that you can't love me more than she does."

"I don't believe she is capable of saying any such folly. But we shall see."

"Yes; but not to-day, not to-morrow. Not at all for the present. You must wait a great many months."

"I will wait as long as you please."

"And you must n't say a word to me of the kind you said last night."

"Is that your condition ?"

"Oh, no; my condition is a very different matter, and very difficult. It will probably spoil everything."

"Please, then, let me hear it at once."

"It is very hard for me to mention it; you must give me time." I turned back to my little easel and began to daub again; but I think my hand trembled, for my heart was beating fast. There was a silence of many moments; I could n't make up my mind to speak.

"How in the world has she lost her money ?" Mr. Frank asked, abruptly, as if the question had just come into his mind. "Has n't my brother the charge of her affairs ?"

"Mr. Caliph is her trustee. I can't tell you how the losses have occurred."

He got up quickly. "Do you mean that they have occurred through *him ?*"

I looked up at him, and there was something in his face which made me leave my work and rise also. "I will tell you my condition now," I said. "It is that you should ask no questions — not one!" This was not what I had had in my mind; but I had not courage for more, and this had to serve.

He had turned very pale, and I laid my hand on his arm, while he looked at me as if he wished to wrest my secret out of my eyes. My secret, I call it, by courtesy; God knows I had come terribly near telling it. God will forgive me, but Eunice probably will not. Had I broken my vow, or had I kept it? I asked myself this, and the answer, so far as I read it in Mr. Frank's eyes, was not reassuring. I dreaded his next question; but when it came it was not what I had expected. Something violent took place in his own mind — something I could n't follow.

"If I do what you ask me, what will be my reward?"

"You will make me very happy."

"And what shall I make your cousin? — God help us!"

"Less wretched than she is to-day."

"Is she 'wretched'?" he asked, frowning as he did before — a most distressing change in his fair countenance.

"Ah, when I think that I have to tell you that — that you have never noticed it — I despair!" I exclaimed with a laugh.

I had laid my hand on his arm, and he placed his right hand upon it, holding it there. He kept it a moment in his grasp, and then he said, "Don't despair!"

"Promise me to wait," I answered. "Everything is in your waiting."

"I promise you!" After which he asked me to

kiss him, and I did so, on the lips. It was as if he were starting on a journey — leaving me for a long time.

"Will you come when I send for you ?" I asked.

"I adore you!" he said; and he turned quickly away, to leave the place without going near the house. I watched him, and in a moment he was gone. He has not reappeared; and when I found, at lunch, that neither Eunice nor Mrs. Ermine alluded to his visit, I determined to keep the matter to myself. I said nothing about it, and up to the moment Eunice was taken ill — the next evening — he was not mentioned between us. I believe Mrs. Ermine more than once gave herself up to wonder as to his whereabouts, and declared that he had not the perfect manners of his step-brother, who was a religious observer of the *convenances;* but I think I managed to listen without confusion. Nevertheless, I had a bad conscience, and I have it still. It throbs a good deal as I sit there with Eunice in her darkened room. I *have* given her away; I *have* broken my vow. But what I wrote above is not true; she *will* forgive me! I sat at my easel for an hour after Mr. Frank left me, and then suddenly I found that I had cured myself of my folly by giving it out. It was the result of a sudden passion of desire to do something for Eunice. Passion is blind, and when I opened my eyes I saw ten thousand difficulties; that is, I saw one, which contained all the rest. That evening I wrote to Mr. Frank, to his New York address, to tell him that I had had a fit of madness, and that it had passed away;

but that I was sorry to say it was not any more possible for me to marry him. I have had no answer to this letter; but what answer can he make to that last declaration? He will continue to adore me. How strange are the passions of men!

New York, November 20. I have been silent for three months, for good reasons. Eunice was ill for many weeks, but there was never a moment when I was really alarmed about her; I knew she would recover. In the last days of October she was strong enough to be brought up to town, where she had business to transact, and now she is almost herself again. I say almost, advisedly; for she will never be herself, — her old, sweet, trustful self, as far as I am concerned. She has simply not forgiven me! Strange things have happened — things that I did n't dare to consider too closely, lest I should not forgive myself. Eunice is in complete possession of her property! Mr. Caliph has made over to her everything — everything that had passed away; everything of which, three months ago, he could give no account whatever. He was with her in the country for a long day before we came up to town (during which I took care not to meet her), and after our return he was in and out of this house repeatedly. I once asked Eunice what he had to say to her, and she answered that he was "explaining." A day or two later she told me that he had given a complete account of her affairs; everything was in order; she had been wrong in what she told me before. Beyond this little statement, however, she did no further penance for the impression she had given of Mr. Caliph's earlier conduct. She does n't yet know what to think; she only feels that if she has recovered her property there has been some interference; and she traces, or at least imputes, such interference to me. If I have interfered, I have broken my vow; and for this, as I say, the gentle creature can't forgive me. If the passions of men are strange, the passions of women are stranger still! It was sweeter for her to suffer at Mr. Caliph's hands than to receive her simple dues from them. She looks at me askance, and her coldness shows through a conscientious effort not to let me see the change in her feeling. Then she is puzzled and mystified; she can't tell what has happened, or how and why it has happened. She has waked up from her illness into a different world — a world in which Mr. Caliph's accounts were correct after all; in which, with the washing away of his stains, the color has been quite washed out of his rich physiognomy. She vaguely feels that a sacrifice, a great effort of some kind, has been made for her, whereas her plan of life was to make the sacrifices and efforts herself. Yet she asks me no questions; the property is her right, after all, and I think there are certain things she is afraid to know. But I am more afraid than she, for it comes over me that a great sacrifice has indeed been made. I have not seen Adrian Frank since he parted from me under the trees three months ago. He has gone to Europe, and the day before he left I got a note from him.   It contained only these words: "When you send for me I will come.   I am waiting, as you told me."   It is my belief that up to the moment I spoke of Eunice's loss of money and requested him to ask no questions, he had not definitely suspected his noble kinsman, but that my words kindled a train that lay all ready.   He went away then to his shame, to the intolerable weight of it, and to heaven knows what sickening explanations with his step-brother!   That gentleman has a still more brilliant bloom; he looks to my mind exactly as people look who have accepted a sacrifice; and he has n't had another word to say about Eunice's marrying Mr. Adrian Frank.   Mrs. Ermine sticks to her idea that Mr. Caliph and Eunice will make a match; but my belief is that Eunice is cured.   Oh, yes, she is cured!   But I have done more than I meant to do, and I have not done it as I meant to do it; and I am very weary, and I shall write no more.

November 27.   Oh, yes, Eunice is cured!   And that is what she has not forgiven me.   Mr. Caliph told her yesterday that Mr. Frank meant to spend the winter in Rome.

December 3.   I have decided to return to Europe, and have written about my apartment in Rome.   I shall leave New York, if possible, on the 10th.   Eunice tells me she can easily believe I shall be happier there.

December 7.   I *must* note something I had the satisfaction to-day to say to Mr. Caliph.   He has not been here for three weeks, but this afternoon he came to call. He is no longer the trustee; he is only the visitor. I was alone in the library, into which he was ushered; and it was ten minutes before Eunice appeared. We had some talk, though my disgust for him is now unspeakable. At first it was of a very perfunctory kind; but suddenly he said, with more than his old impudence, "That was a most extraordinary interview of ours, at Cornerville!" I was surprised at his saying only this, for I expected him to take his revenge on me by some means or other for having put his brother on the scent of his misdeeds. I can only account for his silence on that subject by the supposition that Mr. Frank has been able to extract from him some pledge that I shall not be molested. He was, however, such an image of unrighteous success that the sight of him filled me with gall, and I tried to think of something which would make him smart.

"I don't know what you have done, nor how you have done it," I said; "but you took a very roundabout way to arrive at certain ends. There was a time when you might have married Eunice."

It was of course nothing new that we were frank with each other, and he only repeated, smiling, "Married Eunice?"

"She was very much in love with you last spring."

"Very much in love with me?"

"Oh, it's over now. Can't you imagine that? She's cured."

He broke into a laugh, but I felt I had startled him.

" You are the most delightful woman ! " he cried.

" Think how much simpler it would have been — I mean originally, when things were right, if they ever were right. Don't you see my point ? But now it 's too late. She has seen you when you were not on show. I assure you she is cured ! "

At this moment Eunice came in, and just afterwards I left the room. I am sure it was a revelation, and that I have given him a *mauvais quart d'heure.*

Rome, February 23. When I came back to this dear place Adrian Frank was not here, and I learned that he had gone to Sicily. A week ago I wrote to him : " You said you would come if I should send for you. I should be glad if you would come now." Last evening he appeared, and I told him that I could no longer endure my suspense in regard to a certain subject. Would he kindly inform me what he had done in New York after he left me under the trees at Cornerville ? Of what sacrifice had he been guilty; to what high generosity — terrible to me to think of — had he committed himself ? He would tell me very little ; but he is almost a poor man. He has just enough income to live in Italy.

May 9. Mrs. Ermine has taken it into her head to write to me. I have heard from her three times ; and in her last letter, received yesterday, she returns to her old refrain that Eunice and Mr. Caliph will soon be united. I don't know what may be going on ; but can it be possible that I put it into his head ? Truly, I have a felicitous touch !

May 15. I told Adrian yesterday that I would marry him if ever Eunice should marry Mr. Caliph. It was the first time I had mentioned his step-brother's name to him since the explanation I had attempted to have with him after he came back to Rome; and he evidently did n't like it at all.

In the Tyrol, August. I sent Mrs. Ermine a little water-color in return for her last letter, for I can't write to her, and that is easier. She now writes me again, in order to get another water-color. She speaks of course of Eunice and Mr. Caliph, and for the first time there appears a certain reality in what she says. She complains that Eunice is very slow in coming to the point, and relates that poor Mr. Caliph, who has taken her into his confidence, seems at times almost to despair. Nothing would suit him better of course than to appropriate two fortunes: two are so much better than one. But however much he may have explained, he can hardly have explained everything. Adrian Frank is in Scotland; in writing to him three days ago I had occasion to repeat that I will marry him on the day on which a certain other marriage takes place. In that way I am safe. I shall send another water-color to Mrs. Ermine. Water-colors or no, Eunice does n't write to me. It is clear that she has n't forgiven me! She regards me as perjured; and of course I am. Perhaps she will marry him after all.

LADY BARBERINA.

LADY BARBERINA.

———◆———

PART I.

I.

It is well known that there are few sights in the world more brilliant than the main avenues of Hyde Park of a fine afternoon in June. This was quite the opinion of two persons, who on a beautiful day at the beginning of that month, four years ago, had established themselves under the great trees in a couple of iron chairs (the big ones with arms, for which, if I mistake not, you pay twopence), and sat there with the slow procession of the Drive behind them, while their faces were turned to the more vivid agitation of the Row. They were lost in the multitude of observers, and they belonged, superficially, at least, to that class of persons who, wherever they may be, rank rather with the spectators than with the spectacle. They were quiet, simple, elderly, of aspect somewhat neutral; you would have liked them extremely, but you would scarcely have noticed them. Nevertheless, in all that shining host, it is to them,

obscure, that we must give our attention. The reader
is begged to have confidence; he is not asked to make
vain concessions. There was that in the faces of our
friends which indicated that they were growing old together, and that they were fond enough of each other's
company not to object (if it was a condition), even
to that. The reader will have guessed that they were
husband and wife; and perhaps while he is about it,
he will have guessed that they were of that nation-
ality for which Hyde Park at the height of the season
is most completely illustrative. They were familiar
strangers, as it were; and people at once so initiated
and so detached could only be Americans. This reflection, indeed, you would have made only after some
delay; for it must be admitted that they carried few
patriotic signs on the surface. They had the American turn of mind, but that was very subtle; and to
your eye—if your eye had cared about it—they
might have been of English, or even of Continental,
parentage. It was as if it suited them to be color-
less; their color was all in their talk. They were not
in the least verdant; they were gray, rather, of monotonous hue. If they were interested in the riders,
the horses, the walkers, the great exhibition of English wealth and health, beauty, luxury, and leisure, it
was because all this referred itself to other impressions, because they had the key to almost everything
that needed an answer, — because, in a word, they
were able to compare. They had not arrived, they had
only returned; and recognition much more than sur-

prise was expressed in their quiet gaze. It may as
well be said outright that Dexter Freer and his wife
belonged to that class of Americans who are constantly "passing through" London. Possessors of a
fortune of which, from any standpoint, the limits
were plainly visible, they were unable to command
that highest of luxuries, — a habitation in their own
country. They found it much more possible to
economize at Dresden or Florence than at Buffalo or
Minneapolis. The economy was as great, and the
inspiration was greater. From Dresden, from Florence, moreover, they constantly made excursions
which would not have been possible in those other
cities ; and it is even to be feared that they had some
rather expressive methods of saving. They came to
London to buy their portmanteaus, their toothbrushes,
their writing-paper; they occasionally even crossed
the Atlantic to assure themselves that prices over
there were still the same. They were eminently a
social pair; their interests were mainly personal.
Their point of view, always, was so distinctly human,
that they passed for being fond of gossip; and they
certainly knew a good deal about the affairs of other
people. They had friends in every country, in every
town ; and it was not their fault if people told them
their secrets. Dexter Freer was a tall, lean man, with
an interested eye, and a nose that rather drooped than
aspired, yet was salient withal. He brushed his hair,
which was streaked with white, forward over his ears,
in those locks which are represented in the portraits

of clean-shaven gentlemen who flourished fifty years
ago, and wore an old-fashioned neckcloth and gaiters.
His wife, a small, plump person, of superficial freshness, with a white face, and hair that was still perfectly black, smiled perpetually, but had never
laughed since the death of a son whom she had lost
ten years after her marriage. Her husband, on the
other hand, who was usually quite grave, indulged on
great occasions in resounding mirth. People confided in her less than in him; but that mattered
little, as she confided sufficiently in herself. Her
dress, which was always black or dark gray, was so
harmoniously simple, that you could see she was fond
of it; it was never smart by accident. She was full of
intentions of the most judicious sort; and though she
was perpetually moving about the world, she had the
air of being perfectly stationary. She was celebrated
for the promptitude with which she made her sitting-
room at an inn, where she might be spending a night
or two, look like an apartment long inhabited. With
books, flowers, photographs, draperies, rapidly dis-
tributed, — she had even a way, for the most part, of
having a piano, — the place seemed almost hereditary.
The pair were just back from America, where they
had spent three months, and now were able to face
the world with something of the elation which people
feel who have been justified in a prevision. They
had found their native land quite ruinous.

"There he is again!" said Mr. Freer, following
with his eyes a young man who passed along the

Row, riding slowly. "That's a beautiful thoroughbred!"

Mrs. Freer asked idle questions only when she wished for time to think. At present she had simply to look and see who it was her husband meant. "The horse is too big," she remarked, in a moment.

"You mean that the rider is too small," her husband rejoined; "he is mounted on his millions."

"Is it really millions?"

"Seven or eight, they tell me."

"How disgusting!" It was in this manner that Mrs. Freer usually spoke of the large fortunes of the day. "I wish he would see us," she added.

"He does see us, but he does n't like to look at us. He is too conscious; he is n't easy."

"Too conscious of his big horse?"

"Yes, and of his big fortune; he is rather ashamed of it."

"This is an odd place to come, then," said Mrs. Freer.

"I am not sure of that. He will find people here richer than himself, and other big horses in plenty, and that will cheer him up. Perhaps, too, he is looking for that girl."

"The one we heard about? He can't be such a fool."

"He is n't a fool," said Dexter Freer. "If he is thinking of her, he has some good reason."

"I wonder what Mary Lemon would say."

"She would say it was right, if he should do it. She thinks he can do no wrong. He is exceedingly fond of her."

"I sha'n't be sure of that if he takes home a wife that will despise her."

"Why should the girl despise her? She is a delightful woman."

"The girl will never know it, — and if she should, it would make no difference; she will despise everything."

"I don't believe it, my dear; she will like some things very much. Every one will be very nice to her."

"She will despise them all the more. But we are speaking as if it were all arranged; I don't believe in it at all," said Mrs. Freer.

"Well, something of the sort — in this case or in some other — is sure to happen sooner or later," her husband replied, turning round a little toward the part of the delta which is formed, near the entrance to the Park, by the divergence of the two great vistas of the Drive and the Row.

Our friends had turned their backs, as I have said, to the solemn revolution of wheels and the densely-packed mass of spectators who had chosen that part of the show. These spectators were now agitated by a unanimous impulse: the pushing back of chairs, the shuffle of feet, the rustle of garments, and the deepening murmur of voices sufficiently expressed it. Royalty was approaching — royalty was passing — royalty had passed. Freer turned his head and his ear a little; but he failed to alter his position further, and his wife took no notice of the flurry. They had seen royalty pass, all over Europe, and they knew that it passed very quickly. Sometimes it came back; sometimes it did n't; for more than once they had seen it pass for the last time. They were veteran tourists, and they knew perfectly when to get up and when to remain seated. Mr. Freer went on with his proposition: "Some young fellow is certain to do it, and one of these girls is certain to take the risk. They must take risks, over here, more and more."

"The girls, I have no doubt, will be glad enough; they have had very little chance as yet. But I don't want Jackson to begin."

"Do you know I rather think I do," said Dexter Freer; "it will be very amusing."

"For us, perhaps, but not for him; he will repent of it, and be wretched. He is too good for that."

"Wretched, never! He has no capacity for wretchedness; and that 's why he can afford to risk it."

"He will have to make great concessions," Mrs. Freer remarked.

"He won't make one."

"I should like to see."

"You admit, then, that it will be amusing, which is all I contend for. But, as you say, we are talking as if it were settled, whereas there is probably nothing in it after all. The best stories always turn out false. I shall be sorry in this case."

They relapsed into silence, while people passed and repassed them — continuous, successive, mechanical, with strange sequences of faces. They looked at the people, but no one looked at them, though every one

was there so admittedly to see what was to be seen.
It was all striking, all pictorial, and it made a great
composition. The wide, long area of the Row, its
red-brown surface dotted with bounding figures,
stretched away into the distance and became suffused
and misty in the bright, thick air. The deep, dark
English verdure that bordered and overhung it, looked
rich and old, revived and refreshed though it was by
the breath of June. The mild blue of the sky was
spotted with great silvery clouds, and the light
drizzled down in heavenly shafts over the quieter
spaces of the Park, as one saw them beyond the Row.
All this, however, was only a background, for the
scene was before everything personal; superbly so,
and full of the gloss and lustre, the contrasted tones,
of a thousand polished surfaces. Certain things were
salient, pervasive, — the shining flanks of the perfect
horses, the twinkle of bits and spurs, the smoothness
of fine cloth adjusted to shoulders and limbs, the
sheen of hats and boots, the freshness of complexions,
the expression of smiling, talking faces, the flash and
flutter of rapid gallops. Faces were everywhere, and
they were the great effect, — above all, the fair faces
of women on tall horses, flushed a little under their
stiff black hats, with figures stiffened, in spite of
much definition of curve, by their tight-fitting habits.
Their hard little helmets, their neat, compact heads,
their straight necks, their firm, tailor-made armor,
their blooming, competent physique, made them look
doubly like amazons about to ride a charge. The

men, with their eyes before them, with hats of undulating brim, good profiles, high collars, white flowers on their chests, long legs and long feet, had an air more elaboratively decorative, as they jolted beside the ladies, always out of step. These were youthful types; but it was not all youth, for many a saddle was surmounted by a richer rotundity, and ruddy faces, with short white whiskers or with matronly chins, looked down comfortably from an equilibrium which was moral as well as physical. The walkers differed from the riders only in being on foot, and in looking at the riders more than these looked at them; for they would have done as well in the saddle and ridden as the others ride. The women had tight little bonnets and still tighter little knots of hair; their round chins rested on a close swathing of lace, or, in some-cases, of silver chains and circlets. They had flat backs and small waists, they walked slowly, with their elbows out, carrying vast parasols, and turning their heads very little to the right or the left. They were amazons unmounted, quite ready to spring into the saddle. There was a great deal of beauty and a suffused look of successful development, which came from clear, quiet eyes and from well-cut lips, on which syllables were liquid and sentences brief. Some of the young men, as well as the women, had the happiest proportions and oval faces, in which line and color were pure and fresh, and the idea of the moment was not very intense.

"They are very good-looking," said Mr. Freer, at

the end of ten minutes; "they are the finest whites."

"So long as they remain white they do very well; but when they venture upon color!" his wife replied. She sat with her eyes on a level with the skirts of the ladies who passed her; and she had been following the progress of a green velvet robe, enriched with ornaments of steel and much gathered up in the hands of its wearer, who, herself apparently in her teens, was accompanied by a young lady draped in scanty pink muslin, embroidered, æsthetically, with flowers that simulated the iris.

"All the same, in a crowd, they are wonderfully well turned out," Dexter Freer went on; "take the men, and women, and horses together. Look at that big fellow on the light chestnut: what could be more perfect? By the way, it's Lord Canterville," he added in a moment, as if the fact were of some importance.

Mrs. Freer recognized its importance to the degree of raising her glass to look at Lord Canterville. "How do you know it's he?" she asked, with her glass still up.

"I heard him say something the night I went to the House of Lords. It was very few words, but I remember him. A man who was near me told me who he was."

"He is not so handsome as you," said Mrs. Freer, dropping her glass.

"Ah, you're too difficult!" her husband murmured.

"What a pity the girl is n't with him," he went on ; "we might see something."

It appeared in a moment that the girl was with him. The nobleman designated had ridden slowly forward from the start, but just opposite our friends he pulled up to look behind him, as if he had been waiting for some one. At the same moment a gentleman in the Walk engaged his attention, so that he advanced to the barrier which protects the pedestrians, and halted there, bending a little from his saddle and talking with his friend, who leaned against the rail. Lord Canterville was indeed perfect, as his American admirer had said. Upwards of sixty, and of great stature and great presence, he was really a splendid apparition. In exquisite preservation, he had the freshness of middle life, and would have been young to the eye if the lapse of years were not needed to account for his considerable girth. He was clad from head to foot in garments of a radiant gray, and his fine florid countenance was surmounted with a white hat, of which the majestic curves were a triumph of good form. Over his mighty chest was spread a beard of the richest growth, and of a color, in spite of a few streaks, vaguely grizzled, to which the coat of his admirable horse appeared to be a perfect match. It left no opportunity, in his uppermost button-hole, for the customary gardenia ; but this was of comparatively little consequence, as the vegetation of the beard itself was tropical. Astride his great steed, with his big fist, gloved in pearl-gray, on his swelling thigh, his

face lighted up with good-humored indifference, and
all his magnificent surface reflecting the mild sunshine, he was a very imposing man indeed, and visibly,
incontestably, a personage.   People almost lingered
to look at him as they passed.   His halt was brief,
however, for he was almost immediately joined by
two handsome girls, who were as well turned-out, in
Dexter Freer's phrase, as himself.   They had been
detained a moment at the entrance to the Row, and
now advanced side by side, their groom close behind
them.   One was taller and older than the other, and
it was apparent at a glance that they were sisters.
Between them, with their charming shoulders, con-
tracted waists, and skirts that hung without a wrinkle,
like a plate of zinc, they represented in a singularly
complete form the pretty English girl in the position
in which she is prettiest.

"Of course they are his daughters," said Dexter
Freer, as they rode away with Lord Canterville; "and
in that case one of them must be Jackson Lemou's
sweetheart.   Probably the bigger; they said it was
the eldest.   She is evidently a fine creature."

"She would hate it over there," Mrs. Freer remarked, for all answer to this cluster of inductions.

"You know I don't admit that.   But granting she
should, it would do her good to have to accommodate
herself."

"She would n't accommodate herself."

"She looks so confoundedly fortunate, perched up
on that saddle," Dexter Freer pursued, without heeding his wife's rejoinder.

" Are n't they supposed to be very poor ? "

" Yes, they look it ! "   And his eyes followed the distinguished trio, as, with the groom, as distinguished in his way as any of them, they started on a canter.

The air was full of sound, but it was low and diffused ; and when, near our friends, it became articulate, the words were simple and few.

" It 's as good as the circus, is n't it, Mrs. Freer ? " These words correspond to that description, but they pierced the air more effectually than any our friends had lately heard.   They were uttered by a young man who had stopped short in the path, absorbed by the sight of his compatriots.   He was short and stout, he had a round, kind face, and short, stiff-looking hair, which was reproduced in a small bristling beard.   He wore a double-breasted walkiug-coat, which was not, however, buttoned, and on the summit of his round head was perched a hat of exceeding smallness, and of the so-called "pot" category. It evidently fitted him, but a hatter himself would not have known why.   His hands were encased in new gloves, of a dark-brown color, and they hung with an air of unaccustomed inaction at his sides. He sported neither umbrella nor stick.   He extended one of his hands, almost with eagerness, to Mrs. Freer, blushing a little as he became aware that he had been eager.

" Oh, Dr. Feeder ! " she said, smiling at him.   Then she repeated to her husband, " Dr. Feeder, my dear ! " and her husband said, " Oh, Doctor, how d' ye do ? "

I have spoken of the composition of his appearance; but the items were not perceived by these two. They saw only one thing, his delightful face, which was both simple and clever, and unreservedly good. They had lately made the voyage from New York in his company, and it was plain that he would be very genial at sea. After he had stood in front of them a moment, a chair beside Mrs. Freer became vacant, on which he took possession of it, and sat there telling her what he thought of the Park, and how he liked London. As she knew every one, she had known many of his people at home; and while she listened to him she remembered how large their contribution had been to the virtue and culture of Cincinnati. Mrs. Freer's social horizon included even that city; she had been on terms almost familiar with several families from Ohio, and was acquainted with the position of the Feeders there. This family, very numerous, was interwoven into an enormous cousinship. She herself was quite out of such a system, but she could have told you whom Dr. Feeder's great-grandfather had married. Every one, indeed, had heard of the good deeds of the descendants of this worthy, who were generally physicians, excellent ones, and whose name expressed not inaptly their numerous acts of charity. Sidney Feeder, who had several cousins of this name established in the same line at Cincinnati, had transferred himself and his ambition to New York, where his practice, at the end of three years, had begun to grow. He had studied his profession at Vienna, and was impregnated with German science; indeed, if he had only worn spectacles, he might perfectly, as he sat there watching the riders in Rotten Row as if their proceedings were a successful demonstration, have passed for a young German of distinction. He had come over to London to attend a medical congress which met this year in the British capital; for his interest in the healing art was by no means limited to the cure of his patients, it embraced every form of experiment; and the expression of his honest eyes would almost have reconciled you to vivisection. It was the first time he had come to the Park; for social experiments he had little leisure. Being aware, however, that it was a very typical, and as it were symptomatic, sight, he had conscientiously reserved an afternoon, and had dressed himself carefully for the occasion. "It 's quite a brilliant show," he said to Mrs. Freer; "it makes me wish I had a mount." Little as he resembled Lord Canterville, he rode very well.

"Wait till Jackson Lemon passes again, and you can stop him and make him let you take a turn." This was the jocular suggestion of Dexter Freer.

"Why, is he here? I have been looking out for him; I should like to see him."

"Does n't he go to your medical congress?" asked Mrs. Freer.

"Well yes, he attends; but he is n't very regular. I guess he goes out a good deal."

"I guess he does," said Mr. Freer; "and if he is n't very regular, I guess he has a good reason. A beautiful reason, a charming reason," he went on, bending forward to look down toward the beginning of the Row. "Dear me, what a lovely reason!"

Dr. Feeder followed the direction of his eyes, and after a moment understood his allusion. Little Jackson Lemon, on his big horse, passed along the avenue again, riding beside one of the young girls who had come that way shortly before in the company of Lord Canterville. His lordship followed, in conversation with the other, his younger daughter. As they advanced, Jackson Lemon turned his eyes toward the multitude under the trees, and it so happened that they rested upon the Dexter Freers. He smiled, and raised his hat with all possible friendliness; and his three companions turned to see to whom he was bowing with so much cordiality. As he settled his hat on his head, he espied the young man from Cincinnati, whom he had at first overlooked; whereupon he smiled still more brightly, and waved Sidney Feeder an airy salutation with his hand, reining in a little at the same time just for an instant, as if he half expected the Doctor to come and speak to him. Seeing him with strangers, however, Sidney Feeder hung back, staring a little as he rode away.

It is open to us to know that at this moment the young lady by whose side he was riding said to him familiarly enough: "Who are those people you bowed to?"

"Some old friends of mine, — Americans," Jackson Lemon answered.

" Of course they are Americans; there is nothing but Americans nowadays."

" Oh, yes, our turn 's coming round ! " laughed the young man.

" But that does n't say who they are," his companion continued. " It 's so difficult to say who Americans are," she added, before he had time to answer her.

" Dexter Freer and his wife, — there is nothing difficult about that; every one knows them."

" I never heard of them," said the English girl.

" Ah, that 's your fault. I assure you everybody knows them."

" And does everybody know the little man with the fat face whom you kissed your hand to ? "

" I did n't kiss my hand; but I would if I had thought of it. He is a great chum of mine, — a fellow student at Vienna."

" And what 's *his* name ? "

" Dr. Feeder."

Jackson Lemon's companion was silent a moment. " Are *all* your friends doctors ? " she presently inquired.

" No; some of them are in other businesses."

" Are they all in some business ? "

" Most of them; save two or three, like Dexter Freer."

" Dexter Freer ? I thought you said Dr. Freer."

The young man gave a laugh. " You heard me

wrong. You have got doctors on the brain, Lady
Barb."

"I am rather glad," said Lady Barb, giving the
rein to her horse, who bounded away.

"Well yes, she's very handsome, the reason," Dr.
Feeder remarked, as he sat under the trees.

"Is he going to marry her?" Mrs. Freer inquired.

"Marry her? I hope not."

"Why do you hope not?"

"Because I know nothing about her. I want to
know something about the woman that man marries."

"I suppose you would like him to marry in Cincinnati," Mrs. Freer rejoined, lightly.

"Well, I am not particular where it is; but I want
to know her first." Dr. Feeder was very sturdy.

"We were in hopes you would know all about it,"
said Mr. Freer.

"No; I have n't kept up with him there."

"We have heard from a dozen people that he has
been always with her for the last month; and that
kind of thing, in England, is supposed to mean something. Has n't he spoken of her when you have
seen him?"

"No, he has only talked about the new treatment
of spinal meningitis. He is very much interested
in spinal meningitis."

"I wonder if he talks about it to Lady Barb," said
Mrs. Freer.

"Who is she, any way?" the young man inquired.

"Lady Barberina Clement."

" And who is Lady Barberina Clement ? "

" The daughter of Lord Canterville."

" And who is Lord Canterville ? "

" Dexter must tell you that," said Mrs. Freer.

And Dexter accordingly told him that the Marquis of Canterville had been in his day a great sporting nobleman and an ornament to English society, and had held more than once a high post in her Majesty's household. Dexter Freer knew all these things, — how his lordship had married a daughter of Lord Treherne, a very serious, intelligent, and beautiful woman, who had redeemed him from the extravagance of his youth and presented him in rapid succession with a dozen little tenants for the nurseries at Pasterns, — this being, as Mr. Freer also knew, the name of the principal seat of the Cantervilles. The Marquis was a Tory, but very liberal for a Tory, and very popular in society at large ; good-natured, good-looking, knowing how to be genial, and yet to remain a *grand seigneur*, clever enough to make an occasional speech, and much associated with the fine old English pursuits, as well as with many of the new improvements, — the purification of the Turf, the opening of the museums on Sunday, the propagation of coffee-taverns, the latest ideas on sanitary reform. He disapproved of the extension of the suffrage, but he positively had drainage on the brain. It had been said of him at least once (and I think in print) that he was just the man to convey to the popular mind the impression that the British aristocracy is still a living force.

He was not very rich, unfortunately (for a man who
had to exemplify such truths), and of his twelve children, no less than seven were daughters. Lady Barberina, Jackson Lemon's friend, was the second; the
eldest had married Lord Beauchemin. Mr. Freer had
caught quite the right pronunciation of this name:
he called it Bitumen. Lady Lucretia had done very
well, for her husband was rich, and she had brought
him nothing to speak of; but it was hardly to be expected that the others would do as well. Happily
the younger girls were still in the schoolroom; and
before they had come up, Lady Canterville, who was
a woman of resources, would have worked off the two
that were out. It was Lady Agatha's first season;
she was not so pretty as her sister, but she was
thought to be cleverer. Half-a-dozen people had
spoken to him of Jackson Lemon's being a great
deal at the Cantervilles. He was supposed to be
enormously rich.

"Well, so he is," said Sidney Feeder, who had
listened to Mr. Freer's little recital with attention,
with eagerness even, but with an air of imperfect
apprehension.

"Yes, but not so rich as they probably think."

"Do they want his money? Is that what they 're
after?"

"You go straight to the point," Mrs. Freer murmured.

"I have n't the least idea," said her husband. "He
is a very nice fellow in himself."

" Yes, but he's a doctor," Mrs. Freer remarked.

" What have they got against that ? " asked Sidney Feeder.

" Why, over here, you know, they only call them in to prescribe," said Dexter Freer ; " the profession is n't — a — what you'd call aristocratic."

" Well, I don't know it, and I don't know that I want to know it. How do you mean, aristocratic ? What profession is ? It would be rather a curious one. Many of the gentlemen at the congress there are quite charming."

" I like doctors very much," said Mrs. Freer ; " my father was a doctor. But they don't marry the daughters of marquises."

" I don't believe Jackson wants to marry that one."

" Very possibly not — people are such asses," said Dexter Freer. " But he will have to decide. I wish you would find out, by the way ; you can if you will."

" I will ask him — up at the congress ; I can do that. I suppose he has got to marry some one." Sidney Feeder added, in a moment, " And she may be a nice girl."

" She is said to be charming."

" Very well, then ; it won't hurt him. I must say, however, I am not sure I like all that about her family."

" What I told you ? It's all to their honor and glory."

" Are they quite on the square ? It's like those people in Thackeray."

"Oh, if Thackeray could have done this!" Mrs. Freer exclaimed, with a good deal of expression.

"You mean all this scene?" asked the young man.

"No; the marriage of a British noblewoman and an American doctor. It would have been a subject for Thackeray."

"You see you do want it, my dear," said Dexter Freer, quietly.

"I want it as a story, but I don't want it for Dr. Lemon."

"Does he call himself 'Doctor' still?" Mr. Freer asked of young Feeder.

"I suppose he does; I call him so. Of course he does n't practise. But once a doctor, always a doctor."

"That 's doctrine for Lady Barb!"

Sidney Feeder stared. "Has n't she got a title too? What would she expect him to be? President of the United States? He 's a man of real ability; he might have stood at the head of his profession. When I think of that, I want to swear. What did his father want to go and make all that money for!"

"It must certainly be odd to them to see a 'medical man' with six or eight millions," Mr. Freer observed.

"They use the same term as the Choctaws," said his wife.

"Why, some of their own physicians made immense fortunes," Sidney Feeder declared.

"Could n't he be made a baronet by the Queen?" This suggestion came from Mrs. Freer.

"Yes, then he would be aristocratic," said the young man. "But I don't see why he should want to marry over here; it seems to me to be going out of his way. However, if he is happy, I don't care. I like him very much; he has got lots of ability. If it had n't been for his father he would have made a splendid doctor. But, as I say, he takes a great interest in medical science, and I guess he means to promote it all he can — with his fortune. He will always be doing something in the way of research. He thinks we *do* know something, and he is bound we shall know more. I hope she won't prevent him, the young marchioness — is that her rank? And I hope they are really good people. He ought to be very useful. I should want to know a good deal about the family I was going to marry into."

"He looked to me, as he rode there, as if he knew a good deal about the Clements," Dexter Freer said, rising, as his wife suggested that they ought to be going; "and he looked to me pleased with the knowledge. There they come, down on the other side. Will you walk away with us, or will you stay?"

"Stop him and ask him, and then come and tell us — in Jermyn Street." This was Mrs. Freer's parting injunction to Sidney Feeder.

"He ought to come himself — tell him that," her husband added.

"Well, I guess I 'll stay," said the young man, as his companions merged themselves in the crowd that now was tending toward the gates. He went and

stood by the barrier, and saw Dr. Lemon and his
friends pull up at the entrance to the Row, where
they apparently prepared to separate. The separation
took some time, and Sidney Feeder became interested.
Lord Canterville and his younger daughter lingered
to talk with two gentlemen, also mounted, who looked
a good deal at the legs of Lady Agatha's horse. Jackson. Lemon and Lady Barberina were face to face,
very near each other; and she, leaning forward a
little, stroked the overlapping neck of his glossy bay.
At a distance he appeared to be talking, and she to
be listening and saying nothing. "Oh, yes, he's
making love to her," thought Sidney Feeder. Suddenly her father turned away to leave the Park, and
she joined him and disappeared, while Dr. Lemon
came up on the left again, as if for a final gallop. He
had not gone far before he perceived his *confrère*, who
awaited him at the rail; and he repeated the gesture
which Lady Barberina had spoken of as a kissing
of his hand, though it must be added that, to his
friend's eyes, it had not quite that significance.
When he reached the point where Feeder stood,
he pulled up.

"If I had known you were coming here, I would
have given you a mount," he said. There was not
in his person that irradiation of wealth and distinction which made Lord Canterville glow like a picture ; but as he sat there with his little legs stuck out,
he looked very bright, and sharp, and happy, wearing
in his degree the aspect of one of Fortune's favorites.

He had a thin, keen, delicate face, a nose very carefully finished, a rapid eye, a trifle hard in expression, and a small mustache, a good deal cultivated. He was not striking, but he was very positive, and it was easy to see that he was full of purpose.

"How many horses have you got — about forty?" his compatriot inquired, in response to his greeting.

"About five hundred," said Jackson Lemon.

"Did you mount your friends — the three you were riding with?"

"Mount them? They have got the best horses in England."

"Did they sell you this one?" Sidney Feeder continued, in the same humorous strain.

"What do you think of him?" said his friend, not deigning to answer this question.

"He's an awful old screw; I wonder he can carry you."

"Where did you get your hat?" asked Dr. Lemon, in return.

"I got it in New York. What's the matter with it?"

"It's very beautiful; I wish I had bought one like it."

"The head's the thing — not the hat. I don't mean yours, but mine. There is something very deep in your question; I must think it over."

"Don't — don't," said Jackson Lemon; "you will never get to the bottom of it. Are you having a good time?"

"A glorious time. Have you been up to-day?"

"Up among the doctors? No; I have had a lot of things to do."

"We had a very interesting discussion. I made a few remarks."

"You ought to have told me. What were they about?"

"About the intermarriage of races, from the point of view ——." And Sidney Feeder paused a moment, occupied with the attempt to scratch the nose of his friend's horse.

"From the point of view of the progeny, I suppose?"

"Not at all; from the point of view of the old friends."

"Damn the old friends!" Dr. Lemon exclaimed, with jocular crudity.

"Is it true that you are going to marry a young marchioness?"

The face of the young man in the saddle became just a trifle rigid, and his firm eyes fixed themselves on Dr. Feeder.

"Who has told you that?"

"Mr. and Mrs. Freer, whom I met just now."

"Mr. and Mrs. Freer be hanged! And who told them?"

"Ever so many people; I don't know who."

"Gad, how things are tattled!" cried Jackson Lemon, with some asperity.

"I can see it's true, by the way you say that."

"Do Freer and his wife believe it?" Jackson Lemon went on, impatiently.

"They want you to go and see them: you can judge for yourself."

"I will go and see them, and tell them to mind their business."

"In Jermyn Street; but I forget the number. I am sorry the marchioness isn't American," Sidney Feeder continued.

"If I should marry her, she would be," said his friend. "But I don't see what difference it can make to you."

"Why, she'll look down on the profession; and I don't like that from your wife."

"That will touch me more than you."

"Then it *is* true?" cried Feeder, more seriously, looking up at his friend.

"She won't look down; I will answer for that."

"You won't care; you are out of it all now."

"No, I am not; I mean to do a great deal of work."

"I will believe that when I see it," said Sidney Feeder, who was by no means perfectly incredulous, but who thought it salutary to take that tone. "I am not sure that you have any right to work, — you ought n't to have everything; you ought to leave the field to us. You must pay the penalty of being so rich. You would have been celebrated if you had continued to practise, — more celebrated than any one. But you won't be now, — you can't be. Some one else will be, in your place."

Jackson Lemon listened to this, but without meeting the eyes of the speaker; not, however, as if he were avoiding them, but as if the long stretch of the Ride, now less and less obstructed, invited him, and made his companion's talk a little retarding. Nevertheless, he answered, deliberately and kindly enough: "I hope it will be you;" and he bowed to a lady who rode past.

"Very likely it will. I hope I make you feel badly,—that's what I'm trying to do."

"Oh, awfully!" cried Jackson Lemon; "all the more that I am not in the least engaged."

"Well, that's good. Won't you come up to-morrow?" Dr. Feeder went on.

"I'll try, my dear fellow; I can't be sure. By by!"

"Oh, you're lost anyway!" cried Sidney Feeder, as the other started away.

II.

IT was Lady Marmaduke, the wife of Sir Henry Marmaduke, who had introduced Jackson Lemon to Lady Beauchemin; after which Lady Beauchemin had made him acquainted with her mother and sisters. Lady Marmaduke was also transatlantic; she had been for her conjugal baronet the most permanent consequence of a tour in the United States. At present, at the end of ten years, she knew her London as she had never known her New York, so that it had been easy for her to be, as she called herself, Jackson Lemon's social godmother. She had views with regard to his career, and these views fitted into a social scheme which, if our space permitted, I should be glad to lay before the reader in its magnitude. She wished to add an arch or two to the bridge on which she had effected her transit from America ; and it was her belief that Jackson Lemon might furnish the materials. This bridge, as yet a somewhat sketchy and rickety structure, she saw (in the future) boldly stretching from one solid pillar to another. It would have to go both ways, for reciprocity was the keynote of Lady Marmaduke's plan. It was her belief that an ultimate fusion was inevitable, and that those who were the first to understand the situation would gain the most. The first time Jackson Lemon had dined with her, he met Lady Beauchemin, who was her intimate friend. Lady Beauchemin was remarkably gracious ; she asked him to come and see her as if she really meant it. He presented himself, and in her drawing-room met her mother, who happened to be calling at the same moment. Lady Canterville, not less friendly than her daughter, invited him down to Pasterns for Easter week ; and before a month had passed it seemed to him that, though he was not what he would have called intimate at any house in London, the door of the house of Clement opened to him pretty often. This was a considerable good fortune, for it always opened upon a charming picture. The inmates were a blooming and beautiful race, and their interior had an aspect of the ripest comfort. It was not the splendor of New York (as New York had lately begun to appear to the young man), but a splendor in which there was an unpurchasable ingredient of age. He himself had a great deal of money, and money was good, even when it was new; but old money was the best. Even after he learned that Lord Canterville's fortune was more ancient than abundant, it was still the mellowness of the golden element that struck him. It was Lady Beauchemin who had told him that her father was not rich; having told him, besides this, many surprising things, — things that were surprising in themselves, or surprising on her lips. This struck him afresh later that evening — the day he met Sidney Feeder in the Park. He dined out, in the company of Lady Beauchemin, and afterward, as she was alone, — her husband had gone down to listen to a debate, — she offered to "take him on." She was going to several places, and he must be going to some of them. They compared notes; and it was settled that they should proceed together to the Trumpington's, whither, also, it appeared at eleven o'clock that all the world was going, the approach to the house being choked for half a mile with carriages. It was a close, muggy night; Lady Beauchemin's chariot, in its place in the rank, stood still for long periods. In his corner beside her, through the open window, Jackson Lemon, rather hot, rather oppressed, looked out on the moist, greasy pavement, over which was flung, a considerable distance up and down, the flare of a public-house. Lady Beauchemin, however, was not impatient, for she had a purpose in her mind, and now she could say what she wished.

"Do you really love her?" That was the first thing she said.

"Well, I guess so," Jackson Lemon answered, as if he did not recognize the obligation to be serious.

Lady Beauchemin looked at him a moment in silence; he felt her gaze, and turning his eyes, saw her face, partly shadowed, with the aid of a street-lamp. She was not so pretty as Lady Barberina; her countenance had a certain sharpness; her hair, very light in color and wonderfully frizzled, almost covered her eyes, the expression of which, however, together with that of her pointed nose, and the glitter of several diamonds, emerged from the gloom. "You don't seem to know. I never saw a man in such an odd state," she presently remarked.

"You push me a little too much; I must have time to think of it," the young man went on. "You know in my country they allow us plenty of time." He had several little oddities of expression, of which he was perfectly conscious, and which he found convenient, for they protected him in a society in which a lonely American was rather exposed; they gave him the advantage which corresponded with certain drawbacks. He had very few natural Americanisms, but the occasional use of one, discreetly chosen, made him appear simpler than he really was, and he had his

reasons for wishing this result.   He was not simple;
he was subtle, circumspect, shrewd, and perfectly
aware that he might make mistakes.   There was a
danger of his making a mistake at present, — a mistake which would be immensely grave.   He was determined only to succeed.   It is true that for a great
success he would take a certain risk; but the risk
was to be considered, and he gained time while he
multiplied his guesses and talked about his country.

"You may take ten years if you like," said Lady
Beauchemin.   "I am in no hurry whatever to make
you my brother-in-law.   Only you must remember
that you spoke to me first."

"What did I say?"

"You told me that Barberina was the finest girl
you had seen in England."

"Oh, I am willing to stand by that; I like her
type."

"I should think you might!"   ·

"I like her very much, — with all her peculiarities."

"What do you mean by her peculiarities?"

"Well, she has some peculiar ideas," said Jackson
Lemon, in a tone of the sweetest reasonableness,
"and she has a peculiar way of speaking."

"Ah, you can't expect us to speak as well as you!"
cried Lady Beauchemin.

"I don't know why not; you do some things much
better."

"We have our own ways, at any rate, and we think
them the best in the world.   One of them is not to

let a gentleman devote himself to a girl for three or four months without some sense of responsibility. If you don't wish to marry my sister, you ought to go away."

" I ought never to have come," said Jackson Lemon.

" I can scarcely agree to that; for I should have lost the pleasure of knowing you."

" It would have spared you this duty, which you dislike very much."

" Asking you about your intentions? I don't dislike it at all; it amuses me extremely."

" Should you like your sister to marry me ? " asked Jackson Lemon, with great simplicity.

If he expected to take Lady Beauchemin by surprise he was disappointed; for she was perfectly prepared to commit herself. " I should like it very much. I think English and American society ought to be but one — I mean the best of each — a great whole."

" Will you allow me to ask whether Lady Marmaduke suggested that to you ? "

" We have often talked of it."

" Oh yes, that 's her aim."

" Well, it 's my aim too. I think there 's a great deal to be done."

" And you would like me to do it ? "

" To begin it, precisely. Don't you think we ought to see more of each other ?— I mean the best in each country."

Jackson Lemon was silent a moment. " I am afraid I have n't any general ideas. If I should marry an English girl, it would n't be for the good of the species."

"Well, we want to be mixed a little; that I am sure of," Lady Beauchemin said.

"You certainly got that from Lady Marmaduke."

"It 's too tiresome, your not consenting to be serious! But my father will make you so," Lady Beauchemin went on. "I may as well let you know that he intends in a day or two to ask you your intentions. That 's all I wished to say to you. I think you ought to be prepared."

"I am much obliged to you; Lord Canterville will do quite right."

There was, to Lady Beauchemin, something really unfathomable in this little American doctor, whom she had taken up on grounds of large policy, and who, though he was assumed to have sunk the medical character, was neither handsome nor distinguished, but only immensely rich and quite original, for he was not insignificant. It was unfathomable, to begin with, that a medical man should be so rich, or that so rich a man should be a doctor; it was even, to an eye which was always gratified by suitability, rather irritating. Jackson Lemon himself could have explained it better than any one else, but this was an explanation that one could scarcely ask for. There were other things: his cool acceptance of certain situations; his general indisposition to explain; his way of taking refuge in jokes, which at times had not even the merit of being American; his way, too, of appearing to be a suitor without being an aspirant. Lady Beauchemin, however, was, like Jackson Lemon, prepared to run a certain risk. His reserves made him slippery; but that was only when one pressed. She flattered herself that she could handle people lightly. "My father will be sure to act with perfect tact," she said; "of course, if you should n't care to be questioned, you can go out of town." She had the air of really wishing to make everything easy for him.

"I don't want to go out of town; I am enjoying it far too much here," her companion answered. "And would n't your father have a right to ask me what I meant by that?"

Lady Beauchemin hesitated; she was slightly perplexed. But in a moment she exclaimed: "He is incapable of saying anything vulgar!"

She had not really answered his inquiry, and he was conscious of that; but he was quite ready to say to her, a little later, as he guided her steps from the brougham to the strip of carpet which, between a somewhat rickety border of striped cloth and a double row of waiting footmen, policemen, and dingy amateurs of both sexes, stretched from the curbstone to the portal of the Trumpingtons, "Of course I shall not wait for Lord Canterville to speak to me."

He had been expecting some such announcement as this from Lady Beauchemin, and he judged that her father would do no more than his duty. He knew that he ought to be prepared with an answer

to Lord Canterville, and he wondered at himself for
not yet having come to the point. Sidney Feeder's
question in the Park had made him feel rather pointless; it was the first allusion that had been made to
his possible marriage, except on the part of Lady
Beauchemin. None of his own people were in London; he was perfectly independent, and even if his
mother had been within reach he could not have
consulted her on the subject. He loved her dearly,
better than any one; but she was not a woman to
consult, for she approved of whatever he did : it was
her standard. He was careful not to be too serious
when he talked with Lady Beauchemin; but he was
very serious indeed as he thought over the matter
within himself, which he did even among the diver-
sions of the next half hour, while he squeezed obliquely and slowly through the crush in Mrs. Trumpington's drawing-room. At the end of the half-hour
he came away, and at the door he found Lady Beauchemin, from whom he had separated on entering
the house, and who, this time with a companion of
her own sex, was awaiting her carriage and still
"going on." He gave her his arm into the street,
and as she stepped into the vehicle she repeated that
she wished he would go out of town for a few days.

"Who, then, would tell me what to do?" he asked,
for answer, looking at her through the window.

She might tell him what to do, but he felt free,
all the same; and he was determined this should
continue. To prove it to himself he jumped into a

hansom and drove back to Brook Street to his hotel, instead of proceeding to a bright-windowed house in Portland Place, where he knew that after midnight he should find Lady Canterville and her daughters. There had been a reference to the subject between Lady Barberina and himself during their ride, and she would probably expect him; but it made him taste his liberty not to go, and he liked to taste his liberty. He was aware that to taste it in perfection he ought to go to bed; but he did not go to bed, he did not even take off his hat. He walked up and down his sitting-room, with his head surmounted by this ornament, a good deal tipped back, and his hands in his pockets. There were a good many cards stuck into the frame of the mirror over his chimney-piece, and every time he passed the place he seemed to see what was written on one of them, — the name of the mistress of the house in Portland Place, his own name, and, in the lower left-hand corner, the words: "A small Dance." Of course, now, he must make up his mind; he would make it up to the next day: that was what he said to himself as he walked up and down; and according to his decision he would speak to Lord Canterville, or he would take the night-express to Paris. It was better meanwhile that he should not see Lady Barberina. It was vivid to him, as he paused occasionally, looking vaguely at that card in the chimney-glass, that he had come pretty far; and he had come so far because he was under the charm, — yes, he was in love with Lady

Barb. There was no doubt whatever of that; he had a faculty for diagnosis, and he knew perfectly well what was the matter with him. He wasted no time in musing upon the mystery of this passion, in wondering whether he might not have escaped it by a little vigilance at first, or whether it would die out if he should go away. He accepted it frankly, for the sake of the pleasure it gave him, — the girl was the delight of his eyes, — and confined himself to considering whether such a marriage would square with his general situation. This would not at all necessarily follow from the fact that he was in love; too many other things would come in between. The most important of these was the change, not only of the geographical, but of the social, standpoint for his wife, and a certain readjustment that it would involve in his own relation to things. He was not inclined to readjustments, and there was no reason why he should be; his own position was in most respects so advantageous. But the girl tempted him almost irresistibly, satisfying his imagination both as a lover and as a student of the human organism; she was so blooming, so complete, of a type so rarely encountered in that degree of perfection. Jackson Lemon was not an Anglo-maniac, but he admired the physical conditions of the English, — their complexion, their temperament, their tissue; and Lady Barberina struck him in flexible, virginal form, as a wonderful compendium of these elements. There was something simple and robust in her beauty; it had the quietness of an old Greek statue, without the vulgarity of the moderu simper or of contemporary prettiness. Her head was antique; and though her conversation was quite of the present period, Jackson Lemon had said to himself that there was sure to be in her soul a certain primitive sincerity which would match with the outline of her brow. He saw her as she might be in the future, the beautiful mother of beautiful children, in whom the look of race should be conspicuous. He should like his children to have the look of race, and he was not unaware that he must take his precautions accordingly. A great many people had it in England; and it was a pleasure to him to see it, especially as no one had it so unmistakably as the second daughter of Lord Canterville. It would be a great luxury to call such a woman one's own; nothing could be more evident than that, because it made no difference that she was not strikingly clever. Striking cleverness was not a part of harmonious form and the English complexion; it was associated with the modern simper, which was a result of modern nerves. If Jackson Lemon had wanted a nervous wife, of course he could have found her at home; but this tall, fair girl, whose character, like her figure, appeared mainly to have been formed by riding across country, was differently put together. All the same, would it suit his book, as they said in London, to marry her and transport her to New York? He came back to this question; came back to it with a persistency which, had she been admitted to a view

of it, would have tried the patience of Lady Beauchemin.　She had been irritated, more than once, at
his appearing to attach himself so exclusively to this
horn of the dilemma, — as if it could possibly fail to
be a good thing for a little American doctor to marry
the daughter of an English peer.　It would have
been more becoming, in her ladyship's eyes, that he
should take that for granted a little more, and the
consent of her ladyship's — of their ladyships' —
family a little less.　They looked at the matter so
differently !　Jackson Lemon was conscious that if
he should marry Lady Barberina Clement, it would
be because it suited him, and not because it suited
his possible sisters-in-law.　He believed that he acted
in all things by his own will, — an organ for which
he had the highest respect.

It would have seemed, however, that on this occasion it was not working very regularly, for though
he had come home to go to bed, the stroke of half-
past twelve saw him jump, not into his couch, but
into a hansom which the whistle of the porter had
summoned to the door of his hotel, and in which he
rattled off to Portland Place.　Here he found — in a
very large house — an assembly of three hundred
people, and a band of music concealed in a bower of
azaleas.　Lady Canterville had not arrived ; he wandered through the rooms and assured himself of that.
He also discovered a very good conservatory, where
there were banks and pyramids of azaleas.　He
watched the top of the staircase, but it was a long

time before he saw what he was looking for, and his impatience at last was extreme. The reward, however, when it came, was all that he could have desired. It was a little smile from Lady Barberina, who stood behind her mother while the latter extended her finger-tips to the hostess. The entrance of this charming woman, with her beautiful daughters—always a noticeable incident—was effected with a certain brilliancy, and just now it was agreeable to Jackson Lemon to think that it concerned him more than any one else in the house. Tall, dazzling, indifferent, looking about her as if she saw very little, Lady Barberina was certainly a figure round which a young man's fancy might revolve. She was very quiet and simple, had little manner and little movement; but her detachment was not a vulgar art. She appeared to efface herself, to wait till, in the natural course, she should be attended to; and in this there was evidently no exaggeration, for she was too proud not to have perfect confidence. Her sister, smaller, slighter, with a little surprised smile, which seemed to say that in her extreme innocence she was yet prepared for anything, having heard, indirectly, such extraordinary things about society, was much more impatient and more expressive, and projected across a threshold the pretty radiance of her eyes and teeth before her mother's name was announced. Lady Canterville was thought by many persons to be very superior to her daughters; she had kept even more beauty than she had given them; and it was a beauty

which had been called intellectual. She had extraordinary sweetness, without any definite professions;
her manner was mild almost to tenderness; there was
even a kind of pity in it. Moreover, her features
were perfect, and nothing could be more gently gracious than a way she had of speaking, or rather, of
listening, to people, with her head inclined a little
to one side. Jackson Lemon liked her very much,
and she had certainly been most kind to him. He
approached Lady Barberina as soon as he could do so
without an appearance of precipitation, and said to
her that he hoped very much she would not dance.
He was a master of the art which flourishes in New
York above every other, and he had guided her through
a dozen waltzes with a skill which, as she felt, left
absolutely nothing to be desired. But dancing was
not his business to-night. She smiled a little at the
expression of his hope.

"That is what mamma has brought us here for,"
she said; " she does n't like it if we don't dance."

" How does she know whether she likes it or not ?
You have always danced."

" Once I did n't," said Lady Barberina.

He told her that, at any rate, he would settle it
with her mother, and persuaded her to wander with
him into the conservatory, where there were colored
lights suspended among the plants, and a vault of
verdure overhead. In comparison with the other
rooms the conservatory was dusky and remote. But
they were not alone; half a dozen other couples

were in possession. The gloom was rosy with the slopes of azalea, and suffused with mitigated music, which made it possible to talk without consideration of one's neighbors. Nevertheless, though it was only in looking back on the scene later that Lady Barberina perceived this, these dispersed couples were talking very softly. She did not look at them; it seemed to her that, virtually, she was alone with Jackson Lemon. She said something about the flowers, about the fragrance of the air; for all answer to which he asked her, as he stood there before her, a question by which she might have been exceedingly startled.

"How do people who marry in England ever know each other before marriage? They have no chance."

"I am sure I don't know," said Lady Barberina; "I never was married."

"It 's very different in my country. There a man may see much of a girl; he may come and see her, he may be constantly alone with her. I wish you allowed that over here."

Lady Barberina suddenly examined the less ornamental side of her fan, as if it had never occurred to her before to look at it. "It must be so very odd, America," she murmured at last.

"Well, I guess in that matter we are right; over here it 's a leap in the dark."

"I am sure I don't know," said the girl. She had folded her fan; she stretched out her arm mechanically, and plucked a sprig of azalea.

"I guess it does n't signify, after all," Jackson

Lemon remarked. " They say that love is blind at the best." His keen young face was bent upon hers; his thumbs were in the pockets of his trousers; he smiled a little, showing his fine teeth. She said nothing, but only pulled her azalea to pieces. She was usually so quiet, that this small movement looked restless.

" This is the first time I have seen you in the least without a lot of people," he went on.

" Yes, it's very tiresome," she said.

"I have been sick of it; I did n't want to come here to-night."

She had not met his eyes, though she knew they were seeking her own. But now she looked at him a moment. She had never objected to his appearance, and in this respect she had no repugnance to overcome. She liked a man to be tall and handsome, and Jackson Lemon was neither; but when she was sixteen, and as tall herself as she was to be at twenty, she had been in love (for three weeks) with one of her cousins, a little fellow in the Hussars, who was. shorter even than the American, shorter, consequently, than herself. This proved that distinction might be independent of stature — not that she ever reasoned it out. Jackson Lemon's facial spareness, his bright little eye, which seemed always to be measuring things, struck her as original, and she thought them very cutting, which would do very well for a husband of hers. As she made this reflection, of course it never occurred to her that she herself might be cut; she was not a sacrificial lamb. She perceived that his features expressed a mind — a mind that would be rather superior. She would never have taken him for a doctor; though, indeed, when all was said, that was very negative, and did n't account for the way he imposed himself.

" Why, then, did you come ? " she asked, in answer to his last speech.

" Because it seems to me after all better to see you in this way than not to see you at all; I want to know you better."

" I don't think I ought to stay here," said Lady Barberina, looking round her.

" Don't go till I have told you I love you," murmured the young man.

She made no exclamation, indulged in no start; he could not see even that she changed color. She took his request with a noble simplicity, with her head erect and her eyes lowered.

" I don't think you have a right to tell me that."

" Why not ? " Jackson Lemon demanded. " I wish to claim the right; I wish you to give it to me."

" I can't — I don't know you. You have said it yourself."

" Can't you have a little faith ? That will help us to know each other better. It 's disgusting, the want of opportunity; even at Pasterns I could scarcely get a walk with you. But I have the greatest faith in you. I feel that I love you, and I could n't do more than that at the end of six months. I love your beauty — I love you from head to foot. Don't move, please don't move." He lowered his tone; but it went straight to her ear, and it must be believed that it had a certain eloquence. For himself, after he had heard himself say these words, all his being was in a glow. It was a luxury to speak to her of her beauty; it brought him nearer to her than he had ever been. But the color had come into her face, and it seemed to remind him that her beauty was not all. "Everything about you is sweet and noble," he went on; "everything is dear to me. I am sure you are good. I don't know what you think of me; I asked Lady Beauchemin to tell me, and she told me to judge for myself. Well, then, I judge you like me. Haven't I a right to assume that till the contrary is proved? May I speak to your father? That's what I want to know. I have been waiting; but now what should I wait for longer? I want to be able to tell him that you have given me some hope. I suppose I ought to speak to him first. I meant to, to-morrow, but meanwhile, to-night, I thought I would just put this in. In my country it would n't matter particularly. You must see all that over there for yourself. If you should tell me not to speak to your father, I would n't; I would wait. But I like better to ask your leave to speak to him than to ask his to speak to you."

His voice had sunk almost to a whisper; but, though it trembled, his emotion gave it peculiar intensity. He had the same attitude, his thumbs in his trousers, his attentive head, his smile, which was a matter of course; no one would have imagined what he was saying. She had listened without moving, and at the end she raised her eyes. They rested on his a moment, and he remembered, a good while later, the look which passed her lids.

"You may say anything that you please to my father, but I don't wish to hear any more. You have said too much, considering how little idea you have given me before."

"I was watching you," said Jackson Lemon.

Lady Barberina held her head higher, looking straight at him. Then, quite seriously, "I don't like to be watched," she remarked.

"You shouldn't be so beautiful, then. Won't you give me a word of hope?" he added.

"I have never supposed I should marry a foreigner," said Lady Barberiua.

"Do you call me a foreigner?"

"I think your ideas are very different, and your country is different; you have told me so yourself."

"I should like to show it to you; I would make you like it."

"I am not sure what you would make me do," said Lady Barberina, very honestly.

"Nothing that you don't want."

"I am sure you would try," she declared, with a smile.

"Well," said Jackson Lemon, "after all, I am trying now."

To this she simply replied she must go to her

mother, and he was obliged to lead her out of the conservatory. Lady Canterville was not immediately found, so that he had time to murmur as they went, " Now that I have spoken, I am very happy."

" Perhaps you are happy too soon," said the girl.

" Ah, don't say that, Lady Barb."

" Of course I must think of it."

" Of course you must!" said Jackson Lemon; " I will speak to your father to-morrow."

" I can't fancy what he will say."

" How can he dislike me ?" the young man asked, in a tone which Lady Beauchemin, if she had heard him, would have been forced to attribute to his general affectation of the jocose. What Lady Beauchemin's sister thought of it is not recorded ; but there is perhaps a clue to her opinion in the answer she made him after a moment's silence: " Really, you know, you *are* a foreigner!" With this she turned her back upon him, for she was already in her mother's hands. Jackson Lemon said a few words to Lady Canterville ; they were chiefly about its being very hot. She gave him her vague, sweet attention, as if he were saying something ingenious, of which she missed the point. He could see that she was thinking of the doings of her daughter Agatha, whose attitude toward the contemporary young man was wanting in the perception of differences, — a madness without method; she was evidently not occupied with Lady Barberina, who was more to be trusted. This young woman never met her suitor's eyes again; she let her own rest, rather ostentatiously, upon other objects. At last he was going away without a glance from her. Lady Canterville had asked him to come to lunch on the morrow, and he had said he would do so if she would promise him he should see his lordship. "I can't pay you another visit until I have had some talk with him," he said.

"I don't see why not; but if I speak to him, I dare say he will be at home," she answered.

"It will be worth his while!"

Jackson Lemon left the house reflecting that as he had never proposed to a girl before, he could not be expected to know how women demean themselves in this emergency. He had heard, indeed, that Lady Barb had had no end of offers; and though he thought it probable that the number was exaggerated, as it always is, it was to be supposed that her way of appearing suddenly to have dropped him was but the usual behavior for the occasion.

III.

AT her mother's the next day she was absent from luncheon, and Lady Canterville mentioned to him (he did n't ask) that she had gone to see a dear old great-aunt, who was also her godmother, and who lived at Roehampton. Lord Canterville was not present, but our young man was informed by his hostess that he

had promised her he would come in exactly at three
o'clock. Jackson Lemon lunched with Lady Canterville and the children, who appeared in force at this
repast, all the younger girls being present, and two
little boys, the juniors of the two sons who were in
their teens. Jackson, who was very fond of children,
and thought these absolutely the finest in the world,—
magnificent specimens of a magnificent brood, such
as it would be so satisfactory in future days to see
about his own knee, — Jackson felt that he was being
treated as one of the family, but was not frightened
by what he supposed the privilege to imply. Lady
Canterville betrayed no consciousness whatever of
his having mooted the question of becoming her son-
in-law, and he believed that her eldest daughter had
not told her of their talk the night before. This
idea gave him pleasure; he liked to think that Lady
Barb was judging him for herself. Perhaps, indeed, she
was taking counsel of the old lady at Roehampton :
he believed that he was the sort of lover of whom a
godmother would approve. Godmothers in his mind
were mainly associated with fairy-tales (he had had
no baptismal sponsors of his own); and that point of
view would be favorable to a young man with a great
deal of gold who had suddenly arrived from a foreign
country, — an apparition, surely, sufficiently elfish.
He made up his mind that he should like Lady Canterville as a mother-in-law; she would be too well-
bred to meddle. Her husband came in at three
o'clock, just after they had left the table, and said to

Jackson Lemon that it was very good in him to have waited.

"I have n't waited," Jackson replied, with his watch in his hand; "you are punctual to the minute."

I know not how Lord Canterville may have judged his young friend, but Jackson Lemon had been told more than once in his life that he was a very good fellow, but rather too literal. After he had lighted a cigarette in his lordship's "den," a large brown apartment on the ground-floor, which partook at once of the nature of an office and of that of a harness-room (it could not have been called in any degree a library), he went straight to the point in these terms: " Well now, Lord Canterville, I feel as if I ought to let you know without more delay that I am in love with Lady Barb, and that I should like to marry her." So he spoke, puffing his cigarette, with his conscious but unextenuating eye fixed on his host.

No man, as I have intimated, bore better being looked at than this noble personage; he seemed to bloom in the envious warmth of human contemplation, and never appeared so faultless as when he was most exposed. "My dear fellow, my dear fellow," he murmured, almost in disparagement, stroking his ambrosial beard from before the empty fireplace. He lifted his eyebrows, but he looked perfectly good-natured.

"Are you surprised, sir?" Jackson Lemon asked.

"Why, I suppose any one is surprised at a man wanting one of his children. He sometimes feels the weight of that sort of thing so much, you know. He wonders what the devil another man wants of them." And Lord Canterville laughed pleasantly out of the copious fringe of his lips.

"I only want one of them," said Jackson Lemon, laughing too, but with a lighter organ.

" Polygamy would be rather good for the parents. However, Lucy told me the other night that she thought you were looking the way you speak of."

" Yes, I told Lady Beauchemin that I love Lady Barb, and she seemed to think it was natural."

" Oh, yes, I suppose there 's no want of nature in it! But, my dear fellow, I really don't know what to say."

" Of course you 'll have to think of it." Jackson Lemon, in saying this, felt that he was making the most liberal concession to the point of view of his interlocutor; being perfectly aware that in his own country it was not left much to the parents to think of.

" I shall have to talk it over with my wife."

" Lady Canterville has been very kind to me; I hope she will continue."

" My dear fellow, we are excellent friends. No one could appreciate you more than Lady Canterville. Of course we can only consider such a question on the — a — the highest grounds. You would never want to marry without knowing, as it were, exactly what you are doing. I, on my side, naturally, you know, am bound to do the best I can for my own child. At the same time, of course, we don't want to spend our time in — a — walking round the horse. We want to keep to the main lines." It was settled between them after a little that the main lines were that Jackson Lemon knew to a certainty the state of his affections, and was in a position to pretend to the hand of a young lady who Lord Canterville might say — of course, you know, without swaggering about it — had a right to expect to do well, as the women call it.

"I should think she had," Jackson Lemon said; "she's a beautiful type."

Lord Canterville stared a moment. "She is a clever, well-grown girl, and she takes her fences like a grasshopper. Does she know all this, by the way?" he added.

"Oh yes, I told her last night."

Again Lord Canterville had the air, unusual with him, of returning his companion's regard. "I am not sure that you ought to have done that, you know."

"I could n't have spoken to you first — I could n't," said Jackson Lemon. "I meant to; but it stuck in my crop."

"They don't in your country, I guess," his lordship returned, smiling.

"Well, not as a general thing; however, I find it very pleasant to discuss with you now." And in truth it was very pleasant. Nothing could be easier, friendlier, more informal, than Lord Canterville's manner, which implied all sorts of equality, especially that of age and fortune, and made Jackson Lemon feel at the end of three minutes almost as if he too were a beautifully preserved and somewhat straitened nobleman of sixty, with the views of a man of the world about his own marriage. The young American perceived that Lord Canterville waived the point of his having spoken first to the girl herself, and saw in this indulgence a just concession to the ardor of young affection. For Lord Canterville seemed perfectly to appreciate the sentimental side, — at least so far as it was embodied in his visitor, — when he said without deprecation: "Did she give you any encouragement ? "

"Well, she did n't box my ears. She told me that she would think of it, but that I must speak to you. But naturally I should n't have said what I did to her if I had n't made up my mind during the last fortnight that I am not disagreeable to her."

"Ah, my dear young man, women are odd cattle ! " Lord Canterville exclaimed, rather unexpectedly. "But of course you know all that," he added in an instant; "you take the general risk."

"I am perfectly willing to take the general risk; the particular risk is small."

"Well, upon my honor I don't really know my girls. You see a man's time, in England, is tremendously taken up; but I dare say it 's the same in your country. Their mother knows them — I think I had better send for their mother. If you don't mind I 'll just suggest that she join us here."

"I 'm rather afraid of you both together, but if it will settle it any quicker —" said Jackson Lemon. Lord Canterville rang the bell, and, when a servant appeared, despatched him with a message to her ladyship. While they were waiting, the young man remembered that it was in his power to give a more definite account of his pecuniary basis. He had simply said before that he was abundantly able to marry; he shrank from putting himself forward as a billionnaire. He had a fine taste, and he wished to appeal to Lord Canterville primarily as a gentleman. But now that he had to make a double impression, he bethought himself of his millions, for millions were always impressive. "I think it only fair to let you know that my fortune is really very considerable," he remarked.

"Yes, I dare say you are beastly rich," said Lord Canterville.

"I have about seven millions."

"Seven millions?"

"I count in dollars; upwards of a million and a half sterling."

Lord Canterville looked at him from head to foot, with an air of cheerful resignation to a form of grossness which threatened to become common. Then he said, with a touch of that inconsequence of which he had already given a glimpse: "What the deuce, then, possessed you to turn doctor?"

Jackson Lemon colored a little, hesitated, and then said quickly: "Because I had the talent for it."

"Of course, I don't for a moment doubt of your ability; but don't you find it rather a bore?"

"I don't practise much. I am rather ashamed to say that."

"Ah, well, of course, in your country it's different. I dare say you've got a door-plate, eh?"

"Oh yes, and a tin sign tied to the balcony!" said Jackson Lemon, smiling.

"What did your father say to it?"

"To my going into medicine? He said he would be hanged if he'd take any of my doses. He didn't think I should succeed; he wanted me to go into the house."

"Into the House — a —" said Lord Canterville, hesitating a little. "Into your Congress — yes, exactly."

"Ah, no, not so bad as that. Into the store," Jackson Lemon replied, in the candid tone in which he expressed himself when, for reasons of his own, he wished to be perfectly national.

Lord Canterville stared, not venturing, even for the moment, to hazard an interpretation; and before a solution had presented itself, Lady Canterville came into the room.

"My dear, I thought we had better see you. Do you know he wants to marry our second girl?" It was in these simple terms that her husband acquainted her with the question.

Lady Canterville expressed neither surprise nor elation; she simply stood there, smiling, with her head a little inclined to the side, with all her customary graciousness. Her charming eyes rested on those of Jackson Lemon; and though they seemed to show that she had to think a little of so serious a proposition, his own discovered in them none of the coldness of calculation. "Are you talking about Barberina?" she asked in a moment, as if her thoughts had been far away.

Of course they were talking about Barberina, and Jackson Lemon repeated to her ladyship what he had said to the girl's father. He had thought it all over, and his mind was quite made up. Moreover, he had spoken to Lady Barb.

"Did she tell you that, my dear?" asked Lord Canterville, while he lighted another cigar.

She gave no heed to this inquiry, which had been vague and accidental on his lordship's part, but simply said to Jackson Lemon that the thing was very serious, and that they had better sit down for a moment. In an instant he was near her on the sofa on which she had placed herself, still smiling and looking up at her husband with an air of general meditation, in which a sweet compassion for every one concerned was apparent.

"Barberina has told me nothing," she said after a little.

"That proves she cares for me!" Jackson Lemon exclaimed, eagerly.

Lady Canterville looked as if she thought this almost too ingenious, almost professional; but her husband said cheerfully, jovially: "Ah well, if she cares for you, I don't object."

This was a little ambiguous; but before Jackson Lemon had time to look into it, Lady Canterville asked, gently: "Should you expect her to live in America?"

"Oh, yes; that's my home, you know."

"Shouldn't you be living sometimes in England?"

"Oh, yes, we'll come over and see you." The young man was in love, he wanted to marry, he wanted to be genial, and to commend himself to the parents of Lady Barb; at the same time it was in his nature not to accept conditions, save in so far as they exactly suited him, to tie himself, or, as they said in New York, to give himself away. In any transaction he preferred his own terms to those of any one else. Therefore, the moment Lady Canterville gave signs of wishing to extract a promise, he was on his guard.

"She'll find it very different; perhaps she won't like it," her ladyship suggested.

"If she likes me, she'll like my country," said Jackson Lemon, with decision.

"He tells me he has got a plate on his door," Lord Canterville remarked, humorously.

"We must talk to her, of course; we must understand how she feels," said his wife, looking more serious than she had done as yet.

"Please don't discourage her, Lady Canterville," the young man begged; "and give me a chance to talk to her a little more myself. You haven't given me much chance, you know."

"We don't offer our daughters to people, Mr. Lemon." Lady Canterville was always gentle, but now she was a little majestic.

"She is n't like some women in London, you know," said Jackson Lemon's host, who seemed to remember that to a discussion of such importance he ought from time to time to contribute a word of wisdom. And Jackson Lemon, certainly, if the idea had been presented to him, would have said that, No, decidedly, Lady Barberina had not been thrown at him.

"Of course not," he declared, in answer to her mother's remark. "But, you know, you must n't refuse them too much, either; you must n't make a poor fellow wait too long. I admire her, I love her, more than I can say; I give you my word of honor for that."

"He seems to think that settles it," said Lord Canterville, smiling down at the young American, very pleasantly, from his place before the cold chimney-piece.

"Of course that's what we desire, Phillip," her ladyship returned, very nobly.

"Lady Barb believes it; I am sure she does!" Jackson Lemon exclaimed. "Why should I pretend to be in love with her if I am not?"

Lady Canterville received this inquiry in silence, and her husband, with just the least air in the world of repressed impatience, began to walk up and down the room. He was a man of many engagements, and he had been closeted for more than a quarter of an hour with the young American doctor. "Do you imagine you should come often to England?" Lady Canterville demanded, with a certain abruptness, returning to that important point.

"I'm afraid I can't tell you that; of course we shall do whatever seems best." He was prepared to suppose they should cross the Atlantic every summer: that prospect was by no means displeasing to him; but he was not prepared to give any such pledge to Lady Canterville, especially as he did not believe it would really be necessary. It was in his mind, not as an overt pretension, but as a tacit implication that he should treat with Barberina's parents on a footing of perfect equality; and there would somehow be nothing equal if he should begin to enter into engagements which did n't belong to the essence of the matter. They were to give their daughter, and he was to take her: in this arrangement there would be as much on one side as on the other. But beyond this he had nothing to ask of them; there was nothing he wished them to promise, and his own pledges, therefore, would have no equivalent. Whenever his wife should wish it, she should come over and see her people. Her home was to be in New York; but he was tacitly conscious that on the question of absences he should be very liberal. Nevertheless, there was something in the very grain of his character which forbade that he should commit himself at present in respect to times and dates.

Lady Canterville looked at her husband, but her

husband was not attentive; he was taking a peep at his watch. In a moment, however, he threw out a remark to the effect that he thought it a capital thing that the two countries should become more united, and there was nothing that would bring it about better than a few of the best people on both sides pairing off together. The English, indeed, had begun it; a lot of fellows had brought over a lot of pretty girls, and it was quite fair play that the Americans should take their pick. They were all one race, after all; and why should n't they make one society, — the best on both sides, of course? Jackson Lemon smiled as he recognized Lady Marmaduke's philosophy, and he was pleased to think that Lady Beauchemin had some influence with her father; for he was sure the old gentleman (as he mentally designated his host) had got all this from her, though he expressed himself less happily than the cleverest of his daughters. Our hero had no objection to make to it, especially if there was anything in it that would really help his case. But it was not in the least on these high grounds that he had sought the hand of Lady Barb. He wanted her not in order that her people and his (the best on both sides!) should make one society; he wanted her simply because he wanted her. Lady Canterville smiled; but she seemed to have another thought.

"I quite appreciate what my husband says; but I don't see why poor Barb should be the one to begin."

"I dare say she 'll like it," said Lord Canterville,

as if he were attempting a short cut. " They say you spoil your women awfully."

" She 's not one of their women yet," her ladyship remarked, in the sweetest tone in the world; and then she added, without Jackson Lemon's knowing exactly what she meant, " It seems so strange."

He was a little irritated ; and perhaps these simple words added to the feeling. There had been no positive opposition to his suit, and Lord and Lady Canterville were most kind; but he felt that they held back a little ; and though he had not expected them to throw themselves on his neck, he was rather disappointed; his pride was touched. Why should they hesitate ? He considered himself such a good *parti.* It was not so much the old gentleman, it was Lady Canterville. As he saw the old gentleman look, covertly, a second time at his watch, he could have believed he would have been glad to settle the matter on the spot. Lady Canterville seemed to wish her daughter's lover to come forward more, to give certain assurances and guaranties. He felt that he was ready to say or do anything that was a matter of proper form ; but he could n't take the tone of trying to purchase her ladyship's consent, penetrated as he was with the conviction that such a man as he could be trusted to care for his wife rather more than an impecunious British peer and *his* wife could be supposed (with the lights he had acquired in English society) to care even for the handsomest of a dozen children. It was a mistake on Lady Canterville's part not to recognize that. He humored her mistake to the extent of saying, just a little dryly, " My wife shall certainly have everything she wants."

" He tells me he is disgustingly rich," Lord Canterville added, pausing before their companion with his hands in his pockets.

" I am glad to hear it; but it is n't so much that," she answered, sinking back a little on her sofa. If it was not that, she did not say what it was, though she had looked for a moment as if she were going to. She only raised her eyes to her husband's face, as if to ask for inspiration. I know not whether she found it, but in a moment she said to Jackson Lemon, seeming to imply that it was quite another point: " Do you expect to continue your profession ?"

He had no such intention, so far as his profession meant getting up at three o'clock in the morning to assuage the ills of humanity; but here, as before, the touch of such a question instantly stiffened him. " Oh, my profession ! I am rather ashamed of that matter. I have neglected my work so much, I don't know what I shall be able to do, once I am really settled at home."

Lady Canterville received these remarks in silence; fixing her eyes again upon her husband's face. But this nobleman was really not helpful; still with his hands in his pockets, save when he needed to remove his cigar from his lips, he went and looked out of the window. " Of course we know you don't practise, and when you 're a married man you will have less

time even than now. But I should really like to
know if they call you Doctor over there."

"Oh, yes, universally. We are nearly as fond of
titles as your people."

"I don't call that a title."

"It's not so good as duke or marquis, I admit;
but we have to take what we have got."

"Oh, bother, what does it signify?" Lord Canterville demanded, from his place at the window. "I
used to have a horse named Doctor, and a devilish
good one too."

"You may call me bishop, if you like," said Jackson Lemon, laughing.

Lady Canterville looked grave, as if she did not enjoy this pleasantry. "I don't care for any titles," she
observed; "I don't see why a gentleman should n't
be called Mr."

It suddenly appeared to Jackson Lemon that there
was something helpless, confused, and even slightly
comical, in the position of this noble and amiable
lady. The impression made him feel kindly; he too,
like Lord Canterville, had begun to long for a short
cut. He relaxed a moment, and leaning toward his
hostess, with a smile and his hands on his little
knees, he said, softly, "It seems to me a question of
no importance; all I desire is that you should call
me your son-in-law."

Lady Canterville gave him her hand, and he pressed
it almost affectionately. Then she got up, remarking
that before anything was decided she must see her

daughter, she must learn from her own lips the state of her feelings. "I don't like at all her not having spoken to me already," she added.

"Where has she gone — to Roehampton? I dare say she has told it all to her godmother," said Lord Canterville.

"She won't have much to tell, poor girl!" Jackson Lemon exclaimed. "I must really insist upon seeing with more freedom the person I wish to marry."

"You shall have all the freedom you want, in two or three days," said Lady Canterville. She smiled with all her sweetness; she appeared to have accepted him, and yet still to be making tacit assumptions. "Are there not certain things to be talked of first?"

"Certain things, dear lady?"

Lady Canterville looked at her husband, and though he was still at his window, this time he felt it in her silence, and had to come away and speak. "Oh, she means settlements, and that kind of thing." This was an allusion which came with a much better grace from him.

Jackson Lemon looked from one of his companions to the other; he colored a little, and gave a smile that was perhaps a trifle fixed. "Settlements? We don't make them in the United States. You may be sure I shall make a proper provision for my wife."

"My dear fellow, over here — in our class, you know, it 's the custom," said Lord Canterville, with a richer brightness in his face at the thought that the discussion was over.

" I have my own ideas," Jackson answered, smiling.

" It seems to me it 's a question for the solicitors to discuss," Lady Canterville suggested.

" They may discuss it as much as they please," said Jackson Lemon, with a laugh. He thought he saw his solicitors discussing it ! He had indeed his own ideas. He opened the door for Lady Canterville, and the three passed out of the room together, walking into the hall in a silence in which there was just a tinge of awkwardness. A note had been struck which grated and scratched a little. A pair of brilliant footmen, at their approach, rose from a bench to a great altitude, and stood there like sentinels presenting arms. Jackson Lemon stopped, looking for a moment into the interior of his hat, which he had in his hand. Then, raising his keen eyes, he fixed them a moment on those of Lady Canterville, addressing her, instinctively, rather than her husband. " I guess you and Lord Canterville had better leave it to me ! "

" We have our traditions, Mr. Lemon," said her ladyship, with nobleness. " I imagine you don't know——" she murmured.

Lord Canterville laid his hand on the young man's shoulder. " My dear boy, those fellows will settle it in three minutes."

" Very likely they will ! " said Jackson Lemon. Then he asked of Lady Canterville when he might see Lady Barb.

She hesitated a moment, in her gracious way. " I will write you a note."

One of the tall footmen, at the end of the impressive vista, had opened wide the portals, as if even he were aware of the dignity to which the little visitor had virtually been raised. But Jackson lingered a moment; he was visibly unsatisfied, though apparently so little unconscious that he was unsatisfying. " I don't think you understand me."

"Your ideas are certainly different," said Lady Canterville.

" If the girl understands you, that 's enough !" Lord Canterville exclaimed in a jovial, detached, irrelevant way.

"May not *she* write to me ? " Jackson asked of her mother. "I certainly must write to her, you know, if you won't let me see her."

"Oh, yes, you may write to her, Mr. Lemon."

There was a point for a moment in the look that he gave Lady Canterville, while he said to himself that if it were necessary he would transmit his notes through the old lady at Roehampton. "All right, good by ; you know what I want, at any rate." Then, as he was going, he turned and added : "You need n't be afraid that I won't bring her over in the hot weather ! "

"In the hot weather ? " Lady Canterville murmured, with vague visions of the torrid zone, while the young American quitted the house with the sense that he had made great concessions.

His host and hostess passed into a small morning-room, and (Lord Canterville having taken up his hat

and stick to go out again) stood there a moment, face
to face.

"It 's clear enough he wants her," said his lordship,
in a summary manner.

"There 's something so odd about him," Lady Canterville answered. "Fancy his speaking so about
settlements ! "

"You had better give him his head; he 'll go
much quieter."

"He 's so obstinate — very obstinate; it 's easy to
see that. And he seems to think a girl in your
daughter's position can be married from one day to
the other — with a ring and a new frock — like a
housemaid."

"Well, of course, over there, that 's the kind of
thing. But he seems really to have a most extraordinary fortune ; and every one does say their women
have *carte blanche.*"

" *Carte blanche* is not what Barb wishes ; she wishes
a settlement. She wants a definite income ; she wants
to be safe."

Lord Canterville stared a moment. "Has she told
you so ? I thought you said———." And then he
stopped. " I beg your pardon," he added.

Lady Canterville gave no explanation of her inconsistency. She went on to remark that American fortunes were notoriously insecure ; one heard of nothing
else ; they melted away like smoke. It was their
duty to their child to demand that something should
be fixed.

"He has a million and a half sterling," said Lord Canterville. "I can't make out what he does with it."

" She ought to have something very handsome," his wife remarked.

" Well, my dear, you must settle it: you must consider it; you must send for Hilary. Only take care you don't put him off; it may be a very good opening, you know. There is a great deal to be done out there; I believe in all that," Lord Canterville went on, in the tone of a conscientious parent.

" There is no doubt that he *is* a doctor — in those places," said Lady Canterville, musingly.

" He may be a pedler for all I care."

" If they should go out, I think Agatha might go with them," her ladyship continued, in the same tone, a little disconnectedly.

" You may send them all out if you like. Good by !" And Lord Canterville kissed his wife.

But she detained him a moment, with her hand on his arm. " Don't you think he is very much in love ? "

" Oh, yes, he 's very bad; but he 's a clever little beggar."

" She likes him very much," Lady Canterville announced, rather formally, as they separated.

PART SECOND.

IV.

JACKSON LEMON had said to Sidney Feeder in the
Park that he would call on Mr. and Mrs. Freer; but
three weeks elapsed before he knocked at their door
in Jermyn Street. In the meantime he had met
them at dinner, and Mrs. Freer had told him that she
hoped very much he would find time to come and see
her. She had not reproached him, nor shaken her
finger at him; and her clemency, which was calcu-
lated, and very characteristic of her, touched him so
much (for he was in fault; she was one of his
mother's oldest and best friends), that he very soon
presented himself. It was on a fine Sunday afternoon, rather late, and the region of Jermyn Street
looked forsaken and inanimate; the native dulness of
the landscape appeared in all its purity. Mrs. Freer,
however, was at home, resting on a lodging-house
sofa — an angular couch, draped in faded chintz —
before she went to dress for dinner. She made the
young man very welcome; she told him she had
been thinking of him a great deal; she had wished
to have a chance to talk with him. He immediately
perceived what she had in mind, and then he remembered that Sidney Feeder had told him what it was

that Mr. and Mrs. Freer took upon themselves to say. This had provoked him at the time, but he had forgotten it afterward; partly because he became aware, that same evening, that he did wish to marry the "young marchioness," and partly because since then he had had much greater annoyances. Yes, the poor young man, so conscious of liberal intentions, of a large way of looking at the future, had had much to irritate and disgust him. He had seen the mistress of his affections but three or four times, and he had received letters from Mr. Hilary, Lord Canterville's solicitor, asking him, in terms the most obsequious, it is true, to designate some gentleman of the law with whom the preliminaries of his marriage to Lady Barberina Clement might be arranged. He had given Mr. Hilary the name of such a functionary, but he had written by the same post to his own solicitor (for whose services in other matters he had had much occasion, Jackson Lemon being distinctly contentious), instructing him that he was at liberty to meet Mr. Hilary, but not at liberty to entertain any proposals as to this odious English idea of a settlement. If marrying Jackson Lemon were not settlement enough, then Lord and Lady Canterville had better alter their point of view. It was quite out of the question that he should alter his. It would perhaps be difficult to explain the strong aversion that he entertained to the introduction into his prospective union of this harsh diplomatic element; it was as if they mistrusted him, suspected him; as if his

hands were to be tied, so that he could not handle
his own fortune as he thought best. It was not the
idea of parting with his money that displeased him,
for he flattered himself that he had plans of expenditure for his wife beyond even the imagination of her
distinguished parents. It struck him even that they
were fools not to have perceived that they should
make a much better thing of it by leaving him perfectly free. This intervention of the solicitor was
a nasty little English tradition — totally at variance
with the large spirit of American habits — to which
he would not submit. It was not his way to submit
when he disapproved : why should he change his way
on this occasion, when the matter lay so near him ?
These reflections, and a hundred more, had flowed
freely through his mind for several days before he
called in Jermyn Street, and they had engendered a
lively indignation and a really bitter sense of wrong.
As may be imagined, they had infused a certain awkwardness into his relations with the house of Canterville, and it may be said of these relations that they
were for the moment virtually suspended. His first
interview with Lady Barb, after his conference with
the old couple, as he called her august elders, had
been as tender as he could have desired. Lady Canterville, at the end of three days, had sent him an
invitation — five words on a card — asking him to
dine with them to-morrow, quite *en famille*. This
had been the only formal intimation that his engagement to Lady Barb was recognized ; for even at the

family banquet, which included half a dozen outsiders, there had been no allusion on the part either of his host or his hostess to the subject of their conversation in Lord Canterville's den. The only allusion was a wandering ray, once or twice, in Lady Barberina's eyes. When, however, after dinner, she strolled away with him into the music-room, which was lighted and empty, to play for him something out of *Carmen,* of which he had spoken at table, and when the young couple were allowed to enjoy for upwards of an hour, unmolested, the comparative privacy of this rich apartment, he felt that Lady Canterville definitely counted upon him. She did n't believe in any serious difficulties. Neither did he, then; and that was why it was a nuisance there should be a vain appearance of them. The arrangements, he supposed Lady Canterville would have said, were pending, and indeed they were; for he had already given orders in Bond Street for the setting of an extraordinary number of diamonds. Lady Barb, at any rate, during that hour he spent with her, had had nothing to say about arrangements; and it had been an hour of pure satisfaction. She had seated herself at the piano and had played perpetually, in a soft, incoherent manner, while he leaned over the instrument, very close to her, and said everything that came into his head. She was very bright and serene, and she looked at him as if she liked him very much.

This was all he expected of her, for it did not belong to the cast of her beauty to betray a vulgar infatuation. That beauty was more delightful to him than ever; and there was a softness about her which seemed to say to him that from this moment she was quite his own. He felt more than ever the value of such a possession; it came over him more than ever that it had taken a great social outlay to produce such a mixture. Simple and girlish as she was, and not particularly quick in the give and take of conversation, she seemed to him to have a part of the history of England in her blood; she was a *résumé* of generations of privileged people, and of centuries of rich country-life. Between these two, of course, there was no allusion to the question which had been put into the hands of Mr. Hilary, and the last thing that occurred to Jackson Lemon was that Lady Barb had views as to his settling a fortune upon her before their marriage. It may appear singular, but he had not asked himself whether his money operated upon her in any degree as a bribe; and this was because, instinctively, he felt that such a speculation was idle,—the point was not to be ascertained,—and because he was willing to assume that it was agreeable to her that she should continue to live in luxury. It was eminently agreeable to him that he might enable her to do so. He was acquainted with the mingled character of human motives, and he was glad that he was rich enough to pretend to the hand of a young woman who, for the best of reasons, would be very expensive. After that happy hour in the music-room he had ridden with her twice; but he had not found her otherwise accessible. She had let him know, the second time they rode, that Lady Canterville had directed her to make, for the moment, no further appointment with him ; and on his presenting himself, more than once at the house, he had been told that neither the mother nor the daughter was at home ; it had been added that Lady Barberina was staying at Roehampton. On giving him that information in the Park, Lady Barb had looked at him with a mute reproach, — there was always a certain superior dumbness in her eyes, — as if he were exposing her to an annoyance that she ought to be spared ; as if he were taking an eccentric line on a question that all well-bred people treated in the conventional way. His induction from this was not that she wished to be secure about his money, but that, like a dutiful English daughter, she received her opinions (on points that were indifferent to her) ready-made from a mamma whose fallibility had never been exposed. He knew by this that his solicitor had answered Mr. Hilary's letter, and that Lady Canterville's coolness was the fruit of this correspondence. The effect of it was not in the least to make him come round, as he phrased it ; he had not the smallest intention of doing that. Lady Canterville had spoken of the traditions of her family ; but he had no need to go to his family for his own. They resided within himself ; anything that he had definitely made up his mind to, acquired in an hour the force of a tradition. Meanwhile, he was in the detestable position of not knowing whether or no he were engaged. He wrote to Lady Barb to inquire,—it being so strange that she should not receive him; and she answered, in a very pretty little letter, which had to his mind a sort of bygone quality, an old-fashioned freshness, as if it might have been written in the last century by Clarissa or Amelia: she answered that she did not in the least understand the situation; that, of course, she would never give him up; that her mother had said that there were the best reasons for their not going too fast; that, thank God, she was yet young, and could wait as long as he would; but that she begged he would n't write her anything about money-matters, as she could never comprehend them. Jackson felt that he was in no danger whatever of making this last mistake; he only noted how Lady Barb thought it natural that there should be a discussion; and this made it vivid to him afresh that he had got hold of a daughter of the Crusaders. His ingenious mind could appreciate this hereditary assumption perfectly, at the same time that, to light his own footsteps, it remained entirely modern. He believed—or he thought he believed—that in the end he should marry Barberina Clement on his own terms; but in the interval there was a sensible indignity in being challenged and checked. One effect of it, indeed, was to make him desire the girl more keenly. When she was not before his eyes in the flesh, she hovered before him as an image; and this image had reasons of its own for being a radiant picture. There were moments, however, when he wearied of looking at it; it was so impalpable and thankless, and then Jackson Lemon, for the first time in his life, was melancholy. He felt alone in London, and very much out of it, in spite of all the acquaintances he had made, and the bills he had paid; he felt the need of a greater intimacy than any he had formed (save, of course, in the case of Lady Barb). He wanted to vent his disgust, to relieve himself, from the American point of view. He felt that in engaging in a contest with the great house of Canterville, he was, after all, rather single. That singleness was, of course, in a great measure an inspiration; but it pinched him a little at moments. Then he wished his mother had been in London, for he used to talk of his affairs a great deal with this delightful parent, who had a soothing way of advising him in the sense he liked best. He had even gone so far as to wish he had never laid eyes on Lady Barb, and had fallen in love with some transatlantic maiden of a similar composition. He presently came back, of course, to the knowledge that in the United States there was — and there could be — nothing similar to Lady Barb; for was it not precisely as a product of the English climate and the British constitution that he valued her? He had relieved himself, from his American point of view, by speaking his mind to Lady Beauchemin, who confessed that she was very much vexed with her parents. She agreed with him that they had made a great mistake; they ought to have left

him free; and she expressed her confidence that
that freedom would be for her family, as it were,
like the silence of the sage, golden. He must excuse
them; he must remember that what was asked of
him had been their custom for centuries. She did
not mention her authority as to the origin of customs,
but she assured him that she would say three words
to her father and mother, which would make it all
right. Jackson answered that customs were all very
well, but that intelligent people recognized, when
they saw it, the right occasion for departing from
them; and with this he awaited the result of Lady
Beauchemin's remonstrance. It had not as yet been
perceptible, and it must be said that this charming
woman was herself much bothered. When, on her
venturing to say to her mother that she thought a
wrong line had been taken with regard to her sister's
prétendant, Lady Canterville had replied that Mr.
Lemon's unwillingness to settle anything was in itself a proof of what they had feared, the unstable
nature of his fortune (for it was useless to talk —
this gracious. lady could be very decided — there
could be no serious reason but that one —) on meeting this argument, as I say, Jackson's protectress felt
considerably baffled. It was perhaps true, as her
mother said, that if they did n't insist upon proper
guaranties, Barberina might be left in a few years
with nothing but the stars and stripes (this odd
phrase was a quotation from Mr. Lemon) to cover her.
Lady Beauchemin tried to reason it out with Lady

Marmaduke; but these were complications unforeseen by Lady Marmaduke in her project of an Anglo-American society. She was obliged to confess that Mr. Lemon's fortune could not have the solidity of long-established things; it was a very new fortune indeed. His father had made the greater part of it all in a lump, a few years before his death, in the extraordinary way in which people made money in America; that, of course, was why the son had those singular professional attributes. He had begun to study to be a doctor very young, before his expectations were so great. Then he had found he was very clever, and very fond of it; and he had kept on, because, after all, in America, where there were no country gentlemen, a young man had to have something to do, don't you know? And Lady Marmaduke, like an enlightened woman, intimated that in such a case she thought it in much better taste not to try to sink anything. "Because, in America, don't you see," she reasoned, "you can't sink it — nothing *will* sink. Everything is floating about — in the newspapers." And she tried to console her friend by remarking that if Mr. Lemon's fortune was precarious, it was at all events so big. That was just the trouble for Lady Beauchemin; it was so big, and yet they were going to lose it. He was as obstinate as a mule; she was sure he would never come round. Lady Marmaduke declared that he would come round; she even offered to bet a dozen pair of *gants de Suède* on it; and she added that this consummation lay quite in the hands of Barberina. Lady Beauchemin promised herself to converse with her sister; for it was not for nothing that she herself had felt the international contagion.

Jackson Lemon, to dissipate his chagrin, had returned to the sessions of the medical congress, where, inevitably, he had fallen into the hands of Sidney Feeder, who enjoyed in this disinterested assembly a high popularity. It was Dr. Feeder's earnest desire that his old friend should share it, which was all the more easy as the medical congress was really, as the young physician observed, a perpetual symposium. Jackson Lemon entertained the whole body — entertained it profusely, and in a manner befitting one of the patrons of science rather than its humbler votaries; but these dissipations only made him forget for a moment that his relations with the house of Canterville were anomalous. His great difficulty punctually came back to him, and Sidney Feeder saw it stamped upon his brow. Jackson Lemon, with his acute inclination to open himself, was on the point, more than once, of taking the sympathetic Sidney into his confidence. His friend gave him easy opportunity; he asked him what it was he was thinking of all the time, and whether the young marchioness had concluded she could n't swallow a doctor. These forms of speech were displeasing to Jackson Lemon, whose fastidiousness was nothing new; but it was for even deeper reasons that he said to himself that, for such complicated cases as his, there was no assistance in Sidney Feeder. To understand his situation one must know the world; and the child of Cincinnati did n't know the world,—at least the world with which his friend was now concerned.

"Is there a hitch in your marriage? Just tell me that," Sidney Feeder had said, taking everything for granted, in a manner which was in itself a proof of great innocence. It is true he had added that he supposed he had no business to ask; but he had been anxious about it ever since hearing from Mr. and Mrs. Freer that the British aristocracy was down on the medical profession. "Do they want you to give it up? Is that what the hitch is about? Don't desert your colors, Jackson. The repression of pain, the mitigation of misery, constitute surely the noblest profession in the world."

"My dear fellow, you don't know what you are talking about," Jackson observed, for answer to this. "I have n't told any one I was going to be married; still less have I told any one that any one objected to my profession. I should like to see them do it. I have got out of the swim to-day, but I don't regard myself as the sort of person that people object to. And I do expect to do something, yet."

"Come home, then, and do it. And excuse me if I say that the facilities for getting married are much greater over there."

"You don't seem to have found them very great."

"I have never had time. Wait till my next vacation, and you will see."

"The facilities over there are too great. Nothing is good but what is difficult," said Jackson Lemon, in a tone of artificial sententiousness that quite tormented his interlocutor.

"Well, they have got their backs up, I can see that. I'm glad you like it. Only if they despise your profession, what will they say to that of your friends? If they think you are queer, what would they think of me?" asked Sidney Feeder, the turn of whose mind was not, as a general thing, in the least sarcastic, but who was pushed to this sharpness by a conviction that (in spite of declarations which seemed half an admission and half a denial) his friend was suffering himself to be bothered for the sake of a good which might be obtained elsewhere without bother. It had come over him that the bother was of an unworthy kind.

"My dear fellow, all that is idiotic." That had been Jackson Lemon's reply; but it expressed but a portion of his thoughts. The rest was inexpressible, or almost; being connected with a sentiment of rage at its having struck even so genial a mind as Sidney Feeder's, that in proposing to marry a daughter of the highest civilization he was going out of his way — departing from his natural line. Was he then so ignoble, so pledged to inferior things, that when he saw a girl who (putting aside the fact that she had not genius, which was rare, and which, though he prized rarity, he didn't want) seemed to him the most complete feminine nature he had known, he was to think himself too different, too incongruous, to mate with her? He would mate with whom he chose; that was the upshot of Jackson Lemon's reflections. Several days elapsed, during which everybody — even the pure-minded, like Sidney Feeder — seemed to him very abject.

I relate all this to show why it was that in going to see Mrs. Freer he was prepared much less to be angry with people who, like the Dexter Freers, a month before, had given it out that he was engaged to a peer's daughter, than to resent the insinuation that there were obstacles to such a prospect. He sat with Mrs. Freer alone for half an hour, in the sabbatical stillness of Jermyn Street. Her husband had gone for a walk in the Park; he always walked in the Park on Sunday. All the world might have been there, and Jackson and Mrs. Freer in sole possession of the district of St. James's. This perhaps had something to do with making him at last rather confidential; the influences were conciliatory, persuasive. Mrs. Freer was extremely sympathetic; she treated him like a person she had known from the age of ten; asked his leave to continue recumbent; talked a great deal about his mother; and seemed almost, for a while, to perform the kindly functions of that lady. It had been wise of her from the first not to allude, even indirectly, to his having neglected so long to call; her silence on this point was in the best taste. Jackson Lemon had forgotten that it was a habit with her, and indeed a high accomplishment, never to reproach

people with these omissions. You might have left
her alone for two years, her greeting was always the
same; she was never either too delighted to see you,
or not delighted enough. After a while, however, he
perceived that her silence had been to a certain extent a reference; she appeared to take for granted that
he devoted all his hours to a certain young lady. It
came over him, for a moment, that his country people took a great deal for granted; but when Mrs.
Freer, rather abruptly, sitting up on her sofa, said to
him, half simply, half solemnly, "And now, my dear
Jackson, I want you to tell me something!" — he
perceived that, after all, she did n't pretend to know
more about the impending matter than he himself
did. In the course of a quarter of an hour — so ap-
preciatively she listened — he had told her a good
deal about it. It was the first time he had said so
much to any one, and the process relieved him even
more than he would have supposed. It made certain
things clear to him, by bringing them to a point —
above all, the fact that he had been wronged. He
made no allusion whatever to its being out of the
usual way that, as an American doctor, he should sue
for the hand of a marquis's daughter; and this reserve
was not voluntary, it was quite unconscious. His
mind was too full of the offensive conduct of the Cantervilles, and the sordid side of their want of confidence. He could not imagine that while he talked
to Mrs. Freer — and it amazed him afterward that
he should have chattered so; he could account for it

only by the state of his nerves — she should be thinking only of the strangeness of the situation he sketched
for her. She thought Americans as good as other
people, but she did n't see where, in American life,
the daughter of a marquis would, as she phrased it,
work in. To take a simple instance, — they coursed
through Mrs. Freer's mind with extraordinary speed,—
would she not always expect to go in to dinner first?
As a novelty, over there, they might like to see her
do it, at first; there might be even a pressure for
places for the spectacle. But with the increase of
every kind of sophistication that was taking place in
America, the humorous view to which she would owe
her safety might not continue to be taken; and then
where would Lady Barberina be? This was but a
small instance; but Mrs. Freer's vivid imagination —
much as she had lived in Europe, she knew her native
land so well — saw a host of others massing themselves behind it. The consequence of all of which
was that after listening to him in the most engaging
silence, she raised her clasped hands, pressed them
against her breast, lowered her voice to a tone of
entreaty, and, with her perpetual little smile, uttered
three words: " My dear Jackson, don't — don't —
don't."

" Don't what ? " he asked, staring.

" Don't neglect the chance you have of getting out
of it; it would never do."

He knew what she meant by his chance of getting
out of it; in his many meditations he had, of course,

not overlooked that.   The ground the old couple had taken about settlements (and the fact that Lady Beauchemin had not come back to him to tell him, as she promised, that she had moved them, proved how firmly they were rooted) would have offered an all-sufficient pretext to a man who should have repented of his advances.   Jackson Lemon knew that; but he knew at the same time that he had not repented.   The old couple's want of imagination did not in the least alter the fact that Barberina was, as he had told her father, a beautiful type.   Therefore he simply said to Mrs. Freer that he did n't in the least wish to get out of it; he was as much in it as ever, and he intended to remain there.   But what did she mean, he inquired in a moment, by her statement that it would never do? Why wouldn't it do?   Mrs. Freer replied by another inquiry, — Should he really like her to tell him?   It would n't do, because Lady Barb would not be satisfied with her place at dinner.   She would not be content — in a society of commoners — with any but the best; and the best she could not expect (and it was to be supposed that he did not expect her) always to have.

"What do you mean by commoners?" Jackson Lemon demanded, looking very serious.

"I mean you, and me, and my poor husband, and Dr. Feeder," said Mrs. Freer.

"I don't see how there can be commoners where there are not lords.   It is the lord that makes the commoner; and *vice versâ.*"

"Won't a lady do as well? Lady Barberina — a single English girl — can make a million inferiors."

" She will be, before anything else, my wife; and she will not talk about inferiors any more than I do. I never do; it 's very vulgar."

" I don't know what she 'll talk about, my dear Jackson, but she will think; and her thoughts won't be pleasant, — I mean for others. Do you expect to sink her to your own rank?"

Jackson Lemon's bright little eyes were fixed more brightly than ever upon his hostess. "I don't understand you; and I don't think you understand yourself." This was not absolutely candid, for he did understand Mrs. Freer to a certain extent; it has been related that before he asked Lady Barb's hand of her parents there had been moments when he himself was not very sure that the flower of the British aristocracy would flourish in American soil. But an intimation from another person that it was beyond his power to pass off his wife — whether she were the daughter of a peer or of a shoemaker — set all his blood on fire. It quenched on the instant his own perception of difficulties of detail, and made him feel only that he was dishonored — he, the heir of all the ages, — by such insinuations. It was his belief — though he had never before had occasion to put it forward — that his position, one of the best in the world, was one of those positions that make everything possible. He had had the best education the age could offer, for if he had rather wasted his time at Harvard, where he entered very young, he had, as he believed, been tremendously serious at Heidelberg and at Vienna. He had devoted himself to one of the noblest of professions, — a profession recognized as such everywhere but in England, — and he had inherited a fortune far beyond the expectation of his earlier years, the years when he cultivated habits of work, which alone — or rather in combination with talents that he neither exaggerated nor minimized — would have conduced to distinction. He was one of the most fortunate inhabitants of an immense, fresh, rich country, a country whose future was admitted to be incalculable, and he moved with perfect ease in a society in which he was not overshadowed by others. It seemed to him, therefore, beneath his dignity to wonder whether he could afford, socially speaking, to marry according to his taste. Jackson Lemon pretended to be strong; and what was the use of being strong if you were not prepared to undertake things that timid people might find difficult? It was his plan to marry the woman he liked, and not to be afraid of her afterward. The effect of Mrs. Freer's doubt of his success was to represent to him that his own character would not cover his wife's; she could n't have made him feel otherwise if she had told him that he was marrying beneath him, and would have to ask for indulgence. "I don't believe you know how much I think that any woman who marries me will be doing very well," he added, directly.

"I am very sure of that; but it is n't so simple —

one's being an American," Mrs. Freer rejoined, with a little philosophic sigh.

"It 's whatever one chooses to make it."

"Well, you 'll make it what no one has done yet, if you take that young lady to America and make her happy there."

"Do you think it 's such a very dreadful place?"

"No, indeed; but she will."

Jackson Lemon got up from his chair, and took up his hat and stick. He had actually turned a little pale, with the force of his emotion; it had made him really quiver that his marriage to Lady Barberina should be looked at as too high a flight. He stood a moment leaning against the mantelpiece, and very much tempted to say to Mrs. Freer that she was a vulgar-minded old woman. But he said something that was really more to the point: "You forget that she will have her consolations."

"Don't go away, or I shall think I have offended you. You can't console a wounded marchioness."

"How will she be wounded? People will be charming to her."

"They will be charming to her — charming to her!" These words fell from the lips of Dexter Freer, who had opened the door of the room and stood with the knob in his hand, putting himself into relation to his wife's talk with their visitor. This was accomplished in an instant. "Of course I know whom you mean," he said, while he exchanged greetings with Jackson Lemon. "My wife and I — of

course you know we are great busybodies — have
talked of your affair, and we differ about it completely: she sees only the dangers, and I see the
advantages."

"By the advantages he means the fun for us," Mrs.
Freer remarked, settling her sofa-cushions.

Jackson looked with a certain sharp blankness
from one of these disinterested judges to the other;
and even yet they did not perceive how their misdi-
rected familiarities wrought upon him. It was hardly
more agreeable to him to know that the husband
wished to see Lady Barb in America, than to know
that the wife had a dread of such a vision; for there
was that in Dexter Freer's face which seemed to say
that the thing would take place somehow for the
benefit of the spectators. "I think you both see too
much — a great deal too much," he answered, rather
coldly.

"My dear young man, at my age I can take certain
liberties," said Dexter Freer. "Do it — I beseech
you to do it; it has never been done before." And
then, as if Jackson's glance had challenged this last
assertion, he went on: "Never, I assure you, this
particular thing. Young female members of the
British aristocracy have married coachmen and fish-
mongers, and all that sort of thing; but they have
never married you and me."

"They certainly have n't married you," said Mrs.
Freer.

"I am much obliged to you for your advice." It

may be thought that Jackson Lemon took himself rather seriously; and indeed I am afraid that if he had not done so there would have been no occasion for my writing this little history. But it made him almost sick to hear his engagement spoken of as a curious and ambiguous phenomenon. He might have his own ideas about it — one always had about one's engagement; but the ideas that appeared to have peopled the imagination of his friends ended by kindling a little hot spot in each of his cheeks. "I would rather not talk any more about my little plans," he added to Dexter Freer. "I have been saying all sorts of absurd things to Mrs. Freer."

"They have been most interesting," that lady declared. "You have been very stupidly treated."

"May she tell me when you go?" her husband asked of the young man.

"I am going now; she may tell you whatever she likes."

"I am afraid we have displeased you," said Mrs. Freer; "I have said too much what I think. You must excuse me, it's all for your mother."

"It's she whom I want Lady Barberina to see!" Jackson Lemon exclaimed, with the inconsequence of filial affection.

"Deary me!" murmured Mrs. Freer.

"We shall go back to America to see how you get on," her husband said; "and if you succeed, it will be a great precedent."

"Oh, I shall succeed!" And with this he took his

departure.   He walked away with the quick step of
a man laboring under a certain excitement; walked
up to Piccadilly and down past Hyde Park Corner.
It relieved him to traverse these distances, for he was
thinking hard, under the influence of irritation; and
locomotion helped him to think.   Certain suggestions
that had been made him in the last half-hour rankled
in his mind, all the more that they seemed to have
a kind of representative value, to be an echo of the
common voice.   If his prospects wore that face to
Mrs. Freer, they would probably wear it to others;
and he felt a sudden need of showing such others that
they took a pitiful measure of his position.   Jackson
Lemon walked and walked till he found himself on
the highway of Hammersmith.   I have represented
him as a young man of much strength of purpose,
and I may appear to undermine this plea when I
relate that he wrote that evening to his solicitor that
Mr. Hilary was to be informed that he would agree to
any proposals for settlements that Mr. Hilary should
make.   Jackson's strength of purpose was shown in
his deciding to marry Lady Barberina on any terms.
It seemed to him, under the influence of his desire to
prove that he was not afraid — so odious was the
imputation — that terms of any kind were very
superficial things.   What was fundamental, and of
the essence of the matter, would be to marry Lady
Barb and carry everything out.

V.

"On Sundays, now, you might be at home," Jackson Lemon said to his wife in the following month of March, more than six months after his marriage.

"Are the people any nicer on Sundays than they are on other days?" Lady Barberina replied, from the depths of her chair, without looking up from a stiff little book.

He hesitated a single instant before answering: "I don't know whether they are, but I think you might be."

"I'm as nice as I know how to be. You must take me as I am. You knew when you married me that I was not an American."

Jackson Lemon stood before the fire, towards which his wife's face was turned and her feet were extended; stood there some time, with his hands behind him and his eyes dropped a little obliquely upon the bent head and richly-draped figure of Lady Barberina. It may be said without delay that he was irritated, and it may be added that he had a double cause. He felt himself to be on the verge of the first crisis that had occurred between himself and his wife, — the reader will perceive that it had occurred rather promptly, — and he was annoyed at his annoyance. A glimpse of his state of mind before his marriage has been given to the reader, who will remember that at that period Jackson Lemon

somehow regarded himself as lifted above possibilities
of irritation.   When one was strong, one was not irri-
table ; and a union with a kind of goddess would of
course be an element of strength.   Lady Barb was a
goddess still, and Jackson Lemon admired his wife as
much as the day he led her to the altar ; but I am
not sure that he felt as strong.

"How do you know what people are ? " he said in
a moment.   "You have seen so few ; you are perpetually denying yourself.   If you should leave New
York to-morrow, you would know wonderfully little
about it."

"It 's all the same," said Lady Barb ; "the people
are all exactly alike."

"How can you tell ?   You never see them."

"Did n't I go out every night for the first two
months we were here ? "

"It was only to about a dozen houses, — always
the same ; people, moreover, you had already met in
London.   You have got no general impressions."

"That 's just what I have got ; I had them before
I came.   Every one is just the same ; they have just
the same names — just the same manners."

Again, for an instant, Jackson Lemon hesitated ;
then he said, in that apparently artless tone of which
mention has already been made, and which he sometimes used in London during his wooing : "Don't you
like it over here ? "

Lady Barb raised her eyes from her book.   "Did
you expect me to like it ? "

"I hoped you would, of course. I think I told you so."

"I don't remember. You said very little about it; you seemed to make a kind of mystery. I knew, of course, you expected me to live here, but I didn't know you expected me to like it."

"You thought I asked of you the sacrifice, as it were."

"I am sure I don't know," said Lady Barb. She got up from her chair and tossed the volume she had been reading into the empty seat. "I recommend you to read that book," she added.

"Is it interesting?"

"It 's an American novel."

"I never read novels."

"You had better look at that one; it will show you the kind of people you want me to know."

"I have no doubt it 's very vulgar," said Jackson Lemon; "I don't see why you read it."

"What else can I do? I can't always be riding in the Park; I hate the Park," Lady Barb remarked.

"It 's quite as good as your own," said her husband.

She glanced at him with a certain quickness, her eyebrows slightly lifted. "Do you mean the park at Pasterns?"

"No; I mean the park in London."

"I don't care about London. One was only in London a few weeks."

"I suppose you miss the country," said Jackson

Lemon. It was his idea of life that he should not be afraid of anything, not be afraid, in any situation, of knowing the worst that was to be known about it; and the demon of a courage with which discretion was not properly commingled prompted him to take soundings which were perhaps not absolutely necessary for safety, and yet which revealed unmistakable rocks. It was useless to know about rocks if he could n't avoid them; the only thing was to trust to the wind.

"I don't know what I miss. I think I miss everything!" This was his wife's answer to his too-curious inquiry. It was not peevish, for that is not the tone of a goddess; but it expressed a good deal — a good deal more than Lady Barb, who was rarely eloquent, had expressed before. Nevertheless, though his question had been precipitate, Jackson Lemon said to himself that he might take his time to think over what his wife's little speech contained; he could not help seeing that the future would give him abundant opportunity for that. He was in no hurry to ask himself whether poor Mrs. Freer, in Jermyn Street, might not, after all, have been right in saying that, in regard to marrying the product of an English caste, it was not so simple to be an American doctor — might avail little even, in such a case, to be the heir of all the ages. The transition was complicated, but in his bright mind it was rapid, from the brush of a momentary contact with such ideas to certain considerations which led him to say, after an instant,

to his wife, " Should you like to go down into Connecticut ? "

" Into Connecticut ? "

" That's one of our States; it 's about as large as
Ireland.   I 'll take you there if you like."

" What does one do there ? "

" We can try and get some hunting."

" You and I alone ? "

" Perhaps we can get a party to join us."

" The people in the State ? "

" Yes; we might propose it to them."

" The tradespeople in the towns? "

" Very true; they will have to mind their shops,"
said Jackson Lemon.   " But we might hunt alone."

" Are there any foxes? "

" No; but there are a few old cows."

Lady Barb had already perceived that her husband
took it into his head once in a while to laugh at her,
and she was aware that the present occasion was
neither worse nor better than some others. She did n't
mind it particularly now, though in England it would
have disgusted her; she had the consciousness of virtue,—an immense comfort,—and flattered herself that
she had learned the lesson of an altered standard of
fitness; there were, moreover, so many more disagreeable things in America than being laughed at by
one's husband. But she pretended to mind it, because
it made him stop, and above all it stopped discussion,
which with Jackson was so often jocular, and none
the less tiresome for that.   " I only want to be left

alone," she said, in answer — though, indeed, it had
not the manner of an answer — to his speech about
the cows. With this she wandered away to one of
the windows which looked out in the Fifth Avenue.
She was very fond of these windows, and she had
taken a great fancy to the Fifth Avenue, which, in
the high-pitched winter weather, when everything
sparkled, was a spectacle full of novelty. It will be
seen that she was not wholly unjust to her adoptive
country : she found it delightful to look out of the
window. This was a pleasure she had enjoyed in
London only in the most furtive manner; it was not
the kind of thing that girls did in England. Besides,
in London, in Hill Street, there was nothing particular to see ; but in the Fifth Avenue everything and
every one went by, and observation was made consistent with dignity by the quantities of brocade and
lace in which the windows were draped, which, somehow, would not have been tidy in England, and which
made an ambush, without concealing the brilliant
day. Hundreds of women — the curious women of
New York, who were unlike any that Lady Barb had
hitherto seen — passed the house every hour; and her
ladyship was infinitely entertained and mystified by
the sight of their clothes. She spent a good deal
more time than she was aware of in this amusement ;
and if she had been addicted to returning upon herself, or asking herself for an account of her conduct
—an inquiry which she did not, indeed, completely
neglect, but treated very cursorily, — it would have

made her smile sadly to think what she appeared
mainly to have come to America for, conscious though
she was that her tastes were very simple, and that so
long as she did n't hunt, it did n't much matter what
she did.

Her husband turned about to the fire, giving a push
with his foot to a log that had fallen out of its place.
Then he said, — and the connection with the words
she had just uttered was apparent enough, — " You
really must be at home on Sundays, you know. I
used to like that so much in London. All the best
women here do it. You had better begin to-day. I
am going to see my mother; if I meet any one I will
tell them to come."

"Tell them not to talk so much," said Lady Barb,
among her lace curtains.

"Ah, my dear," her husband replied, "it is n't every
one that has your concision." And he went and
stood behind her in the window, putting his arm
round her waist. It was as much of a satisfaction to
him as it had been six months before, at the time the
solicitors were settling the matter, that this flower of
an ancient stem should be worn upon his own breast;
he still thought its fragrance a thing quite apart, and
it was as clear as day to him that his wife was the
handsomest woman in New York. He had begun,
after their arrival, by telling her this very often; but
the assurance brought no color to her cheek, no light
to her eyes; to be the handsomest woman in New
York evidently did not seem to her a position in life.

Moreover, the reader may be informed that, oddly enough, Lady Barb did not particularly believe this assertion. There were some very pretty women in New York, and without in the least wishing to be like them — she had seen no woman in America whom she desired to resemble — she envied some of their looks. It is probable that her own finest points were those of which she was most unconscious. But her husband was aware of all of them; nothing could exceed the minuteness of his appreciation of his wife. It was a sign of this that after he had stood behind her a moment he kissed her very tenderly. "Have you any message for my mother?" he asked.

"Please give her my love. And you might take her that book."

"What book?"

"That nasty one I have been reading."

"Oh, bother your books," said Jackson Lemon, with a certain irritation, as he went out of the room.

There had been a good many things in her life in New York that cost Lady Barb an effort; but sending her love to her mother-in-law was not one of these. She liked Mrs. Lemon better than any one she had seen in America; she was the only person who seemed to Lady Barb really simple, as she understood that quality. Many people had struck her as homely and rustic, and many others as pretentious and vulgar; but in Jackson's mother she had found the golden mean of a simplicity which, as she would have said, was really nice. Her sister, Lady Agatha, was even fonder of Mrs. Lemon; but then Lady Agatha had taken the most extraordinary fancy to every one and everything, and talked as if America were the most delightful country in the world. She was having a lovely time (she already spoke the most beautiful American), and had been, during the winter that was just drawing to a close, the most prominent girl in New York. She had gone out at first with her sister; but for some weeks past Lady Barb had let so many occasions pass, that Agatha threw herself into the arms of Mrs. Lemon, who found her extraordinarily quaint and amusing, and was delighted to take her into society. Mrs. Lemon, as an old woman, had given up such vanities; but she only wanted a motive, and in her good nature she ordered a dozen new caps, and sat smiling against the wall while her little English maid, on polished floors, to the sound of music, cultivated the American step as well as the American tone. There was no trouble, in New York, about going out, and the winter was not half over before the little English maid found herself an accomplished diner, rolling about, without any chaperon at all, to banquets where she could count upon a bouquet at her plate. She had had a great deal of correspondence with her mother on this point, and Lady Canterville at last withdrew her protest, which in the meantime had been perfectly useless. It was ultimately Lady Canterville's feeling that if she had married the handsomest of her daughters to an American doctor, she might let another

become a professional *raconteuse* (Agatha had written
to her that she was expected to talk so much), strange
as such a destiny seemed for a girl of nineteen.   Mrs.
Lemon was even a much simpler woman than Lady·
Barberina thought her; for she had not noticed that
Lady Agatha danced much oftener with Herman
Longstraw than with any one else.   Jackson Lemon,
though he went little to balls, had discovered this
truth, and he looked slightly preoccupied when, after
he had sat five minutes with his mother on the Sunday afternoon through which I have invited the
reader to trace so much more than (I am afraid) is
easily apparent of the progress of this simple story,
he learned that his sister-in-law was entertaining
Mr. Longstraw in the library.   He had called half
an hour before, and she had taken him into the other
room to show him the seal of the Cantervilles, which
she had fastened to one of her numerous trinkets (she
was adorned with a hundred bangles and chains), and
the proper exhibition of which required a taper and
a stick of wax.   Apparently he was examining it
very carefully, for they had been absent a good while.
Mrs. Lemon's simplicity was further shown by the
fact that she had not measured their absence; it
was only when Jackson questioned her that she
remembered.

Herman Longstraw was a young Californian who
had turned up in New York the winter before, and
who travelled on his mustache, as they were understood to say in his native State.   This mustache,

and some of the accompanying features, were very
ornamental; several ladies in New York had been
known to declare that they were as beautiful as a
dream.   Taken in connection with his tall stature,
his familiar good-nature, and his remarkable Western
vocabulary, they constituted his only social capital;
for of the two great divisions, the rich Californians
and the poor Californians, it was well known to
which he belonged.   Jackson Lemon looked at him
as a slightly mitigated cowboy, and was somewhat
vexed at his dear mother, though he was aware that
she could scarcely figure to herself what an effect
such an account as that would produce in the halls
of Canterville.   He had no desire whatever to play
a trick on the house to which he was allied, and
knew perfectly that Lady Agatha had not been sent
to America to become entangled with a Californian
of the wrong denomination.   He had been perfectly
willing to bring her; he thought, a little vindictively,
that this would operate as a hint to her parents as to
what he might have been inclined to do if they had
not sent Mr. Hilary after him.   Herman Longstraw,
according to the legend, had been a trapper, a squat-
ter, a miner, a pioneer, — had been everything that
one could be in the romantic parts of America, and
had accumulated masses of experience before the age
of thirty.   He had shot bears in the Rockies and buffaloes on the plains; and it was even believed that
he had brought down animals of a still more dangerous kind, among the haunts of men.   There had been

a story that he owned a cattle-ranch in Arizona; but
a later and apparently more authentic version of it,
though it represented him as looking after the cattle,
did not depict him as their proprietor. Many of the
stories told about him were false; but there is no
doubt that his mustache, his good-nature, and his
accent were genuine. He danced very badly; but
Lady Agatha had frankly told several persons that
that was nothing new to her; and she liked (this,
however, she did not tell) Mr. Herman Longstraw.
What she enjoyed in America was the revelation of
freedom; and there was no such proof of freedom as
conversation with a gentleman who dressed in skins
when he was not in New York, and who, in his usual
pursuits, carried his life (as well as that of other
people) in his hand. A gentleman whom she had
sat next to at dinner in the early part of her stay in
New York, remarked to her that the United States
were the paradise of women and mechanics; and this
had seemed to her at the time very abstract, for she
was not conscious, as yet, of belonging to either class.
In England she had been only a girl; and the principal idea connected with that was simply that, for
one's misfortune, one was not a boy. But presently
she perceived that New York was a paradise; and this
helped her to know that she must be one of the people mentioned in the axiom of her neighbor — people
who could do whatever they wanted, had a voice in
everything, and made their taste and their ideas felt.
She saw that it was great fun to be a woman in

America, and that that was the best way to enjoy the New York winter, — the wonderful, brilliant New York winter, the queer, long-shaped, glittering city, the heterogeneous hours, among which you could n't tell the morning from the afternoon, or the night from either of them, the perpetual liberties and walks, the rushings-out and the droppings-in, the intimacies, the endearments, the comicalities, the sleigh-bells, the cutters, the sunsets on the snow, the ice-parties in the frosty clearness, the bright, hot, velvety houses, the bouquets, the bonbons, the little cakes, the big cakes, the irrepressible inspirations of shopping, the innumerable luncheons and dinners that were offered to youth and innocence, the quantities of chatter of quantities of girls, the perpetual motion of the German, the suppers at restaurants after the play, the way in which life was pervaded by Delmonico and Delmonico by the sense that though one's hunting was lost, and this so different, it was almost as good — and in all, through all, a kind of suffusion of bright, loud, friendly sound, which was very local, but very human.

Lady Agatha at present was staying, for a little change, with Mrs. Lemon, and such adventures as that were part of the pleasure of her American season. The house was too close; but, physically, the girl could bear anything, and it was all she had to complain of; for Mrs. Lemon, as we know, thought her a quaint little damsel, and had none of those old-world scruples in regard to spoiling young people to which

Lady Agatha now perceived that she herself, in the past, had been unduly sacrificed. In her own way — it was not at all her sister's way — she liked to be of importance; and this was assuredly the case when she saw that Mrs. Lemon had apparently nothing in the world to do (after spending a part of the morning with her servants) but invent little distractions (many of them of the edible sort) for her guest. She appeared to have certain friends, but she had no society to speak of, and the people who came into her house came principally to see Lady Agatha. This, as we have seen, was strikingly the case with Herman Longstraw. The whole situation gave Lady Agatha a great feeling of success, — success of a new and unexpected kind. Of course, in England, she had been born successful, in a manner, in coming into the world in one of the most beautiful rooms at Pasterns; but her present triumph was achieved more by her own effort (not that she had tried very hard) and by her merit. It was not so much what she said (for she could never say half as much as the girls in New York), as the spirit of enjoyment that played in her fresh young face, with its pointless curves, and shone in her gray English eyes. She enjoyed everything, even the street-cars, of which she made liberal use; and more than everything she enjoyed Mr. Longstraw and his talk about buffaloes and bears. Mrs. Lemon promised to be very careful, as soon as her son had begun to warn her; and this time she had a certain understanding of what she promised. She thought people ought to make the matches they liked; she had given proof of this in her late behavior to Jackson, whose own union was, in her opinion, marked with all the arbitrariness of pure love. Nevertheless, she could see that Herman Longstraw would probably be thought rough in England; and it was not simply that he was so inferior to Jackson, for, after all, certain things were not to be expected. Jackson Lemon was not oppressed with his mother-in-law, having taken his precautions against such a danger; but he was aware that he should give Lady Canterville a permanent advantage over him if while she was in America, her daughter Agatha should attach herself to a mere mustache.

It was not always, as I have hinted, that Mrs. Lemon entered completely into the views of her son, though in form she never failed to subscribe to them devoutly. She had never yet, for instance, apprehended his reason for marrying Lady Barberina Clement. This was a great secret, and Mrs. Lemon was determined that no one should ever know it. For herself, she was sure that, to the end of time, she should not discover Jackson's reason. She could never ask about it, for that, of course, would betray her. From the first she had told him she was delighted; there being no need of asking for explanations then, as the young lady herself, when she should come to know her, would explain. But the young lady had not yet explained; and after this, evidently, she never would. She was very tall, very handsome, she answered exactly to Mrs. Lemon's prefigurement of the daughter of a lord, and she wore her clothes, which were peculiar, but, to her, remarkably becoming, very well. But she did not elucidate; we know ourselves that there was very little that was explanatory about Lady Barb. So Mrs. Lemon continued to wonder, to ask herself, "Why that one, more than so many others, who would have been more natural?" The choice appeared to her, as I have said, very arbitrary. She found Lady Barb very different from other girls she had known, and this led her almost immediately to feel sorry for her daughter-in-law. She said to herself that Barb was to be pitied if she found her husband's people as peculiar as his mother found *her;* for the result of that would be to make her very lonesome. Lady Agatha was different, because she seemed to keep nothing back; you saw all there was of her, and she was evidently not homesick. Mrs. Lemon could see that Barberina was ravaged by this last passion, and that she was too proud to show it. She even had a glimpse of the ultimate truth; namely, that Jackson's wife had not the comfort of crying, because that would have amounted to a confession that she had been idiotic enough to believe in advance that, in an American town, in the society of doctors, she should escape such pangs. Mrs. Lemon treated her with the greatest gentleness, —all the gentleness that was due to a young woman who was in the unfortunate position of having been married one could n't tell why. The world, to Mrs.

Lemon's view, contained two great departments,—
that of people, and that of things; and she believed
that you must take an interest either in one or the
other. The incomprehensible thing in Lady Barb
was that she cared for neither side of the show. Her
house apparently inspired her with no curiosity and no
enthusiasm, though it had been thought magnificent
enough to be described in successive columns of the
American newspapers; and she never spoke of her
furniture or her domestics, though she had a prodi-
gious quantity of such possessions. She was the same
with regard to her acquaintance, which was immense,
inasmuch as every one in the place had called on her.
Mrs. Lemon was the least critical woman in the
world; but it had sometimes exasperated her just a
little that her daughter-in-law should receive every
one in New York in exactly the same way. There
were differences, Mrs. Lemon knew, and some of them
were of the highest importance; but poor Lady Barb
appeared never to suspect them. She accepted every
one and everything, and asked no questions. She
had no curiosity about her fellow citizens, and as
she never assumed it for a moment, she gave Mrs.
Lemon no opportunity to enlighten her. Lady Barb
was a person with whom you could do nothing unless
she gave you an opening; and nothing would have
been more difficult than to enlighten her against her
will. Of course she picked up a little knowledge;
but she confounded and transposed American attributes in the most extraordinary way. She had a

way of calling every one Doctor; and Mrs. Lemon
could scarcely convince her that this distinction was
too precious to be so freely bestowed. She had once
said to her mother-in-law that in New York there
was nothing to know people by, their names were
so very monotonous; and Mrs. Lemon had entered
into this enough to see that there was something that
stood out a good deal in Barberina's own prefix. It
is probable that during her short stay in New York
complete justice was not done Lady Barb; she never
got credit, for instance, for repressing her annoyance
at the aridity of the social nomenclature, which
seemed to her hideous. That little speech to her
mother was the most reckless sign she gave of it;
and there were few things that contributed more to
the good conscience she habitually enjoyed, than her
self-control on this particular point.

Jackson Lemon was making some researches, just
now, which took up a great deal of his time; and, for
the rest, he passed his hours abundantly with his
wife. For the last three months, therefore, he had
seen his mother scarcely more than once a week. In
spite of researches, in spite of medical societies,
where Jackson, to her knowledge, read papers, Lady
Barb had more of her husband's company than she
had counted upon at the time she married. She had
never known a married pair to be so much together
as she and Jackson; he appeared to expect her to sit
with him in the library in the morning. He had
none of the occupations of gentlemen and noblemen

in England, for the element of politics appeared to
be as absent as the hunting. There were politics in
Washington, she had been told, and even at Albany,
and Jackson had proposed to introduce her to these
cities; but the proposal, made to her once at dinner
before several people, had excited such cries of horror
that it fell dead on the spot. "We don't want you
to see anything of that kind," one of the ladies had
said, and Jackson had appeared to be discouraged,—
that is if, in regard to Jackson, she could really tell.

"Pray, what is it you want me to see?" Lady
Barb had asked on this occasion.

"Well, New York; and Boston, if you want to
very much — but not otherwise ; and Niagara; and,
more than anything, Newport."

Lady Barb was tired of their eternal Newport; she
had heard of it a thousand times, and felt already as
if she had lived there half her life; she was sure,
moreover, that she should hate it. This is perhaps
as near as she came to having a lively conviction on
any American subject. She asked herself whether
she was then to spend her life in the Fifth Avenue,
with alternations of a city of villas (she detested
villas), and wondered whether that was all the great
American country had to offer her. There were times
when she thought that she should like the back-
woods, and that the Far West might be a resource;
for she had analyzed her feelings just deep enough
to discover that when she had — hesitating a good
deal — turned over the question of marrying Jackson

Lemon, it was not in the least of American barbarism that she was afraid; her dread was of American civilization. She believed the little lady I have just quoted was a goose; but that did not make New York any more interesting. It would be reckless to say that she suffered from an overdose of Jackson's company, because she had a view of the fact that he was much her most important social resource. She could talk to him about England; about her own England, and he understood more or less what she wished to say, when she wished to say anything, which was not frequent. There were plenty of other people who talked about England; but with them the range of allusion was always the hotels, of which she knew nothing, and the shops, and the opera, and the photographs : they had a mania for photographs. There were other people who were always wanting her to tell them about Pasterns, and the manner of life there, and the parties; but if there was one thing* Lady Barb disliked more than another, it was describing Pasterns. She had always lived with people who knew, of themselves, what such a place would be, without demanding these pictorial efforts, proper only, as she vaguely felt, to persons belonging to the classes whose trade was the arts of expression. Lady Barb, of course, had never gone into it; but she knew that in her own class the business was not to express, but to enjoy; not to represent, but to be represented, — though, indeed, this latter liability might convey offence; for it may be noted that even

for an aristocrat Jackson Lemon's wife was aristocratic.

Lady Agatha and her visitor came back from the
library in course of time, and Jackson Lemon felt it
his duty to be rather cold to Herman Longstraw. It
was not clear to him what sort of a husband his sister-in-law would do well to look for in America, — if
there were to be any question of husbands; but as
to this he was not bound to be definite, provided he
should rule out Mr. Longstraw. This gentleman,
however, was not given to perceive shades of manner; he had little observation, but very great confidence.

"I think you had better come home with me,"
Jackson said to Lady Agatha; "I guess you have
stayed here long enough."

"Don't let him say that, Mrs. Lemon!" the girl
cried. "I like being with you so very much."

"I try to make it pleasant," said Mrs. Lemon.
"I should really miss you now; but perhaps it's
your mother's wish." If it was a question of defending her guest from ineligible suitors, Mrs. Lemon felt,
of course, that her son was more competent than she;
though she had a lurking kindness for Herman Longstraw, and a vague idea that he was a gallant, genial
specimen of young America.

"Oh, mamma would n't see any difference!" Lady
Agatha exclaimed, looking at Jackson with pleading
blue eyes. "Mamma wants me to see every one;
you know she does. That's what she sent me to

America for; she knew it was not like England. She would n't like it if I did n't sometimes stay with people; she always wanted us to stay at other houses. And she knows all about you, Mrs. Lemon, and she likes you immensely. She sent you a message the other day, and I am afraid I forgot to give it you, — to thank you for being so kind to me and taking such a lot of trouble. Really she did, but I forgot it. If she wants me to see as much as possible of America, it 's much better I should be here than always with Barb, — it 's much less like one's own country. I mean it 's much nicer — for a girl," said Lady Agatha, affectionately, to Mrs. Lemon, who began also to look at Jackson with a kind of tender argumentativeness.

"If you want the genuine thing, you ought to come out on the plains," Mr. Longstraw interposed, with smiling sincerity. "I guess that was your mother's idea. Why don't you all come out?" He had been looking intently at Lady Agatha while the remarks I have just repeated succeeded each other on her lips, — looking at her with a kind of fascinated approbation, for all the world as if he had been a slightly slow-witted English gentleman, and the girl had been a flower of the West, — a flower that knew how to talk. He made no secret of the fact that Lady Agatha's voice was music to him, his ear being much more susceptible than his own inflections would have indicated. To Lady Agatha those inflections were not displeasing, partly because, like Mr. Herman him-

self, in general, she had not a perception of shades ;
and partly because it never occurred to her to compare them with any other tones. He seemed to her
to speak a foreign language altogether, — a romantic
dialect, through which the most comical meanings
gleamed here and there.

"I should like it above all things," she said, in answer to his last observation.

"The scenery's superior to anything round here,"
Mr. Longstraw went on.

Mrs. Lemon, as we know, was the softest of women ;
but, as an old New Yorker, she had no patience with
some of the new fashions. Chief among these was
the perpetual reference, which had become common
only within a few years, to the outlying parts of the
country, the States and Territories of which children,
in her time, used to learn the names, in their order,
at school, but which no one ever thought of going to
or talking about. Such places, in Mrs. Lemon's opinion, belonged to the geography-books, or at most to
the literature of newspapers, but not to society
nor to conversation ; and the change — which, so
far as it lay in people's talk, she thought at bottom
a mere affectation — threatened to make her native
land appear vulgar and vague. For this amiable
daughter of Manhattan, the normal existence of man,
and, still more, of woman, had been "located," as she
would have said, between Trinity Church and the
beautiful Reservoir at the top of the Fifth Avenue,
— monuments of which she was personally proud ;

and if we could look into the deeper parts of her
mind, I am afraid we should discover there an impression that both the countries of Europe and the
remainder of her own continent were equally far from
the centre and the light.

"Well, scenery is n't everything," she remarked,
mildly, to Mr. Longstraw; "and if Lady Agatha
should wish to see anything of that kind, all she has
got to do is to take the boat up the Hudson."

Mrs. Lemon's recognition of this river, I should
say, was all that it need have been; she thought
that it existed for the purpose of supplying New
Yorkers with poetical feelings, helping them to face
comfortably occasions like the present, and, in general, meet foreigners with confidence, — part of the
oddity of foreigners being their conceit about their
own places.

"That's a good idea, Lady Agatha; let's take the
boat," said Mr. Longstraw. "I've had great times on
the boats."

Lady Agatha looked at her cavalier a little with
those singular, charming eyes of hers, — eyes of
which it was impossible to say, at any moment,
whether they were the shyest or the frankest in
the world; and she was not aware, while this contemplation lasted, that her brother-in-law was observing her. He was thinking of certain things while
he did so, of things he had heard about the English;
who still, in spite of his having married into a family
of that nation, appeared to him very much through

the medium of hearsay. They were more passionate than the Americans, and they did things that would never have been expected; though they seemed steadier and less excitable, there was much social evidence to show that they were more impulsive.

"It's so very kind of you to propose that," Lady Agatha said in a moment to Mrs. Lemon. "I think I have never been in a ship, — except, of course, coming from England. I am sure mamma would wish me to see the Hudson. We used to go in immensely for boating in England."

"Did you boat in a ship?" Herman Longstraw asked, showing his teeth hilariously, and pulling his mustaches.

"Lots of my mother's people have been in the navy." Lady Agatha perceived vaguely and good-naturedly that she had said something which the odd Americans thought odd, and that she must justify herself. Her standard of oddity was getting dreadfully dislocated.

"I really think you had better come back to us," said Jackson; "your sister is very lonely without you."

"She is much more lonely with me. We are perpetually having differences. Barb is dreadfully vexed because I like America, instead of — instead of — " And Lady Agatha paused a moment; for it just occurred to her that this might be a betrayal.

"Instead of what?" Jackson Lemon inquired.

"Instead of perpetually wanting to go to England,

as she does," she went on, only giving her phrase a little softer turn; for she felt the next moment that her sister could have nothing to hide, and must, of course, have the courage of her opinions. "Of course England's best, but I dare say I like to be bad," said Lady Agatha, artlessly.

"Oh, there's no doubt you are awfully bad," Mr. Longstraw exclaimed, with joyous eagerness. Of course he could not know that what she had principally in mind was an exchange of opinions that had taken place between her sister and herself just before she came to stay with Mrs. Lemon. This incident, of which Longstraw was the occasion, might indeed have been called a discussion, for it had carried them quite into the realms of the abstract. Lady Barb had said she did n't see how Agatha could look at such a creature as that, — an odious, familiar, vulgar being, who had not about him the rudiments of a gentleman. Lady Agatha had replied that Mr. Longstraw was familiar and rough, and that he had a twang, and thought it amusing to talk of her as "the Princess;" but that he was a gentleman for all that, and that at any rate he was tremendous fun. Her sister to this had rejoined that if he was rough and familiar he couldn't be a gentleman, inasmuch as that was just what a gentleman meant, — a man who was civil, and well-bred, and well-born. Lady Agatha had argued that this was just where she differed; that a man might perfectly be a gentleman, and yet be rough, and even ignorant, so long as he was really nice. The only thing was that he should be really nice, which was the case with Mr. Longstraw, who, moreover, was quite extraordinarily civil — as civil as a man could be. And then Lady Agatha made the strongest point she had ever made in her life, she had never been so inspired, in saying that Mr. Longstraw was rough, perhaps, but not rude, — a distinction altogether wasted on her sister, who declared that she had not come to America, of all places, to learn what a gentleman was. The discussion, in short, had been lively. I know not whether it was the tonic effect on them, too, of the fine winter weather, or, on the other hand, that of Lady Barb's being bored and having nothing else to do; but Lord Canterville's daughters went into the question with the moral earnestness of a pair of Bostonians. It was part of Lady Agatha's view of her admirer that he, after all, much resembled other tall people, with smiling eyes and mustaches, who had ridden a good deal in rough countries, and whom she had seen in other places. If he was more familiar, he was also more alert; still, the difference was not in himself, but in the way she saw him, — the way she saw everybody in America. If she should see the others in the same way, no doubt they would be quite the same; and Lady Agatha sighed a little over the possibilities of life; for this peculiar way, especially regarded in connection with gentlemen, had become very pleasant to her.

She had betrayed her sister more than she thought, even though Jackson Lemon did not particularly show it in the tone in which he said: " Of course she knows that she is going to see your mother in the summer." His tone, rather, was that of irritation at the repetition of a familiar idea.

"Oh, it is n't only mamma," replied Lady Agatha.

"I know she likes a cool house," said Mrs. Lemon, suggestively.

"When she goes, you had better bid her good-by," the girl went on.

"Of course I shall bid her good-by," said Mrs. Lemon, to whom, apparently, this remark was addressed.

"I shall never bid you good-by, Princess," Herman Longstraw interposed. "I can tell you that you never will see the last of me."

"Oh, it does n't matter about me, for I shall come back; but if Barb once gets to England, she will never come back."

"Oh, my dear child," murmured Mrs. Lemon, addressing Lady Agatha, but looking at her son.

Jackson looked at the ceiling, at the floor; above all, he looked very conscious.

"I hope you don't mind my saying that, Jackson dear," Lady Agatha said to him, for she was very fond of her brother-in-law.

"Ah, well, then, she sha'n't go, then," he remarked, after a moment, with a dry little laugh.

"But you promised mamma, you know," said the girl, with the confidence of her affection.

Jackson looked at her with an eye which expressed none even of his very moderate hilarity. "Your mother, then, must bring her back."

"Get some of your navy people to supply an iron-clad!" cried Mr. Longstraw.

"It would be very pleasant if the Marchioness could come over," said Mrs. Lemon.

"Oh, she would hate it more than poor Barb," Lady Agatha quickly replied. It did not suit her mood at all to see a marchioness inserted into the field of her vision.

"Does n't she feel interested, from what you have told her?" Herman Longstraw asked of Lady Agatha. But Jackson Lemon did not heed his sister-in-law's answer; he was thinking of something else. He said nothing more, however, about the subject of his thought, and before ten minutes were over, he took his departure, having, meanwhile, neglected also to revert to the question of Lady Agatha's bringing her visit to his mother to a close. It was not to speak to him of this (for, as we know, she wished to keep the girl; and, somehow, could not bring herself to be afraid of Herman Longstraw) that when Jackson took leave she went with him to the door of the house, detaining him a little, while she stood on the steps, as people had always done in New York in her time, though it was another of the new fashions she did not like, not to come out of the parlor. She placed her hand on his arm to keep him on the "stoop," and looked up and down into the brilliant afternoon and the beautiful city, — its chocolate-colored houses, so extraordinarily smooth, — in which it seemed to her that even the most fastidious people

ought to be glad to live. It was useless to attempt
to conceal it; her son's marriage had made a difference, had put up a kind of barrier. It had
brought with it a problem much more difficult than
his old problem of how to make his mother feel that
she was still, as she had been in his childhood, the
dispenser of his rewards. The old problem had been
easily solved; the new one was a visible preoccupa-
tion. Mrs. Lemon felt that her daughter-in-law did
not take her seriously; and that was a part of the
barrier. Even if Barberina liked her better than any
one else, this was mostly because she liked every one
else so little. Mrs. Lemon had not a grain of resent-
ment in her nature; and it was not to feed a sense of
wrong that she permitted herself to criticise her son's
wife. She could not help feeling that his marriage
was not altogether fortunate if his wife did n't take
his mother seriously. She knew she was not otherwise remarkable than as being his mother; but that
position, which was no merit of hers (the merit was
all Jackson's, in being her son), seemed to her one
which, familiar as Lady Barb appeared to have been
in England with positions of various kinds, would
naturally strike the girl as a very high one, to be accepted as freely as a fine morning. If she did n't
think of his mother as an indivisible part of him,
perhaps she did n't think of other things either; and
Mrs. Lemon vaguely felt that, remarkable as Jackson
was, he was made up of parts, and that it would
never do that these parts should be rated lower one

by one, for there was no knowing what that might end in. She feared that things were rather cold for him at home when he had to explain so much to his wife, — explain to her, for instance, all the sources of happiness that were to be found in New York. This struck her as a new kind of problem altogether for a husband. She had never thought of matrimony without a community of feeling in regard to religion and country; one took those great conditions for granted, just as one assumed that one's food was to be cooked; and if Jackson should have to discuss them with his wife, he might, in spite of his great abilities, be carried into regions where he would get entangled and embroiled,—from which, even, possibly, he would not come back at all. Mrs. Lemon had a horror of losing him in some way; and this fear was in her eyes as she stood on the steps of her house, and, after she had glanced up and down the street, looked at him a moment in silence. He simply kissed her again, and said she would take cold.

"I am not afraid of that, I have a shawl!" Mrs. Lemon, who was very small and very fair, with pointed features and an elaborate cap, passed her life in a shawl, and owed to this habit her reputation for being an invalid, — an idea which she scorned, naturally enough, inasmuch as it was precisely her shawl that (as she believed) kept her from being one. "Is it true Barberina won't come back?" she asked of her son.

"I don't know that we shall ever find out; I don't know that I shall take her to England."

"Did n't you promise, dear ? "

"I don't know that I promised; not absolutely."

"But you would n't keep her here against her will ?" said Mrs. Lemon, inconsequently.

"I guess she 'll get used to it," Jackson answered, with a lightness he did not altogether feel.

Mrs. Lemon looked up and down the street again, and gave a little sigh. "What a pity she is n't American !" She did not mean this as a reproach, a hint of what might have been; it was simply embarrassment resolved into speech.

"She could n't have been American," said Jackson, with decision.

"Could n't she, dear ?" Mrs. Lemon spoke with a kind of respect; she felt that there were imperceptible reasons in this.

"It was just as she is that I wanted her," Jackson added.

"Even if she won't come back?" his mother asked, with a certain wonder.

"Oh, she has got to come back !" Jackson said, going down the steps.

VI.

Lady Barb, after this, did not decline to see her New York acquaintances on Sunday afternoons, though she refused for the present to enter into a project of her husband's, who thought it would be a pleasant thing that she should entertain his friends on the evening of that day. Like all good Americans, Jackson Lemon devoted much consideration to the great question how, in his native land, society should be brought into being. It seemed to him that it would help the good cause, for which so many Americans are ready to lay down their lives, if his wife should, as he jocularly called it, open a saloon. He believed, or he tried to believe, the *salon* now possible in New York, on condition of its being reserved entirely for adults; and in having taken a wife out of a country in which social traditions were rich and ancient, he had done something towards qualifying his own house — so splendidly qualified in all strictly material respects — to be the scene of such an effort. A charming woman, accustomed only to the best in each country, as Lady Beauchemin said, what might she not achieve by being at home (to the elder generation) in an easy, early, inspiring, comprehensive way, on the evening in the week on which worldly engagements were least numerous? He laid this philosophy before Lady Barb, in pursuance of a theory that if she disliked New York on a short acquaintance, she could not fail to like it on a long one. Jackson Lemon believed in the New York mind, — not so much, indeed, in its literary, artistic, or political achievements, as in its general quickness and nascent adaptability. He clung to this belief, for it was a very important piece of material in the structure that he was attempting to rear. The New York mind would throw its glamour over Lady Barb if she

would only give it a chance; for it was exceedingly
bright, entertaining, and sympathetic. If she would
only have a *salon*, where this charming organ might
expand, and where she might inhale its fragrance in
the most convenient and luxurious way, without, as
it were, getting up from her chair; if she would only
just try this graceful, good-natured experiment (which
would make every one like *her* so much, too), — he
was sure that all the wrinkles in the gilded scroll of
his fate would be smoothed out. But Lady Barb did
not rise at all to his conception, and had not the least
curiosity about the New York mind. She thought it
would be extremely disagreeable to have a lot of people tumbling in on Sunday evening without being
invited; and altogether her husband's sketch of the
Anglo-American saloon seemed to her to suggest
familiarity, high-pitched talk (she had already made
a remark to him about " screeching women "), and
exaggerated laughter. She did not tell him — for this,
somehow, it was not in her power to express, and,
strangely enough, he never completely guessed it, —
that she was singularly deficient in any natural, or
indeed acquired, understanding of what a saloon
might be. She had never seen one, and for the most
part she never thought of things she had not seen.
She had seen great dinners, and balls, and meets, and
runs, and races; she had seen garden-parties, and a
lot of people, mainly women (who, however, did n't
screech), at dull, stuffy teas, and distinguished com-
panies collected in splendid castles; but all this gave

her no idea of a tradition of conversation, of a social agreement that its continuity, its accumulations from season to season, should not be lost. Conversation, in Lady Barb's experience, had never been continuous; in such a case it would surely have been a bore. It had been occasional and fragmentary, a trifle jerky, with allusions that were never explained; it had a dread of detail; it seldom pursued anything very far, or kept hold of it very long.

There was something else that she did not say to her husband in reference to his visions of hospitality, which was, that if she should open a saloon (she had taken up the joke as well, for Lady Barb was eminently good-natured), Mrs. Vanderdecken would straightway open another, and Mrs. Vanderdecken's would be the more successful of the two. This lady, for reasons that Lady Barb had not yet explored, was supposed to be the great personage in New York; there were legends of her husband's family having behind them a fabulous antiquity. When this was alluded to, it was spoken of as something incalculable, and lost in the dimness of time. Mrs. Vanderdecken was young, pretty, clever, incredibly pretentious (Lady Barb thought), and had a wonderfully artistic house. Ambition, also, was expressed in every rustle of her garments; and if she was the first person in America (this had an immense sound), it was plain that she intended to remain so. It was not till after she had been several months in New York that it came over Lady Barb

that this brilliant native had flung down the glove;
and when the idea presented itself, lighted up by an
incident which I have no space to relate, she simply
blushed a little (for Mrs. Vanderdecken), and held
her tongue. She had not come to America to bandy
words about precedence with such a woman as that.
She had ceased to think about it much (of course
one thought about it in England); but an instinct of
self-preservation led her not to expose herself to
occasions on which her claim might be tested. This,
at bottom, had much to do with her having, very
soon after the first flush of the honors paid her on
her arrival, and which seemed to her rather grossly
overdone, taken the line of scarcely going out.
"They can't keep *that* up!" she had said to herself;
and, in short, she would stay at home. She had a
feeling that whenever she should go forth she would
meet Mrs. Vanderdecken, who would withhold, or
deny, or contest something, — poor Lady Barb could
never imagine what. She did not try to, and gave
little thought to all this; for she was not prone to
confess to herself fears, especially fears from which
terror was absent. But, as I have said, it abode
within her as a presentiment, that if she should set
up a drawing-room in the foreign style (it was
curious, in New York, how they tried to be foreign), Mrs. Vanderdecken would be beforehand with
her. The continuity of conversation, oh! that idea
she would certainly have; there was no one so continuous as Mrs. Vanderdecken. Lady Barb, as I

have related, did not give her husband the surprise of telling him of these thoughts, though she had given him some other surprises. He would have been very much astonished, and perhaps, after a bit, a little encouraged, at finding that she was liable to this particular form of irritation.

On the Sunday afternoon she was visible; and on one of these occasions, going into her drawing-room late, he found her entertaining two ladies and a gentleman. The gentleman was Sidney Feeder, and one of the ladies was Mrs. Vanderdecken, whose ostensible relations with Lady Barb were of the most cordial nature. If she intended to crush her (as two or three persons, not conspicuous for a narrow accuracy, gave out that she privately declared), Mrs. Vanderdecken wished at least to study the weak points of the invader, to penetrate herself with the character of the English girl. Lady Barb, indeed, appeared to have a mysterious fascination for the representative of the American patriciate. Mrs. Vanderdecken could not take her eyes off her victim; and whatever might be her estimate of her importance, she at least could not let her alone. "Why does she come to see me?" poor Lady Barb asked herself. "I am sure I don't want to see her; she has done enough for civility long ago." Mrs. Vanderdecken had her own reasons; and one of them was simply the pleasure of looking at the Doctor's wife, as she habitually called the daughter of the Cantervilles. She was not guilty of the folly of depreciating this lady's appearance, and professed an unbounded admiration for it, defending it on many occasions against superficial people, who said there were fifty women in New York that were handsomer. Whatever might have been Lady Barb's weak points, they were not the curve of her cheek and chin, the setting of her head on her throat, or the quietness of her deep eyes, which were as beautiful as if they had been blank, like those of antique busts. "The head is enchanting — perfectly enchanting," Mrs. Vanderdecken used to say irrelevantly, as if there were only one head in the place. She always used to ask about the Doctor; and that was another reason why she came. She brought up the Doctor at every turn; asked if he were often called up at night; found it the greatest of luxuries, in a word, to address Lady Barb as the wife of a medical man, more or less *au courant* of her husband's patients. The other lady, on this Sunday afternoon, was a certain little Mrs. Chew, who had the appearance of a small, but very expensive doll, and was always asking Lady Barb about England, which Mrs. Vanderdecken never did. The latter visitor conversed with Lady Barb on a purely American basis, with that continuity (on her own side) of which mention has already been made, while Mrs. Chew engaged Sidney Feeder on topics equally local. Lady Barb liked Sidney Feeder; she only hated his name, which was constantly in her ears during the half-hour the ladies sat with her, Mrs. Chew having the habit, which annoyed Lady Barb,

of repeating perpetually the appellation of her interlocutor.

Lady Barb's relations with Mrs. Vanderdecken
consisted mainly in wondering, while she talked,
what she wanted of her, and in looking, with her
sculptured eyes, at her visitor's clothes, in which
there was always much to examine. "Oh, Dr.
Feeder!" "Now, Dr. Feeder!" "Well, Dr. Feeder,"
—these exclamations, on the lips of Mrs. Chew,
were an undertone in Lady Barb's consciousness.
When I say that she liked her husband's *confrère*,
as he used to call himself, I mean that she smiled
at him when he came, and gave him her hand,
and asked him if he would have some tea. There
was nothing nasty (as they said in London) in Lady
Barb, and she would have been incapable of inflicting
a deliberate snub upon a man who had the air of
standing up so squarely to any work that he might
have in hand. But she had nothing to say to Sidney Feeder. He apparently had the art of making
her shy, more shy than usual; for she was always a
little so; she discouraged him, discouraged him completely. He was not a man who wanted drawing
out, there was nothing of that in him, he was remarkably copious; but Lady Barb appeared unable
to follow him, and half the time, evidently, did not
know what he was saying. He tried to adapt his
conversation to her needs; but when he spoke of the
world, of what was going on in society, she was more
at sea even than when he spoke of hospitals and

laboratories, and the health of the city, and the progress of science. She appeared, indeed, after her first smile, when he came in, which was always charming, scarcely to see him, looking past him, and above him, and below him, and everywhere but at him, until he got up to go again, when she gave him another smile, as expressive of pleasure and of casual acquaintance as that with which she had greeted his entry; it seemed to imply that they had been having delightful talk for an hour. He wondered what the deuce Jackson Lemon could find interesting in such a woman, and he believed that his perverse, though gifted, colleague was not destined to feel that she illuminated his life. He pitied Jackson, he saw that Lady Barb, in New York, would neither assimilate nor be assimilated; and yet he was afraid to betray his incredulity, thinking it might be depressing to poor Lemon to show him how his marriage — now so dreadfully irrevocable — struck others. Sidney Feeder was a man of a strenuous conscience, and he did his duty overmuch by his old friend and his wife, from the simple fear that he should not do it enough. In order not to appear to neglect them, he called upon Lady Barb heroically, in spite of pressing engagements, week after week, enjoying his virtue himself as little as he made it fruitful for his hostess, who wondered at last what she had done to deserve these visitations. She spoke of them to her husband, who wondered also what poor Sidney had in his head, and yet was unable, of course, to hint to him that he need not think it necessary to come so often. Between Dr. Feeder's wish not to let Jackson see that his marriage had made a difference, and Jackson's hesitation to reveal to Sidney that his standard of friendship was too high, Lady Barb passed a good many of those numerous hours during which she asked herself if she had come to America for that. Very little had ever passed between her and her husband on the subject of Sidney Feeder; for an instinct told her that if they were ever to have scenes, she must choose the occasion well; and this odd person was not an occasion. Jackson had tacitly admitted that his friend Feeder was anything he chose to think him; he was not a man to be guilty, in a discussion, of the disloyalty of damning him with praise that was faint. If Lady Agatha had usually been with her sister, Dr. Feeder would have been better entertained; for the younger of the English visitors prided herself, after several months of New York, on understanding everything that was said, and catching every allusion, it mattered not from what lips it fell. But Lady Agatha was never at home; she had learned how to describe herself perfectly by the time she wrote to her mother that she was always "on the go." None of the innumerable victims of old-world tyranny who have fled to the United States as to a land of freedom, have ever offered more lavish incense to that goddess than this emancipated London *débutante*. She had enrolled herself in an amiable band which was known by the

humorous name of "the Tearers," — a dozen young
ladies of agreeable appearance, high spirits, and good
wind, whose most general characteristic was that,
when wanted, they were to be sought anywhere in
the world but under the roof that was supposed to
shelter them.   They were never at home; and when
Sidney Feeder, as sometimes happened, met Lady
Agatha at other houses, she was in the hands of
the irrepressible Longstraw.   She had come back to
her sister, but Mr. Longstraw had followed her to the
door.   As to passing it, he had received direct dis-
couragement from her brother-in-law; but he could
at least hang about and wait for her.   It may be
confided to the reader, at the risk of diminishing the
effect of the only incident which in the course of this
very level narrative may startle him, that he never
had to wait very long.

When Jackson Lemon came in, his wife's visitors
were on the point of leaving her; and he did not ask
even Sidney Feeder to remain, for he had something
particular to say to Lady Barb.

"I have n't asked you half what I wanted — I
have been talking so much to Dr. Feeder," the
dressy Mrs. Chew said, holding the hand of her
hostess in one of her own, and toying with one of
Lady Barb's ribbons with the other.

"I don't think I have anything to tell you; I
think I have told people everything," Lady Barb
answered, rather wearily.

"You have n't told *me* much!" Mrs. Vanderdecken said, smiling brightly.

"What could one tell you?—you know every-thing," Jackson Lemon interposed.

"Ah, no; there are some things that are great mysteries for me," the lady returned. "I hope you are coming to me on the 17th," she added, to Lady Barb.

"On the 17th? I think we are going somewhere."

"Do go to Mrs. Vanderdecken's," said Mrs. Chew; "you'll see the cream of the cream."

"Oh, gracious!" Mrs. Vanderdecken exclaimed.

"Well, I don't care; she will, won't she, Dr. Feed-er?—the very pick of American society." Mrs. Chew stuck to her point.

"Well, I have no doubt Lady Barb will have a good time," said Sidney Feeder. "I'm afraid you miss the bran," he went on, with irrelevant jocosity, to Lady Barb. He always tried the jocose, when other elements had failed.

"The bran?" asked Lady Barb, staring.

"Where you used to ride in the Park."

"My dear fellow, you speak as if it were the cir-cus," Jackson Lemon said, smiling; "I have n't mar-ried a mountebank!"

"Well, they put some stuff on the road," Sidney Feeder explained, not holding much to his joke.

"You must miss a great many things," said Mrs. Chew, tenderly.

"I don't see what," Mrs. Vanderdecken remarked, "except the fogs and the Queen. New York is getting more and more like London. It's a pity; you ought to have known us thirty years ago."

"You are the queen, here," said Jackson Lemon; "but I don't know what you know about thirty years ago."

"Do you think she doesn't go back?—she goes back to the last century!" cried Mrs. Chew.

"I dare say I should have liked that," said Lady Barb; "but I can't imagine." And she looked at her husband—a look she often had—as if she vaguely wished him to do something.

He was not called upon, however, to take any violent steps, for Mrs. Chew presently said: "Well, Lady Barberina, good-by;" and Mrs. Vanderdecken smiled in silence at her hostess, and addressed a farewell, accompanied very audibly with his title, to her host; and Sidney Feeder made a joke about stepping on the trains of the ladies' dresses as he accompanied them to the door. Mrs. Chew had always a great deal to say at the last; she talked till she was in the street, and then she did not cease. But at the end of five minutes Jackson Lemon was alone with his wife; and then he told her a piece of news. He prefaced it, however, by an inquiry as he came back from the hall.

"Where is Agatha, my dear?"

"I haven't the least idea. In the streets somewhere, I suppose."

"I think you ought to know a little more."

"How can I know about things here? I have given her up; I can do nothing with her. I don't care what she does."

"She ought to go back to England," Jackson Lemon said, after a pause.

"She ought never to have come."

"It was not my proposal, God knows!" Jackson answered, rather sharply.

"Mamma could never know what it really is," said his wife.

"No, it has not been as yet what your mother supposed! Herman Longstraw wants to marry her. He has made me a formal proposal. I met him half an hour ago in Madison Avenue, and he asked me to come with him into the Columbia Club. There, in the billiard-room, which to-day is empty, he opened himself — thinking evidently that in laying the matter before me he was behaving with extraordinary propriety. He tells me he is dying of love, and that she is perfectly willing to go and live in Arizona."

"So she is," said Lady Barb. "And what did you tell him?"

"I told him that I was sure it would never do, and that at any rate I could have nothing to say to it. I told him explicitly, in short, what I had told him virtually before. I said that we should send Agatha straight back to England, and that if they had the courage they must themselves broach the question over there."

"When shall you send her back?" asked Lady Barb.

"Immediately; by the very first steamer."

"Alone, like an American girl?"

"Don't be rough, Barb," said Jackson Lemon. "I shall easily find some people; lots of people are sailing now."

"I must take her myself," Lady Barb declared in a moment. "I brought her out, and I must restore her to my mother's hands."

Jackson Lemon had expected this, and he believed he was prepared for it. But when it came he found his preparation was not complete; for he had no answer to make — none, at least, that seemed to him to go to the point. During these last weeks it had come over him, with a quiet, irresistible, unmerciful force, that Mrs. Dexter Freer had been right when she said to him, that Sunday afternoon in Jermyn Street, the summer before, that he would find it was not so simple to be an American. Such an identity was complicated, in just the measure that she had foretold, by the difficulty of domesticating one's wife. The difficulty was not dissipated by his having taken a high tone about it; it pinched him from morning till night, like a misfitting shoe. His high tone had given him courage when he took the great step; but he began to perceive that the highest tone in the world cannot change the nature of things. His ears tingled when he reflected that if the Dexter Freers, whom he had thought alike abject in their hopes and their fears, had been by ill-luck spending the winter in New York, they would have found his predicament as entertaining as they could desire. Drop by drop the conviction had entered his mind — the first drop had

come in the form of a word from Lady Agatha —
that if his wife should return to England she would
never again cross the Atlantic to the west. That
word from Lady Agatha had been the touch from the
outside, at which, often, one's fears crystallize. What
she would do, how she would resist, — this he was not
yet prepared to tell himself; but he felt, every time
he looked at her, that this beautiful woman whom he
had adored was filled with a dumb, insuperable, inera-
dicable purpose. He knew that if she should plant
herself, no power on earth would move her; and her
blooming, antique beauty, and the general loftiness of
her breeding, came to seem to him — rapidly — but
the magnificent expression of a dense, patient, imper-
turbable obstinacy. She was not light, she was not
supple, and after six months of marriage he had made
up his mind that she was not clever; but nevertheless she would elude him. She had married him, she
had come into his fortune and his consideration —
for who was she, after all? Jackson Lemon was once
so angry as to ask himself, reminding himself that in
England Lady Claras and Lady Florences were as
thick as blackberries — but she would have nothing
to do, if she could help it, with his country. She had
gone in to dinner first in every house in the place,
but this had not satisfied her. It *had* been simple to
be an American, in this sense, that no one else in
New York had made any difficulties; the difficulties
had sprung from her peculiar feelings, which were
after all what he had married her for, thinking they

would be a fine temperamental heritage for his brood.
So they would, doubtless, in the coming years, after
the brood should have appeared; but meanwhile they
interfered with the best heritage of all — the nation-
ality of his possible children. Lady Barb would do
nothing violent; he was tolerably certain of that.
She would not return to England without his consent; only, when she should return, it would be once
for all. His only possible line, then, was not to take
her back, — a position replete with difficulties, because,
of course, he had, in a manner, given his word, while
she had given no word at all, beyond the general
promise she murmured at the altar. She had been
general, but he had been specific; the settlements he
had made were a part of that. His difficulties were
such as he could not directly face. He must tack in
approaching so uncertain a coast. He said to Lady
Barb presently that it would be very inconvenient
for him to leave New York at that moment: she must
remember that their plans had been laid for a later
departure. He could not think of letting her make
the voyage without him, and, on the other hand, they
must pack her sister off without delay. He would
therefore make instant inquiry for a chaperon, and
he relieved his irritation by expressing considerable
disgust at Herman Longstraw.

Lady Barb did not trouble herself to denounce this
gentleman; her manner was that of having for a long
time expected the worst. She simply remarked dryly,
after having listened to her husband for some minutes

in silence: "I would as lief she should marry Dr. Feeder!"

The day after this, Jackson Lemon closeted himself for an hour with Lady Agatha, taking great pains to set forth to her the reasons why she should not marry her Californian. Jackson was kind, he was affectionate; he kissed her and put his arm round her waist, he reminded her that he and she were the best of friends, and that she had always been awfully nice to him; therefore he counted upon her. She would break her mother's heart, she would deserve her father's curse, and she would get him, Jackson, into a pickle from which no human power could ever disembroil him. Lady Agatha listened and cried, and returned his kiss very affectionately, and admitted that her father and mother would never consent to such a marriage; and when he told her that he had made arrangements for her to sail for Liverpool (with some charming people) the next day but one, she embraced him again and assured him that she could never thank him enough for all the trouble he had taken about her. He flattered himself that he had convinced, and in some degree comforted her, and reflected with complacency that even should his wife take it into her head, Barberina would never get ready to embark for her native land between a Monday and a Wednesday. The next morning Lady Agatha did not appear at breakfast; but as she usually rose very late, her absence excited no alarm. She had not rung her bell, and she was supposed still to be sleeping.

But she had never yet slept later than mid-day; and as this hour approached her sister went to her room. Lady Barb then discovered that she had left the house at seven o'clock in the morning, and had gone to meet Herman Longstraw at a neighboring corner. A little note on the table explained it very succinctly, and put beyond the power of Jackson Lemon and his wife to doubt that by the time this news reached them their wayward sister had been united to the man of her preference as closely as the laws of the State of New York could bind her. Her little note set forth that as she knew she should never be permitted to marry him, she had determined to marry him without permission, and that directly after the ceremony, which would be of the simplest kind, they were to take a train for the Far West. Our history is concerned only with the remote consequences of this incident, which made, of course, a great deal of trouble for Jackson Lemon. He went to the Far West in pursuit of the fugitives, and overtook them in California; but he had not the audacity to propose to them to separate, as it was easy for him to see that Herman Longstraw was at least as well married as himself. Lady Agatha was already popular in the new States, where the history of her elopement, emblazoned in enormous capitals, was circulated in a thousand newspapers. This question of the newspapers had been for Jackson Lemon one of the most definite results of his sister-in-law's *coup de tête.* His first thought had been of the public prints, and his first exclamation a prayer that they should not get hold of the story. But they did get hold of it, and they treated the affair with their customary energy and eloquence. Lady Barb never saw them; but an affectionate friend of the family, travelling at that time in the United States, made a parcel of some of the leading journals, and sent them to Lord Canterville. This missive elicited from her ladyship a letter addressed to Jackson Lemon which shook the young man's position to the base. The phials of an unnamable vulgarity had been opened upon the house of Canterville, and his mother-in-law demanded that in compensation for the affronts and injuries that were being heaped upon her family, and bereaved and dishonored as she was, she should at least be allowed to look on the face of her other daughter. "I suppose you will not, for very pity, be deaf to such a prayer as that," said Lady Barb; and though shrinking from recording a second act of weakness on the part of a man who had such pretensions to be strong, I must relate that poor Jackson, who blushed dreadfully over the newspapers, and felt afresh, as he read them, the force of Mrs. Freer's terrible axiom, — poor Jackson paid a visit to the office of the Cunarders. He said to himself afterward that it was the newspapers that had done it; he could not bear to appear to be on their side; they made it so hard to deny that the country was vulgar, at a time when one was in such need of all one's arguments. Lady Barb, before sailing, definitely refused to mention any week or month as the date of their pre-arranged return to New York. Very many weeks and months have elapsed since then, and she gives no sign of coming back. She will never fix a date. She is much missed by Mrs. Vanderdecken, who still alludes to her — still says the line of the shoulders was superb; putting the statement, pensively, in the past tense. Lady Beauchemin and Lady Marmaduke are much disconcerted; the international project has not, in their view, received an impetus.

Jackson Lemon has a house in London, and he rides in the Park with his wife, who is as beautiful as the day, and a year ago presented him with a little girl, with features that Jackson already scans for the look of race, — whether in hope or fear, to-day, is more. than my muse has revealed. He has occasional scenes with Lady Barb, during which the look of race is very visible in her own countenance; but they never terminate in a visit to the Cunarders. He is exceedingly restless, and is constantly crossing to the Continent; but he returns with a certain abruptness, for he cannot bear to meet the Dexter Freers, and they seem to pervade the more comfortable parts of Europe. He dodges them in every town. Sidney Feeder feels very badly about him; it is months since Jackson has sent him any "results." The excellent fellow goes very often, in a consolatory spirit, to see Mrs. Lemon; but he has not yet been able to answer her standing question: "Why that girl more than another?" Lady Agatha Longstraw and her husband arrived a year ago in England, and Mr. Longstraw's personality had immense success during the last London season. It is not exactly known what they live on, though it is perfectly known that he is looking for something to do. Meanwhile it is as good as known that Jackson Lemon supports them.

A NEW ENGLAND WINTER.

A NEW ENGLAND WINTER.

I.

MRS. DAINTRY stood on her steps a moment, to address a parting injunction to her little domestic, whom she had induced a few days before, by earnest and friendly argument, — the only coercion or persuasion this enlightened mistress was ever known to use, — to crown her ruffled tresses with a cap; and then, slowly and with deliberation, she descended to the street. As soon as her back was turned, her maid-servant closed the door, not with violence, but inaudibly, quickly, and firmly; so that when she reached the bottom of the steps and looked up again at the front, — as she always did before leaving it, to assure herself that everything was well, — the folded wings of her portal were presented to her, smooth and shining, as wings should be, and ornamented with the large silver plate on which the name of her late husband was inscribed, — which she had brought with her when, taking the inevitable course of good Bostonians, she had transferred her household goods from the "hill" to the "new land," and the exhibition of which, as an act of conjugal fidelity, she preferred — how much, those who knew her could easily understand — to the more distinguished modern fashion of suppressing the domiciliary label. She stood still for a minute on the pavement, looking at the closed aperture of her dwelling and asking herself a question; not that there was anything extraordinary in that, for she never spared herself in this respect. She would greatly have preferred that her servant should not shut the door till she had reached the sidewalk, and dismissed her, as it were, with that benevolent, that almost maternal, smile with which it was a part of Mrs. Daintry's religion to encourage and reward her domestics. She liked to know that her door was being held open behind her until she should pass out of sight of the young woman standing in the hall. There was a want of respect in shutting her out so precipitately; it was almost like giving her a push down the steps. What Mrs. Daintry asked herself was, whether she should not do right to ascend the steps again, ring the bell, and request Beatrice, the parlor-maid, to be so good as to wait a little longer. She felt that this would have been a proceeding of some importance, and she presently decided against it. There were a good many reasons, and she thought them over as she took her way slowly up Newbury Street, turning as soon as possible into Commonwealth Avenue; for she was very fond of the south side of this beautiful prospect, and the autumn sunshine to-day was delightful. During the moment that she paused, looking up at her house, she had had time to see that everything was as fresh and bright as she could desire. It looked a little too new, perhaps, and Florimond would not like that; for of course his great fondness was for the antique, which was the reason for his remaining year after year in Europe, where, as a young painter of considerable, if not of the highest, promise, he had opportunities to study the most dilapidated buildings. It was a comfort to Mrs. Daintry, however, to be able to say to herself that he would be struck with her living really very nicely, — more nicely, in many ways, than he could possibly be accommodated — that she was sure of — in a small dark *appartement de garçon* in Paris, on the uncomfortable side of the Seine. Her state of mind at present was such that she set the highest value on anything that could possibly help to give Florimond a pleasant impression. Nothing could be too small to count, she said to herself; for she knew that Florimond was both fastidious and observant. Everything that would strike him agreeably would contribute to detain him, so that if there were only enough agreeable things he would perhaps stay four or five months, instead of three, as he had promised, — the three that were to date from the day of his arrival in Boston, not from that (an important difference) of his departure from Liverpool, which was about to take place.

It was Florimond that Mrs. Daintry had had in

mind when, on emerging from the little vestibule, she gave the direction to Beatrice about the position of the door-mat, — in which the young woman, so carefully selected, as a Protestant, from the British Provinces, had never yet taken the interest that her mistress expected from such antecedents. It was Florimond also that she had thought of in putting before her parlor-maid the question of donning a badge of servitude in the shape of a neat little muslin coif, adorned with pink ribbon and stitched together by Mrs. Daintry's own beneficent fingers. Naturally there was no obvious connection between the parlor-maid's coiffure and the length of Florimond's stay; that detail was to be only a part of the general effect of American life. It was still Florimond that was uppermost as his mother, on her way up the hill, turned over in her mind that question of the ceremony of the front-door. He had been living in a country in which servants observed more forms, and he would doubtless be shocked at Beatrice's want of patience. An accumulation of such anomalies would at last undermine his loyalty. He would not care for them for himself, of course, but he would care about them for her; coming from France, where, as she knew by his letters, and indeed by her own reading, — for she made a remarkably free use of the Athenæum, — that the position of a mother was one of the most exalted, he could not fail to be *froissé* at any want of consideration for his surviving parent. As an artist, he could not make up his mind to live in

Boston; but he was a good son for all that. He had told her frequently that they might easily live together if she would only come to Paris; but of course she could not do that, with Joanna and her six children round in Clarendon Street, and her responsibilities to her daughter multiplied in the highest degree. Besides, during that winter she spent in Paris, when Florimond was definitely making up his mind, and they had in the evening the most charming conversations, interrupted only by the repeated care of winding up the lamp or applying the bellows to the obstinate little fire, — during that winter she had felt that Paris was not her element. She had gone to the lectures at the Sorbonne, and she had visited the Louvre as few people did it, catalogue in hand, taking the catalogue volume by volume; but all the while she was thinking of Joanna and her new baby, and how the other three (that was the number then) were getting on while their mother was so much absorbed with the last. Mrs. Daintry, familiar as she was with these anxieties, had not the step of a grandmother; for a mind that was always intent had the effect of refreshing and brightening her years. Responsibility with her was not a weariness, but a joy, — at least it was the nearest approach to a joy that she knew, and she did not regard her life as especially cheerless; there were many others that were more denuded than hers. She moved with circumspection, but without reluctance, holding up her head and looking at every one she met with a clear, unaccus-

18

ing gaze. This expression showed that she took an interest, as she ought, in everything that concerned her fellow-creatures; but there was that also in her whole person which indicated that she went no farther than Christian charity required. It was only with regard to Joanna and that vociferous houseful, — so fertile in problems, in opportunities for devotion, — that she went really very far. And now to-day, of course, in this matter of Florimond's visit, after an absence of six years; which was perhaps more on her mind than anything had ever been. People who met Mrs. Daintry after she had traversed the Public Garden — she always took that way — and begun to ascend the charming slope of Beacon Street, would never, in spite of the relaxation of her pace as she measured this eminence, have mistaken her for a little old lady who should have crept out, vaguely and timidly, to inhale one of the last mild days. It was easy to see that she was not without a duty, or at least a reason, — and indeed Mrs. Daintry had never in her life been left in this predicament. People who knew her ever so little would have felt that she was going to call on a relation; and if they had been to the manner born they would have added a mental hope that her relation was prepared for her visit. No one would have doubted this, however, who had been aware that her steps were directed to the habitation of Miss Lucretia Daintry. Her sister-in-law, her husband's only sister, lived in that commodious nook which is known as Mount Vernon

Place; and Mrs. Daintry therefore turned off at Joy Street. By the time she did so, she had quite settled in her mind the question of Beatrice's behavior in connection with the front-door. She had decided that it would never do to make a formal remonstrance, for it was plain that, in spite of the Old-World training which she hoped the girl might have imbibed in Nova Scotia (where, until lately, she learned, there had been an English garrison), she would in such a case expose herself to the danger of desertion; Beatrice would not consent to stand there holding the door open for nothing. And after all, in the depths of her conscience Mrs. Daintry was not sure that she ought to; she was not sure that this was an act of homage that one human being had a right to exact of another, simply because this other happened to wear a little muslin cap with pink ribbons. It was a service that ministered to her importance, to her dignity, not to her hunger or thirst; and Mrs. Daintry, who had had other foreign advantages besides her winter in Paris, was quite aware that in the United States the machinery for that former kind of tribute was very undeveloped. It was a luxury that one ought not to pretend to enjoy, — it was a luxury, indeed, that she probably ought not to presume to desire. At the bottom of her heart Mrs. Daintry suspected that such hankerings were criminal. And yet, turning the thing over, as she turned everything, she could not help coming back to the idea that it would be very pleasant, it would be really

delightful, if Beatrice herself, as a result of the growing refinement of her taste, her transplantation to a
society after all more elaborate than that of Nova
Scotia, should perceive the fitness, the felicity, of
such an attitude. This perhaps was too much to
hope; but it did not much matter, for before she had
turned into Mount Vernon Place Mrs. Daintry had
invented a compromise. She would continue to talk
to her parlor-maid until she should reach the bottom
of her steps, making earnestly one remark after the
other over her shoulder, so that Beatrice would be
obliged to remain on the threshold. It is true that
it occurred to her that the girl might not attach much
importance to these Parthian observations, and would
perhaps not trouble herself to wait for their natural
term; but this idea was too fraught with embarrassment to be long entertained. It must be added that
this was scarcely a moment for Mrs. Daintry to go
much into the ethics of the matter, for she felt that
her call upon her sister-in-law was the consequence
of a tolerably unscrupulous determination.

II.

LUCRETIA DAINTRY was at home, for a wonder;
but she kept her visitor waiting a quarter of an
hour, during which this lady had plenty of time to
consider her errand afresh. She was a little ashamed
of it; but she did not so much mind being put to

shame by Lucretia, for Lucretia did things that were much more ambiguous than any she should have thought of doing. It was even for this that Mrs. Daintry had picked her out, among so many relations, as the object of an appeal in its nature somewhat precarious. Nevertheless, her heart beat a little faster than usual as she sat in the quiet parlor, looking about her for the thousandth time at Lucretia's "things," and observing that she was faithful to her old habit of not having her furnace lighted until long after every one else. Miss Daintry had her own habits, and she was the only person her sister-in-law knew who had more reasons than herself. Her taste was of the old fashion, and her drawing-room embraced neither festoons nor Persian rugs, nor plates and *plaques* upon the wall, nor faded stuffs suspended from unexpected projections. Most of the articles it contained dated from the year 1830; and a sensible, reasonable, rectangular arrangement of them abundantly answered to their owner's conception of the decorative. A rosewood sofa against the wall, surmounted by an engraving from Kaulbach; a neatly drawn carpet, faded, but little worn, and sprigged with a floral figure; a chimney-piece of black marble, veined with yellow, garnished with an empire clock and antiquated lamps; half a dozen large mirrors, with very narrow frames; and an immense glazed screen representing in the livid tints of early worsted-work a ruined temple overhanging a river, — these were some of the more obvious of Miss Daintry's treasures. Her sister-in-law was a votary of the newer school, and had made sacrifices to have everything in black and gilt; but she could not fail to see that Lucretia had some very good pieces. It was a wonder how she made them last, for Lucretia had never been supposed to know much about the keeping of a house, and no one would have thought of asking her how she treated the marble floor of her vestibule, or what measures she took in the spring with regard to her curtains. Her work in life lay outside. She took an interest in questions and institutions, sat on committees, and had views on Female Suffrage, — a movement which she strongly opposed. She even wrote letters sometimes to the "Transcript," not "chatty" and jocular, and signed with a fancy name, but "over" her initials, as the phrase was, — every one recognized them, — and bearing on some important topic. She was not, however, in the faintest degree slipshod or dishevelled, like some of the ladies of the newspaper and the forum; she had no ink on her fingers, and she wore her bonnet as scientifically poised as the dome of the State House. When you rang at her door-bell you were never kept waiting, and when you entered her dwelling you were not greeted with those culinary odors which, pervading halls and parlors, had in certain other cases been described as the right smell in the wrong place. If Mrs. Daintry was made to wait some time before her hostess appeared, there was nothing extraordinary in this, for none of her friends came down directly, and she never did herself. To come·down directly would have seemed to her to betray a frivolous eagerness for the social act. The delay, moreover, not only gave her, as I have said, opportunity to turn over her errand afresh, but enabled her to say to herself, as she had often said before, that though Lucretia had no taste, she had some very good things, and to wonder both how she had kept them so well, and how she had originally got them. Mrs. Daintry knew that they proceeded from her mother and her aunts, who had been supposed to distribute among the children of the second generation the accumulations of the old house in Federal Street, where many Daintrys had been born in the early part of the century. Of course she knew nothing of the principles on which the distribution had been made, but all she could say was that Lucretia had evidently been first in the field. There was apparently no limit to what had come to her. Mrs. Daintry was not obliged to look, to assure herself that there was another clock in the back parlor, — which would seem to indicate that all the clocks had fallen to Lucretia. She knew of four other timepieces in other parts of the house, for of course in former years she had often been up stairs; it was only in comparatively recent times that she had renounced that practice. There had been a period when she ascended to the second story as a matter of course, without asking leave. On seeing that her sister-in-law was in neither of the parlors, she mounted and talked with Lucretia at the door of her bedroom, if it happened to be closed. And there had been another season when she stood at the foot of the staircase, and, lifting her voice, inquired of Miss Daintry — who called down with some shrillness in return — whether she might climb, while the maid-servant, wandering away with a vague cachinnation, left her to her own devices. But both of these phases belonged to the past. Lucretia never came into *her* bedroom to-day, nor did she presume to penetrate into Lucretia's; so that she did not know for a long time whether she had renewed her chintz, nor whether she had hung in that bower the large photograph of Florimond, presented by Mrs. Daintry herself to his aunt, which had been placed in neither of the parlors. Mrs. Daintry would have given a good deal to know whether this memento had been honored with a place in her sister-in-law's " chamber," — it was by this name, on each side, that these ladies designated their sleeping-apartment; but she could not bring herself to ask directly, for it would be embarrassing to learn — what was possible — that Lucretia had not paid the highest respect to Florimond's portrait. The point was cleared up by its being revealed to her accidentally that the photograph, — an expensive and very artistic one, taken in Paris, — had been relegated to the spare-room, or guest-chamber. Miss Daintry was very hospitable, and constantly had friends of her own sex staying with her. They were very apt to be young women in their twenties; and one of them had remarked to Mrs. Daintry that her son's portrait — he must be wonderfully handsome — was the first thing she saw when she woke up in the morning. Certainly Florimond was handsome; but his mother had a lurking suspicion that, in spite of his beauty, his aunt was not fond of him. She doubtless thought he ought to come back and settle down in Boston; he was the first of the Daintrys who had had so much in common with Paris. Mrs. Daintry knew as a fact that, twenty-eight years before, Lucretia, whose opinions even at that period were already wonderfully formed, had not approved of the romantic name which, in a moment of pardonable weakness, she had conferred upon her rosy babe. The spinster (she had been as much of a spinster at twenty as she was to-day) had accused her of making a fool of the child. Every one was reading old ballads in Boston then, and Mrs. Daintry had found the name in a ballad. It doubled any anxiety she might feel with regard to her present business to think that, as certain foreign newspapers which her son sent her used to say about ambassadors, Florimond was perhaps not a *persona grata* to his aunt. She reflected, however, that if his fault were in his absenting himself, there was nothing that would remedy it so effectively as his coming home. She reflected, too, that if she and Lucretia no longer took liberties with each other, there was still something a little indiscreet in her purpose this morning.

But it fortified and consoled her for everything to remember, as she sat looking at the empire clock, which was a very handsome one, that her husband at least had been disinterested.

Miss Daintry found her visitor in this attitude, and thought it was an expression of impatience ; which led her to explain that she had been on the roof of her house with a man who had come to see about repairing it. She had walked all over it, and peeped over the cornice, and not been in the least dizzy ; and had come to the conclusion that one ought to know a great deal more about one's roof than was usual.

"I am sure you have never been over yours," she said to her sister-in-law.

Mrs. Daintry confessed with some embarrassment that she had not, and felt, as she did so, that she was superficial and slothful. It annoyed her to reflect that while she supposed, in her new house, she had thought of everything, she had not thought of this important feature. There was no one like Lucretia for giving one such reminders.

"I will send Florimond up when he comes," she said ; "he will tell me all about it."

"Do you suppose he knows about roofs, except tumbledown ones, in his little pictures ? I am afraid it will make him giddy." This had been Miss Daintry's rejoinder, and the tone of it was not altogether reassuring. She was nearly fifty years old ; she had a plain, fresh, delightful face, and in whatever part of the world she might have been met, an attentive observer of American life would not have had the least difficulty in guessing what phase of it she represented. She represented the various and enlightened activities which cast their rapid shuttle — in the comings and goings of eager workers — from one side to the other of Boston Common. She had in an eminent degree the physiognomy, the accent, the costume, the conscience, and the little eye-glass, of her native place. She had never sacrificed to the graces, but she inspired unlimited confidence. Moreover, if she was thoroughly in sympathy with the New England capital, she reserved her liberty ; she had a great charity, but she was independent and witty ; and if she was as earnest as other people, she was not quite so serious. Her voice was a little masculine ; and it had been said of her that she didn't care in the least how she looked. This was far from true, for she would not for the world have looked better than she thought was right for so plain a woman.

Mrs. Daintry was fond of calculating consequences ; but she was not a coward, and she arrived at her business as soon as possible.

"You know that Florimond sails on the 20th of this month. He will get home by the 1st of December."

"Oh, yes, my dear, I know it ; everybody is talking about it. I have heard it thirty times. That's where Boston is so small," Lucretia Daintry remarked.

"Well, it's big enough for me," said her sister-in-law. "And of course people notice his coming back; it shows that everything that has been said is false, and that he really does like us."

"He likes his mother, I hope; about the rest I don't know that it matters."

"Well, it certainly will be pleasant to have him," said Mrs. Daintry, who was not content with her companion's tone, and wished to extract from her some recognition of the importance of Florimond's advent. "It will prove how unjust so much of the talk has been."

"My dear woman, I don't know anything about the talk. We make too much fuss about everything. Florimond was an infant when I last saw him."

This was open to the interpretation that too much fuss had been made about Florimond, — an idea that accorded ill with the project that had kept Mrs. Daintry waiting a quarter of an hour while her hostess walked about on the roof. But Miss Daintry continued, and in a moment gave her sister-in-law the best opportunity she could have hoped for. "I don't suppose he will bring with him either salvation or the other thing; and if he has decided to winter among the bears, it will matter much more to him than to any one else. But I shall be very glad to see him if he behaves himself; and I need n't tell you that if there is anything I can do for him — " and Miss Daintry, tightening her lips together a little, paused, suiting her action to the idea that professions were usually humbug.

"There is indeed something you can do for him," her sister-in-law hastened to respond; "or something you can do for me, at least," she added, more discreetly.

"Call it for both of you. What is it?" and Miss Daintry put on her eyeglass.

"I know you like to do kindnesses, when they are *real* ones; and you almost always have some one staying with you for the winter."

Miss Daintry stared. "Do you want to put him to live with me?"

"No, indeed! Do you think I could part with him? It's another person, — a lady!"

"A lady! Is he going to bring a woman with him?"

"My dear Lucretia, you won't wait. I want to make it as pleasant for him as possible. In that case he may stay longer. He has promised three months; but I should so like to keep him till the summer. It would make me very happy."

"Well, my dear, keep him, then, if you can."

"But I can't, unless I am helped."

"And you want me to help you? Tell me what I must do. Should you wish me to make love to him?"

Mrs. Daintry's hesitation at this point was almost as great as if she had found herself obliged to say yes. She was well aware that what she had come to suggest was very delicate; but it seemed to her at the present moment more delicate than ever. Still,

her cause was good, because it was the cause of maternal devotion. "What I should like you to do would
be to ask Rachel Torrance to spend the winter with
you."

Miss Daintry had not sat so much on committees
without getting used to queer proposals, and she had
long since ceased to waste time in expressing a vain
surprise. Her method was Socratic; she usually entangled her interlocutor in a net of questions.

"Ah, do you want *her* to make love to him?"

"No, I don't want any love at all. In such a
matter as that I want Florimond to be perfectly free.
But Rachel is such an attractive girl; she is so
artistic and so bright."

"I don't doubt it; but I can't invite all the
attractive girls in the country. Why don't you ask
her yourself?"

"It would be too marked. And then Florimond
might not like her in the same house; he would
have too much of her. Besides, she is no relation of
mine, you know; the cousinship — such as it is, it is
not very close — is on your side. I have reason to
believe she would like to come; she knows so little
of Boston, and admires it so much. It is astonishing
how little idea the New York people have. She
would be different from any one here, and that
would make a pleasant change for Florimond. She
was in Europe so much when she was young. She
speaks French perfectly, and Italian, I think, too;
and she was brought up in a kind of artistic way.

Her father never did anything; but even when he had n't bread to give his children, he always arranged to have a studio, and they gave musical parties. That's the way Rachel was brought up. But they tell me that it has n't in the least spoiled her; it has only made her very familiar with life."

"Familiar with humbug!" Miss Daintry ejaculated.

"My dear Lucretia, I assure you she is a very good girl, or I never would have proposed such a plan as this. She paints very well herself, and tries to sell her pictures. They are dreadfully poor, — I don't mean the pictures, but Mrs. Torrance and the rest, — and they live in Brooklyn, in some second-rate boarding-house. With that, Rachel has everything about her that would enable her to appreciate Boston. Of course it would be a real kindness, because there would be one less to pay for at the boarding-house. You have n't a son, so you can't understand how a mother feels. I want to prepare everything, to have everything pleasantly arranged. I want to deprive him of every pretext for going away before the summer; because in August — I don't know whether I have told you — I have a kind of idea of going back with him myself. I am so afraid he will miss the artistic side. I don't mind saying that to you, Lucretia, for I have heard you say yourself that you thought it had been left out here. Florimond might go and see Rachel Torrance every day if he liked; of course, being his cousin, and calling her Rachel, it could n't

attract any particular attention. I should n't much
care if it did," Mrs. Daintry went on, borrowing a certain bravado, that in calmer moments was eminently
foreign to her nature, from the impunity with which
she had hitherto proceeded. Her project, as she heard
herself unfold it, seemed to hang together so well that
she felt something of the intoxication of success. "I
should n't care if it did," she repeated, "so long as
Florimond had a little of the conversation that he is
accustomed to, and I was not in perpetual fear of his
starting off."

Miss Daintry had listened attentively while her
sister-in-law spoke, with eager softness, passing from
point to point with a *crescendo* of lucidity, like a
woman who had thought it all out, and had the consciousness of many reasons on her side. There had
been momentary pauses, of which Lucretia had not
taken advantage, so that Mrs. Daintry rested at last
in the enjoyment of a security that was almost complete, and that her companion's first question was not
of a nature to dispel.

"It 's so long since I have seen her. Is she pretty?"
Miss Daintry inquired.

"She is decidedly striking; she has magnificent
hair!" her visitor answered, almost with enthusiasm.

"Do you want Florimond to marry her?"

This, somehow, was less pertinent. "Ah, no, my
dear," Mrs. Daintry rejoined, very judicially. "That
is not the kind of education — the kind of *milieu* —
one would wish for the wife of one's son." She knew,

moreover, that her sister-in-law knew her opinion about the marriage of young people. It was a sacrament more high and holy than any words could express, the propriety and timeliness of which lay deep in the hearts of the contracting parties, below all interference from parents and friends; it was an inspiration from above, and she would no more have thought of laying a train to marry her son, than she would have thought of breaking open his letters. More relevant even than this, however, was the fact that she did not believe he would wish to make a wife of a girl from a slipshod family in Brooklyn, however little he might care to lose sight of the artistic side. It will be observed that she gave Florimond the credit of being a very discriminating young man; and she indeed discriminated for him in cases in which she would not have presumed to discriminate for herself.

"My dear Susan, you are simply the most immoral woman in Boston!" These were the words of which, after a moment, her sister-in-law delivered herself.

Mrs. Daintry turned a little pale. "Don't you think it would be right?" she asked quickly.

"To sacrifice the poor girl to Florimond's amusement? What has she done that you should wish to play her such a trick?" Miss Daintry did not look shocked: she never looked shocked, for even when she was annoyed she was never frightened; but after a moment she broke into a loud, uncompro-

mising laugh, — a laugh which her sister-in-law knew
of old, and regarded as a peculiarly dangerous form
of criticism.

"I don't see why she should be sacrificed. She
would have a lovely time if she were to come on.
She would consider it the greatest kindness to be
asked."

"To be asked to come and amuse Florimond?"

Mrs. Daintry hesitated a moment. "I don't see
why she should object to that. Florimond is certainly not beneath a person's notice. Why, Lucretia,
you speak as if there were something disagreeable
about Florimond."

"My dear Susan," said Miss Daintry, "I am willing to believe that he is the first young man of his
time; but, all the same, it is n't a thing to do."

"Well, I have thought of it in every possible way,
and I have n't seen any harm in it. It is n't as if
she were giving up anything to come."

"You have thought of it too much, perhaps. Stop
thinking for a while. I should have imagined you
were more scrupulous."

Mrs. Daintry was silent a moment; she took her
sister-in-law's asperity very meekly, for she felt that
if she had been wrong in what she proposed, she de-
served a severe judgment. But why was she wrong?
She clasped her hands in her lap and rested her eyes
with extreme seriousness upon Lucretia's little *pince-
nez*, inviting her to judge her, and too much interested in having the question of her culpability

settled to care whether or no she were hurt. "It is very hard to know what is right," she said presently. "Of course it is only a plan; I wondered how it would strike you."

"You had better leave Florimond alone," Miss Daintry answered. "I don't see why you should spread so many carpets for him. Let him shift for himself. If he does n't like Boston, Boston can spare him."

"You are not nice about him; no, you are not, Lucretia!" Mrs. Daintry cried, with a slight tremor in her voice.

"Of course I am not as nice as you,—he is not my son; but I am trying to be nice about Rachel Torrance."

"I am sure she would like him,—she would delight in him," Mrs. Daintry broke out.

"That's just what I'm afraid of; I could n't stand that."

"Well, Lucretia, I am not convinced," Mrs. Daintry said, rising, with perceptible coldness. "It is very hard to be sure one is not unjust. Of course I shall not expect you to send for her; but I shall think of her with a good deal of compassion, all winter, in that dingy place in Brooklyn. And if you have some one else with you — and I am sure you will, because you always do, unless you remain alone on purpose, this year, to put me in the wrong, — if you have some one else I shall keep saying to myself: 'Well, after all, it might have been Rachel!'"

Miss Daintry gave another of her loud laughs at the idea that she might remain alone "on purpose." "I shall have a visitor, but it will be some one who will not amuse Florimond in the least. If he wants to go away, it won't be for anything in this house that he will stay."

"I really don't see why you should hate him," said poor Mrs. Daintry.

"Where do you find that? On the contrary, I appreciate him very highly. That's just why I think it very possible that a girl like Rachel Torrance — an odd, uninstructed girl, who has n't had great advantages — may fall in love with him and break her heart."

Mrs. Daintry's clear eyes expanded. "Is *that* what you are afraid of?"

"Do you suppose my solicitude is for Florimond? An accident of that sort — if she were to show him her heels at the end — might perhaps do him good. But I am thinking of the girl, since you say you don't want him to marry her."

"It was not for that that I suggested what I did. I don't want him to marry any one — I have no plans for that," Mrs. Daintry said, as if she were resenting an imputation.

"Rachel Torrance least of all!" and Miss Daintry indulged still again in that hilarity, so personal to herself, which sometimes made the subject look so little jocular to others. "My dear Susan, I don't blame you," she said; "for I suppose mothers are

necessarily unscrupulous. But that is why the rest
of us should hold them in check."

"It's merely an assumption, that she would fall
in love with him," Mrs. Daintry continued, with a
certain majesty; "there is nothing to prove it, and I
am not bound to take it for granted."

"In other words, you don't care if she should!
Precisely; that, I suppose, is your *rôle*. I am glad
I have n't any children; it's very sophisticating.
For so good a woman, you are very bad. Yes, you
are good, Susan; and you *are* bad."

"I don't know that I pretend to be particularly
good," Susan remarked, with the warmth of one who
had known something of the burden of such a
reputation, as she moved toward the door.

"You have a conscience, and it will wake up,"
her companion returned. "It will come over you
in the watches of the night that your idea was — as
I have said — immoral."

Mrs. Daintry paused in the hall, and stood there
looking at Lucretia. It was just possible that she
was being laughed at, for Lucretia's deepest mirth was
sometimes silent, — that is, one heard the laughter
several days later. Suddenly she colored to the roots
of her hair, as if the conviction of her error had come
over her. Was it possible she had been corrupted by
an affection in itself so pure? "I only want to do
right," she said, softly. "I would rather he should
never come home, than that I should go too far."

She was turning away, but her sister-in-law held

her a moment and kissed her. "You are a delightful
woman, but I won't ask Rachel Torrance!" This
was the understanding on which they separated.

III.

Miss Daintry, after her visitor had left her, recognized that she had been a little brutal; for Susan's
proposition did not really strike her as so heinous.
Her eagerness to protect the poor girl in Brooklyn
was not a very positive quantity, inasmuch as she
had an impression that this young lady was on the
whole very well able to take care of herself. What
her talk with Mrs. Daintry had really expressed was
the lukewarmness of her sentiment with regard to
Florimond. She had no wish to help his mother
lay carpets for him, as she said. Rightly or wrongly,
she had a conviction that he was selfish, that he was
spoiled, that he was conceited; and she thought
Lucretia Daintry meant for better things thàn the
service of sugaring for the young man's lips the pill
of a long-deferred visit to Boston. It was quite
indifferent to her that he should be conscious, in
that city, of unsatisfied needs. At bottom, she had
never forgiven him for having sought another way
of salvation. Moreover she had a strong sense of
humor, and it amused her more than a little that her
sister-in-law — of all women in Boston — should have
come to her on that particular errand. It completed

the irony of the situation that one should frighten
Mrs. Daintry — just a little — about what she had
undertaken; and more than once that day Lucretia
had, with a smile, the vision of Susan's countenance
as she remarked to her that she was immoral.   In
reality, and speaking seriously, she did not consider
Mrs. Daintry's inspiration unpardonable; what was
very positive was simply that she had no wish to
invite Rachel Torrance for the benefit of her nephew.
She was by no means sure that she should like the
girl for her own sake, and it was still less apparent
that she should like her for that of Florimond.
With all this, however, Miss Daintry had a high
love of justice; she revised her social accounts from
time to time, to see that she had not cheated any one.
She thought over her interview with Mrs. Daintry
the next day, and it occurred to her that she had
been a little unfair.   But she scarcely knew what
to do to repair her mistake, by which Rachel Torrance also had suffered, perhaps; for after all, if it
had not been wicked of her sister-in-law to ask such
a favor, it had at least been cool; and the penance
that presented itself to Lucretia Daintry did not
take the form of despatching a letter to Brooklyn.
An accident came to her help, and four days after
the conversation I have narrated she wrote her a
note, which explains itself, and which I will presently
transcribe.   Meanwhile Mrs. Daintry, on her side,
had held an examination of her heart; and though
she did not think she had been very civilly treated,

the result of her reflections was to give her a fit of
remorse.   Lucretia was right: she had been anything but scrupulous; she had skirted the edge of
an abyss.   Questions of conduct had long been
familiar to her; and the cardinal rule of life in her
eyes was that before one did anything which in-
volved in any degree the happiness or the interest
of another, one should take one's motives out of the
closet in which they are usually laid away and give
them a thorough airing.   This operation, undertaken
before her visit to Lucretia, had been cursory and
superficial; for now that she repeated it, she discovered among the recesses of her spirit a number
of nut-like scruples which she was astonished to
think she should have overlooked.   She had really
been very wicked, and there was no doubt about *her*
proper penance.   It consisted of a letter to her sister-
in-law, in which she completely disavowed her little
project, attributing it to a momentary intermission of
her reason.   She saw it would never do, and she was
quite ashamed of herself.   She did not exactly thank
Miss Daintry for the manner in which she had ad-
monished her, but she spoke as one saved from a
great danger, and assured her relative of Mount Vernon Place that she should not soon again expose
herself.   This letter crossed with Miss Daintry's
missive, which ran as follows:—

"MY DEAR SUSAN,—I have been thinking over
our conversation of last Tuesday, and I am afraid I

went rather too far in my condemnation of your idea with regard to Rachel Torrance. If I expressed myself in a manner to wound your feelings, I can assure you of my great regret. Nothing could have been farther from my thoughts than the belief that you are wanting in delicacy. I know very well that you were prompted by the highest sense of duty. It is possible, however, I think, that your sense of duty to poor Florimond is a little too high. You think of him too much as that famous dragon of antiquity, — was n't it in Crete, or somewhere ? — to whom young virgins had to be sacrificed. It may relieve your mind, however, to hear that this particular virgin will probably, during the coming winter, be provided for.   Yesterday, at Doll's, where I had gone in to look at the new pictures (there is a striking Appleton Brown) I met Pauline Mesh, whom I had not seen for ages, and had half an hour's talk with her. She seems to me to have come out very much this winter, and to have altogether a higher tone. In short, she is much enlarged, and seems to want to take an interest in something. Of course you will say : Has she not her children ? But, somehow, they don't seem to fill her life. You must remember that they are very small as yet, to fill anything. Anyway, she mentioned to me her great disappointment in having had to give up her sister, who was to have come on from Baltimore to spend the greater part of the winter. Rosalie is very pretty, and Pauline expected to give a lot of Germans, and make things generally pleasant.

I should n't wonder if she thought something might
happen that would make Rosalie a fixture in our
city. She would have liked this immensely; for,
whatever Pauline's faults may be, she has plenty of
family feeling. But her sister has suddenly got engaged in Baltimore (I believe it 's much easier than
here), so that the visit has fallen through. Pauline
seemed to be quite in despair, for she had made all
sorts of beautifications in one of her rooms, on purpose for Rosalie; and not only had she wasted her
labor (you know how she goes into those things,
whatever we may think, sometimes, of her taste), but
she spoke as if it would make a great difference in
her winter; said she should suffer a great deal from
loneliness. She says Boston is no place for a married woman, standing on her own merits; she can't
have any sort of time unless she hitches herself to
some attractive girl who will help her to pull the
social car. You know that is n't what every one
says, and how much talk there has been the last two
or three winters about the frisky young matrons.
Well, however that may be, I don't pretend to know
much about it, not being in the married set. Pauline
spoke as if she were really quite high and dry, and I
felt so sorry for her that it suddenly occurred to me
to say something about Rachel Torrance. I remembered that she is related to Donald Mesh in about
the same degree as she is to me, — a degree nearer,
therefore, than to Florimond. Pauline did n't seem
to think much of the relationship, — it 's so remote;

but when I told her that Rachel (strange as it might appear) would probably be thankful for a season in Boston, and might be a good substitute for Rosalie, why she quite jumped at the idea. She has never seen her, but she knows who she is, — fortunately, for I could never begin to explain. She seems to think such a girl will be quite a novelty in this place. I don't suppose Pauline can do her any particular harm, from what you tell me of Miss Torrance, and, on the other hand, I don't know that she could injure Pauline. She is certainly very kind (Pauline, of course), and I have no doubt she will immediately write to Brooklyn, and that Rachel will come on. Florimond won't, of course, see as much of her as if she were staying with me, and I don't know that he will particularly care about Pauline Mesh, who, you know, is intensely American ; but they will go out a great deal, and he will meet them (if he takes the trouble), and I have no doubt that Rachel will take the edge off the east wind for him. At any rate I have perhaps done her a good turn. I must confess to you — and it won't surprise you — that I was thinking of her, and not of him, when I spoke to Pauline. Therefore I don't feel that I have taken a risk, but I don't much care if I have. I have my views, but I never worry. I recommend you not to do so either, — for you go, I know, from one extreme to the other. I have told you my little story ; it was on my mind. Are n't you glad to see the lovely snow ?   Ever affectionately yours,   L. D.

"P. S.   The more I think of it, the more convinced I am that you *will* worry now about the danger for Rachel.   Why did I drop the poison into your mind?   Of course I did n't say a word about you or Florimond."

This epistle reached Mrs. Daintry, as I have intimated, about an hour after her letter to her sister-in-law had been posted; but it is characteristic of her that she did not for a moment regret having made a retractation rather humble in form, and which proved, after all, scarcely to have been needed.   The delight of having done that duty carried her over the sense of having given herself away.   Her sister-in-law spoke from knowledge when she wrote that phrase about Susan's now beginning to worry from the opposite point of view.   Her conscience, like the good Homer, might sometimes nod; but when it woke, it woke with a start; and for many a day afterward its vigilance was feverish.   For the moment, her emotions were mingled.   She thought Lucretia very strange, and that *she* was scarcely in a position to talk about one's going from one extreme to the other.   It was good news to her that Rachel Torrance would probably be on the ground after all, and she was delighted that on Lucretia the responsibility of such a fact should rest.   This responsibility she now already, after her revulsion, as we know, regarded as grave; she exhaled an almost luxurious sigh when she thought of having herself escaped from it. What she did not quite understand was Lucretia's apology, and her having, even if Florimond's happiness were not her motive, taken almost the very step which three days before she had so severely criticised. This was puzzling, for Lucretia was usually so consistent. But all the same Mrs. Daintry did not repent of her own penance; on the contrary, she took more and more comfort in it. If, with that, Rachel Torrance should be really useful, it would be delightful.

IV.

FLORIMOND DAINTRY had stayed at home for three days after his arrival; he had sat close to the fire in his slippers, every now and then casting a glance over his shoulders at the hard white world which seemed to glare at him from the other side of the window-panes. He was very much afraid of the cold, and he was not in a hurry to go out and meet it. He had met it, on disembarking in New York, in the shape of a wave of frozen air, which had travelled from some remote point in the west (he was told) on purpose, apparently, to smite him in the face. That portion of his organism tingled yet with it, though the gasping, bewildered look which sat upon his features during the first few hours had quite left it. I am afraid it will be

thought he was a young man of small courage;
and on a point so delicate I do not hold myself
obliged to pronounce. It is only fair to add that
it was delightful to him to be with his mother, and
that they easily spent three days in talking. Moreover he had the company of Joanna and her children, who, after a little delay, occasioned apparently
by their waiting to see whether he would not first
come to them, had arrived in a body and had spent
several hours. As regards the majority of them,
they had repeated this visit several times in the
three days, Joanna being obliged to remain at home
with the two younger ones. There were four older
ones, and their grandmother's house was open to
them as a second nursery. The first day, their
Uncle Florimond thought them charming; and as
he had brought a French toy for each, it is probable
that this impression was mutual. The second day,
their little ruddy bodies and woollen clothes seemed
to him to have a positive odor of the cold, — it
was disagreeable to him, and he spoke to his mother
about their "wintry smell." The third day they had
become very familiar; they called him "Florry;"
and he had made up his mind that, to let them
loose in that way on his mother, Joanna must be
rather wanting in delicacy, — not mentioning this
deficiency, however, as yet, for he saw that his
mother was not prepared for it. She evidently
thought it proper, or at least it seemed inevitable,
either that she should be round at Joanna's, or the

children should be round in Newbury Street; for "Joanna's" evidently represented primarily the sound of small, loud voices, and the hard breathing that signalized the intervals of romps. Florimond was rather disappointed in his sister, seeing her after a long separation; he remarked to his mother that she seemed completely submerged. As Mrs. Daintry spent most of her time under the waves with her daughter, she had grown to regard this element as sufficiently favorable to life, and was rather surprised when Florimond said to her that he was sorry to see she and his sister appeared to have been converted into a pair of *bonnes d'enfants*. Afterward, however, she perceived what he meant; she was not aware, until he called her attention to it, that the little Merrimans took up an enormous place in the intellectual economy of two households. "You ought to remember that they exist for you, and not you for them," Florimond said to her in a tone of friendly admonition; and he remarked on another occasion that the perpetual presence of children was a great injury to conversation, — it kept it down so much; and that in Boston they seemed to be present even when they were absent, inasmuch as most of the talk was about them. Mrs. Daintry did not stop to ask herself what her son knew of Boston, leaving it years before as a boy, and not having so much as looked out of the window since his return; she was taken up mainly with noting certain little habits of speech which he evidently had formed, and in wondering how they would strike his fellow-citizens. He was very definite and trenchant; he evidently knew perfectly what he thought; and though his manner was not defiant, — he had, perhaps, even too many of the forms of politeness, as if sometimes, for mysterious reasons, he were playing upon you, — the tone in which he uttered his opinions did not appear exactly to give you the choice. And then apparently he had a great many; there was a moment when Mrs. Daintry vaguely foresaw that the little house in Newbury Street would be more crowded with Florimond's views than it had ever been with Joanna's children. She hoped very much people would like him, and she hardly could see why they should fail to find him agreeable. To herself he was sweeter than any grandchild; he was as kind as if he had been a devoted parent. Florimond had but a small acquaintance with his brother-in-law; but after he had been at home forty-eight hours he found that he bore Arthur Merriman a grudge, and was ready to think rather ill of him, — having a theory that he ought to have held up Joanna and interposed to save her mother. Arthur Merriman was a young and brilliant commission-merchant, who had not married Joanna Daintry for the sake of Florimond, and, doing an active business all day in East Boston, had a perfectly good conscience in leaving his children's mother and grandmother to establish their terms of intercourse.

Florimond, however, did not particularly wonder

why his brother-in-law had not been round to bid him welcome. It was for Mrs. Daintry that this anxiety was reserved; and what made it worse was her uncertainty as to whether she should be justified in mentioning the subject to Joanna. It might wound Joanna to suggest to her that her husband was derelict, — especially if she did not think so, and she certainly gave her mother no opening; and on the other hand, Florimond might have ground for complaint if Arthur should continue not to notice him. Mrs. Daintry earnestly desired that nothing of this sort should happen, and took refuge in the hope that Florimond would have adopted the foreign theory of visiting, in accordance with which the new-comer was to present himself first. Meanwhile the young man, who had looked upon a meeting with his brother-in-law as a necessity rather than a privilege, was simply conscious of a reprieve; and up in Clarendon Street, as Mrs. Daintry said, it never occurred to Arthur Merriman to take this social step, nor to his wife to propose it to him. Mrs. Merriman simply took for granted that her brother would be round early some morning to see the children. A day or two later the couple dined at her mother's, and that virtually settled the question. It is true that Mrs. Daintry, in later days, occasionally recalled the fact that, after all, Joanna's husband never had called upon Florimond; and she even wondered why Florimond, who sometimes said bitter things, had not made more of it. The matter came back at moments when, under the pressure of circumstances which, it must be confessed, were rare, she found herself giving assent to an axiom that sometimes reached her ears. This axiom, it must be added, did not justify her in the particular case I have mentioned, for the full purport of it was that the queerness of Bostonians was collective, not individual.

There was no doubt, however, that it was Florimond's place to call first upon his aunt, and this was a duty of which she could not hesitate to remind him. By the time he took his way across the long expanse of the new land and up the charming hill, which constitutes as it were, the speaking face of Boston, the temperature either had relaxed, or he had got used, even in his mother's hot little house, to his native air. He breathed the bright cold sunshine with pleasure; he raised his eyes to the arching blueness, and thought he had never seen a dome so magnificently painted. He turned his head this way and that, as he walked (now that he had recovered his legs, he foresaw that he should walk a good deal), and freely indulged his most valued organ, the organ that had won him such reputation as he already enjoyed. In the little artistic circle in which he moved in Paris, Florimond Daintry was thought to have a great deal of eye. His power of rendering was questioned, his execution had been called pretentious and feeble; but a conviction had somehow been diffused that he saw things with extraordinary intensity. No one could tell better than he what to

paint, and what not to paint, even though his interpretation were sometimes rather too sketchy. It
will have been guessed that he was an impressionist;
and it must be admitted that this was the character
in which he proceeded on his visit to Miss Daintry.
He was constantly shutting one eye, to see the better
with the other, making a little telescope by curving
one of his hands together, waving these members
in the air with vague pictorial gestures, pointing at
things which, when people turned to follow his direction, seemed to mock the vulgar vision by eluding it.
I do not mean that he practised these devices as he
walked along Beacon Street, into which he had crossed
shortly after leaving his mother's house; but now
that he had broken the ice, he acted quite in ·the
spirit of the reply he had made to a friend in Paris,
shortly before his departure, who asked him why
he was going back to America, — " I am going to see
how it looks." He was of course very conscious of
his eye; and his effort to cultivate it was both intui-
tive and deliberate. He spoke of it freely, as he
might have done of a valuable watch or a horse. He
was always trying to get the visual impression; asking himself, with regard to such and such an object
or a place, of what its " character" would consist.
There is no doubt he really saw with great intensity;
and the reader will probably feel that he was welcome to this ambiguous privilege. It was not important for him that things should be beautiful; what
he sought to discover was their identity, — the signs

by which he should know them. He began this inquiry as soon as he stepped into Newbury Street
from his mother's door, and he was destined to continue it for the first few weeks of his stay in Boston.
As time went on, his attention relaxed; for one
could n't do more than see, as he said to his mother
and another person; and he had seen. Then the novelty wore off, — the novelty which is often so ab-
surdly great in the eyes of the American who returns
to his native land after a few years spent in the foreign element, — an effect to be accounted for only on
the supposition that in the secret parts of his mind
he recognizes the aspect of life in Europe as, through
long heredity, the more familiar; so that superficially,
having no interest to oppose it, it quickly supplants
the domestic type, which, upon his return, becomes
supreme, but with its credit in many cases apprecia-
bly and permanently diminished. Florimond painted
a few things while he was in America, though he
had told his mother he had come home to rest; but
when, several months later, in Paris, he showed his
"notes," as he called them, to a friend, the young
Frenchman asked him if Massachusetts were really
so much like Andalusia.

There was certainly nothing Andalusian in the
prospect as Florimond traversed the artificial bosom
of the Back Bay. He had made his way promptly
into Beacon Street, and he greatly admired that vista.
The long straight avenue lay airing its newness in
the frosty day, and all its individual façades, with

their neat, sharp ornaments, seemed to have been scoured, with a kind of friction, by the hard, salutary light. Their brilliant browns and drabs, their rosy surfaces of brick, made a variety of·fresh, violent tones, such as Florimond liked to memorize, and the large clear windows of their curved fronts faced each other, across the street, like candid, inevitable eyes. There was something almost terrible in the windows; Florimond had forgotten how vast and clean they were, and how, in their sculptured frames, the New England air seemed, like a zealous housewife, to polish and preserve them. A great many ladies were looking out, and groups of children, in the drawing-rooms, were flattening their noses against the transparent plate. Here and there, behind it, the back of a statuette or the symmetry of a painted vase, erect on a pedestal, presented itself to the street, and enabled the passer to construct, more or less, the room within, — its frescoed ceilings, its new silk sofas, its untarnished fixtures. This continuity of glass constituted a kind of exposure, within and without, and gave the street the appearance of an enormous corridor, in which the public and the private were familiar and intermingled. But it was all very cheerful and commodious, and seemed to speak of diffused wealth, of intimate family life, of comfort constantly renewed. All sorts of things in the region of the temperature had happened during the few days that Florimond had been in the country. The cold wave had spent itself, a snowstorm had come

and gone, and the air, after this temporary relaxation, had renewed its keenness. The snow, which
had fallen in but moderate abundance, was heaped
along the side of the pavement; it formed a radiant
cornice on the housetops, and crowned the windows
with a plain white cap. It deepened the color of
everything else, made all surfaces look ruddy, and
at a distance sent into the air a thin, delicate mist,
— a tinted exhalation, — which occasionally softened
an edge. The upper part of Beacon Street seemed to
Florimond charming, — the long, wide, sunny slope,
the uneven line of the older houses, the contrasted,
differing, bulging fronts, the painted bricks, the tidy
facings, the immaculate doors, the burnished silver
plates, the denuded twigs of the far extent of the
Common, on the other side; and to crown the eminence and complete the picture, high in the air, poised
in the right place, over everything that clustered below, the most felicitous object in Boston, — the gilded
dome of the State House. It was in the shadow of
this monument, as we know, that Miss Daintry lived;
and Florimond, who was always lucky, had the good
fortune to find her at home.

V.

It may seem that I have assumed on the part of
the reader too great a curiosity about the impressions
of this young man, who was not very remarkable,
and who has not even the recommendation of being

the hero of our perhaps too descriptive tale. The reader will already have discovered that a hero fails us here; but if I go on at all risks to say a few words about Florimond, he will perhaps understand the better why this part has not been filled. Miss Daintry's nephew was not very original; it was his own illusion that he had in a considerable degree the value of rareness. Even this youthful conceit was not rare, for it was not of heroic proportions, and was liable to lapses and discouragements. He was a fair, slim, civil young man, and you would never have guessed from his appearance that he was an impressionist. He was neat and sleek and quite anti-Bohemian, and in spite of his looking about him as he walked, his figure was much more in harmony with the Boston landscape than he supposed. He was a little vain, a little affected, a little pretentious, a little good-looking, a little amusing, a little spoiled, and at times a little tiresome. If he was disagreeable, however, it was also only a little; he did not carry anything to a very high pitch; he was accomplished, industrious, successful, — all in the minor degree. He was fond of his mother and fond of himself; he also liked the people who liked him. Such people could belong only to the class of good listeners, for Florimond, with the least encouragement (he was very susceptible to that), would chatter by the hour. As he was very observant, and knew a great many stories, his talk was often entertaining, especially to women, many of whom thought him wonderfully sympathetic. It may be added that he was still very young and fluid, and neither his defects nor his virtues had a great consistency. He was fond of the society of women, and had an idea that he knew a great deal about that element of humanity. He believed himself to know everything about art, and almost everything about life, and he expressed himself as much as possible in the phrases that are current in studios. He spoke French very well, and it had rubbed off on his English.

His aunt listened to him attentively, with her nippers on her nose. She had been a little restless at first, and, to relieve herself, had vaguely punched the sofa-cushion which lay beside her, — a gesture that her friends always recognized; they knew it to express a particular emotion. Florimond, whose egotism was candid and confiding, talked for an hour about himself, — about what he had done, and what he intended to do, what he had said and what had been said to him; about his habits, tastes, achievements, peculiarities, which were apparently so numerous; about the decorations of his studio in Paris; about the character of the French, the works of Zola, the theory of art for art, the American type, the "stupidity" of his mother's new house, — though of course it had some things that were knowing, — the pronunciation of Joanna's children, the effect of the commission business on Arthur Merriman's conversation, the effect of everything on his mother, Mrs. Daintry, and the effect of Mrs. Daintry on her son

Florimond. The young man had an epithet, which
he constantly introduced, to express disapproval;
when he spoke of the architecture of his mother's
house, over which she had taken great pains (she
remembered the gabled fronts of Nuremberg), he
said that a certain effect had been dreadfully missed,
that the character of the doorway was simply "crass."
He expressed, however, a lively sense of the bright
cleanness of American interiors. "Oh, as for that,"
he said, "the place is kept, — it's kept;" and, to
give an image of this idea, he put his gathered fingers
to his lips an instant, seemed to kiss them or blow
upon them, and then opened them into the air.
Miss Daintry had never encountered this gesture before; she had heard it described by travelled persons;
but to see her own nephew in the very act of it led
her to administer another thump to the sofa-cushion.
She finally got this article under control, and sat
more quiet, with her hands clasped upon it, while
her visitor continued to discourse. In pursuance of
his character as an impressionist, he gave her a great
many impressions; but it seemed to her that as he
talked, he simply exposed himself, — exposed his egotism, his little pretensions. Lucretia Daintry, as we
know, had a love of justice, and though her opinions
were apt to be very positive, her charity was great
and her judgments were not harsh; moreover, there
was in her composition not a drop of acrimony.
Nevertheless, she was, as the phrase is, rather hard
on poor little Florimond; and to explain her severity

we are bound to assume that in the past he had in some way offended her. To-day, at any rate, it seemed to her that he patronized his maiden aunt. He scarcely asked about her health, but took for granted on her part an unlimited interest in his own sensations. It came over her afresh that his mother had been absurd in thinking that the usual resources of Boston would not have sufficed to maintain him; and she smiled a little grimly at the idea that a special provision should have been made. This idea presently melted into another, over which she was free to regale herself only after her nephew had departed. For the moment she contented herself with saying to him, when a pause in his young eloquence gave her a chance, — "You will have a great many people to go and see. You pay the penalty of being a Bostonian; you have several hundred cousins. One pays for everything."

Florimond lifted his eyebrows. "I pay for that every day of my life. Have I got to go and see them all?"

"All — every one," said his aunt, who in reality did not hold this obligation in the least sacred.

"And to say something agreeable to them all?" the young man went on.

"Oh, no, that is not necessary," Miss Daintry rejoined, with more exactness. "There are one or two, however, who always appreciate a pretty speech." She added in an instant, "Do you remember Mrs. Mesh?"

"Mrs. Mesh?" Florimond apparently did not remember.

"The wife of Donald Mesh; your grandfathers were first cousins. I don't mean her grandfather, but her husband's. If you don't remember her, I suppose he married her after you went away."

"I remember Donald; but I never knew he was a relation. He was single then, I think."

"Well, he's double now," said Miss Daintry; "he's triple, I may say, for there are two ladies in the house."

"If you mean he's a polygamist — are there Mormons even here?" Florimond, leaning back in his chair, with his elbow on the arm, and twisting with his gloved fingers the point of a small fair mustache, did not appear to have been arrested by this account of Mr. Mesh's household; for he almost immediately asked, in a large, detached way, — "Are there any nice women here?"

"It depends on what you mean by nice women; there are some very sharp ones."

"Oh, I don't like sharp ones," Florimond remarked, in a tone which made his aunt long to throw her sofa-cushion at his head. "Are there any pretty ones?"

She looked at him a moment, hesitating. "Rachel Torrance is pretty, in a strange, unusual way, — black hair and blue eyes, a serpentine figure, old coins in her tresses; that sort of thing."

"I have seen a good deal of that sort of thing," said Florimond, a little confusedly.

"That I know nothing about. I mention Pauline Mesh's as one of the houses that you ought to go to, and where I know you are expected."

"I remember now that my mother has said something about that. But who is the woman with coins in her hair? — what has she to do with Pauline Mesh?"

"Rachel is staying with her; she came from New York a week ago, and I believe she means to spend the winter. She is n't a woman, she 's a girl."

"My mother did n't speak of her," said Florimond; "but I don't think she would recommend me a girl with a serpentine figure."

"Very likely not," Miss Daintry answered, dryly. "Rachel Torrance is a far-away cousin of Donald Mesh, and consequently of mine and of yours. She 's an artist, like yourself; she paints flowers on little panels and *plaques.*"

"Like myself? — I never painted a *plaque* in my life!" exclaimed Florimond, staring.

"Well, she 's a model also; you can paint her if you like; she has often been painted, I believe."

Florimond had begun to caress the other tip of his mustache. "I don't care for women who have been painted before. I like to find them out. Besides, I want to rest this winter."

His aunt was disappointed; she wished to put him into relation with Rachel Torrance, and his indifference was an obstacle. The meeting was sure to take place sooner or later, but she would have him glad to precipitate it, and, above all, to quicken her nephew's susceptibilities. " Take care you are not found out yourself ! " she exclaimed, tossing away her sofa-cushion and getting up.

Florimond did not see what she meant, and he accordingly bore her no rancor; but when, before he took his leave, he said to her, rather irrelevantly, that if he should find himself in the mood during his stay in Boston, he should like to do her portrait, — she had such a delightful face, — she almost thought the speech a deliberate impertinence. " Do you mean that you have discovered me, — that no one has suspected it before ? " she inquired with a laugh, and a little flush in the countenance that he was so good as to appreciate.

Florimond replied, with perfect coolness and good-nature, that he did n't know about this, but that he was sure no one had seen her in just the way he saw her; and he waved his hand in the air with strange circular motions, as if to evoke before him the image of a canvas, with a figure just rubbed in. He repeated this gesture, or something very like it, by way of farewell, when he quitted his aunt, and she thought him insufferably patronizing.

This is why she wished him, without loss of time, to make the acquaintance of Rachel Torrance, whose treatment of his pretensions she thought would be salutary. It may now be communicated to the reader — after a delay proportionate to the momentousness of the fact — that this had been the idea

which suddenly flowered in her brain as she sat face
to face with her irritating young visitor. It had
vaguely shaped itself after her meeting with that
strange girl from Brooklyn, whom Mrs. Mesh, all
gratitude, — for she liked strangeness, — promptly
brought to see her; and her present impression of her
nephew rapidly completed it. She had not expected
to take an interest in Rachel Torrance, and could not
see why, through a freak of Susan's, she should have
been called upon to think so much about her; but,
to her surprise, she perceived that Mrs. Daintry's
proposed victim was not the usual forward girl. She
perceived at the same time that it had been ridiculous to think of Rachel as a victim, — to suppose that
she was in danger of vainly fixing her affections upon
Florimond. She was much more likely to triumph
than to suffer; and if her visit to Boston were to produce bitter fruits, it would not be she who should
taste them. She had a striking, oriental head, a
beautiful smile, a manner of dressing which carried
out her exotic type, and a great deal of experience
and wit. She evidently knew the world, as one
knows it when one has to live by its help. If she
had an aim in life, she would draw her bow well
above the tender breast of Florimond Daintry. With
all this, she certainly was an honest, obliging girl,
and had a sense of humor which was a fortunate
obstacle to her falling into a *pose.* Her coins and
amulets and seamless garments were, for her, a part
of the general joke of one's looking like a Circassian

or a Smyrniote,—an accident for which Nature was responsible; and it may be said of her that she took herself much less seriously than other people took her. This was a defect for which Lucretia Daintry had a great kindness; especially as she quickly saw that Rachel was not of an insipid paste, as even triumphant coquettes sometimes are. In spite of her poverty and the opportunities her beauty must have brought her, she had not yet seen fit to marry,—which was a proof that she was clever as well as disinterested. It looks dreadfully cold-blooded as I write it here, but the notion that this capable creature might administer poetic justice to Florimond gave a measurable satisfaction to Miss Daintry. He was in distinct need of a snub, for down in Newbury Street his mother was perpetually swinging the censer; and no young nature could stand that sort of thing,—least of all such a nature as Florimond's. She said to herself that such a "putting in his place" as he might receive from Rachel Torrance would probably be a permanent correction. She wished his good, as she wished the good of every one; and that desire was at the bottom of her vision. She knew perfectly what she should like: she should like him to fall in love with Rachel, as he probably would, and to have no doubt of her feeling immensely honored. She should like Rachel to encourage him just enough— just so far as she might, without being false. A little would do, for Florimond would always take his success for granted. To this point did the study of her nephew's moral regeneration bring the excellent woman, who a few days before had accused his mother of a lack of morality. His mother was thinking only of his pleasure; *she* was thinking of his immortal spirit. She should like Rachel to tell him at the end that he was a presumptuous little boy, and that since it was his business to render "impressions," he might see what he could do with that of having been jilted. This extraordinary flight of fancy on Miss Daintry's part was caused in some degree by the high spirits which sprang from her conviction, after she met the young lady, that Mrs. Mesh's companion was not in danger; for even when she wrote to her sister-in-law in the manner the reader knows, her conscience was not wholly at rest. There was still a risk, and she knew not why she should take risks for Florimond. Now, however, she was prepared to be perfectly happy when she should hear that the young man was constantly in Arlington Street; and at the end of a little month she enjoyed this felicity.

VI.

MRS. MESH sat on one side of the fire, and Florimond on the other; he had by this time acquired the privilege of a customary seat. He had taken a general view of Boston. It was like a first introduction, for before his going to live in Paris he had been too young to judge; and the result of this survey was the conviction that there was nothing better than Mrs. Mesh's drawing-room. She was one of the few persons whom one was certain to find at home after five o'clock; and the place itself was agreeable to Florimond, who was very fastidious about furniture and decorations. He was willing to concede that Mrs. Mesh (the relationship had not yet seemed close enough to justify him in calling her Pauline) knew a great deal about such matters; though it was clear that she was indebted for some of her illumination to Rachel Torrance, who had induced her to make several changes. These two ladies, between them, represented a great fund of taste; with a difference that was a result of Rachel's knowing clearly beforehand what she liked (Florimond called her, at least, by her baptismal name), and Mrs. Mesh's only knowing it after a succession of experiments, of transposings and drapings, all more or less ingenious and expensive. If Florimond liked Mrs. Mesh's drawing-room better than any other corner of Boston, he also had his preference in regard to its phases and hours. It was most charming in the winter twilight, by the glow of the fire, before the lamps had been brought in. The ruddy flicker played over many objects, making them look more mysterious than Florimond had supposed anything could look in Boston, and, among others, upon Rachel Torrance, who, when she moved about the room in a desultory way (never so much *enfoncée*, as Florimond said, in a chair as Mrs. Mesh was) cer-

tainly attracted and detained the eye. The young
man, from his corner (he was almost as much
enfoncé as Mrs. Mesh), used to watch her; and he
could easily see what his aunt had meant by saying
she had a serpentine figure. She was slim and
flexible, she took attitudes which would have been
awkward in other women, but which her charming
pliancy made natural. She reminded him of a celebrated actress in Paris, who was the ideal of tortuous
thinness. Miss Torrance used often to seat herself
for a short time at the piano; and though she never
had been taught this art (she played only by ear),
her musical feeling was such that she charmed the
twilight hour. Mrs. Mesh sat on one side of the fire,
as I have said, and Florimond on the other; the two
might have been found in this relation, — listening,
face to face, — almost any day in the week. Mrs.
Mesh raved about her new friend, as they said in
Boston, — I mean about Rachel Torrance, not about
Florimond Daintry. She had at last got hold of a
mind that understood her own (Mrs. Mesh's mind
contained depths of mystery), and she sacrificed herself, generally, to throw her companion into relief.
Her sacrifice was rewarded, for the girl was universally liked and admired; she was a new type
altogether; she was the lioness of the winter. Florimond had an opportunity to see his native town in
one of its fits of enthusiasm. He had heard of the
infatuations of Boston, literary and social; of its
capacity for giving itself with intensity to a tempo-

rary topic; and he was now conscious, on all sides, of the breath of New England discussion. Some one had said to him, — or had said to some one, who repeated it, — that there was no place like Boston for taking up with such seriousness a second-rate spinster from Brooklyn. But Florimond himself made no criticism ; for, as we know, he speedily fell under the charm of Rachel Torrance's personality. He was perpetually talking with Mrs. Mesh about it; and when Mrs. Mesh herself descanted on the subject, he listened with the utmost attention. At first, on his return, he rather feared the want of topics; he foresaw that he should miss the talk of the studios, of the theatres, of the boulevard, of a little circle of " naturalists " (in literature and art) to which he belonged, without sharing all its views. But he presently perceived that Boston, too, had its actualities, and that it even had this in common with Paris, — that it gave its attention most willingly to a female celebrity. If he had had any hope of being himself the lion of the winter, it had been dissipated by the spectacle of his cousin's success. He saw that while she was there, he could only be a subject of secondary reference. He bore her no grudge for this. I must hasten to declare that from the pettiness of this particular jealousy poor Florimond was quite exempt. Moreover, he was swept along by the general chorus ; and he perceived that when one changes one's sky, one inevitably changes, more or less, one's standard. Rachel Torrance was neither

an actress, nor a singer, nor a beauty, nor one of the
ladies who were chronicled in the " Figaro," nor the
author of a successful book, nor a person of the great
world ; she had neither a future, nor a past, nor a
position, nor even a husband, to make her identity
more solid ; she was a simple American girl, of the
class that lived in *pensions* (a class of which Florimond had ever entertained a theoretic horror) ; and
yet she had profited to the degree of which our
young man was witness, by those treasures of sympathy constantly in reserve in the American public
(as has already been intimated) for the youthful-
feminine. If Florimond was struck with all this, it
may be imagined whether or no his mother thought
she had been clever when it occurred to her (before
any one else) that Rachel would be a resource for the
term of hibernation. She had forgotten all her scruples and hesitations ; she only knew she had seen
very far. She was proud of her prescience, she was
even amused with it ; and for the moment she held her
head rather high. No one knew of it but Lucretia,
— for she had never confided it to Joanna, of whom
she would have been more afraid in such a connection even than of her sister-in-law ; but Mr. and
Mrs. Merriman perceived an unusual lightness in her
step, a fitful sparkle in her eye. It was of course
easy for them to make up their mind that she was
exhilarated to this degree by the presence of her son ;
especially as he seemed to be getting on beautifully
in Boston.

"She stays out longer every day; she is scarcely ever home to tea," Mrs. Mesh remarked, looking up at the clock on the chimney-piece.

Florimond could not fail to know to whom she alluded, for it has been intimated that between these two there was much conversation about Rachel Torrance. "It's funny, the way the girls run about alone here," he said, in the amused, contemplative tone in which he frequently expressed himself on the subject of American life. "Rachel stays out after dark, and no one thinks any the worse of her."

"Oh, well, she's old enough," Mrs. Mesh rejoined, with a little sigh, which seemed to suggest that Rachel's age was really affecting. Her eyes had been opened by Florimond to many of the peculiarities of the society that surrounded her; and though she had spent only as many months in Europe as her visitor had spent years, she now sometimes spoke as if she thought the manners of Boston more odd even than he could pretend to do. She was very quick at picking up an idea, and there was nothing she desired more than to have the last on every subject. This winter, from her two new friends, Florimond and Rachel, she had extracted a great many that were new to her; the only trouble was that, coming from different sources, they sometimes contradicted each other. Many of them, however, were very vivifying; they added a new zest to that prospect of life which had always, in winter, the denuded bushes, the solid pond, and the plank-covered walks, the exaggerated bridge, the patriotic statues, the dry, hard texture of the Public Garden for its foreground, and for its middle distance, the pale, frozen twigs, stiff in the windy sky, that whistled over the Common, the domestic dome of the State House, familiar in the untinted air, and the competitive spires of a liberal faith. Mrs. Mesh had an active imagination, and plenty of time on her hands. Her two children were young, and they slept a good deal; she had explained to Florimond, who observed that she was a great deal less in the nursery than his sister, that she pretended only to give her attention to their waking hours. "I have people for the rest of the time," she said; and the rest of the time was considerable; so that there were very few obstacles to her cultivation of ideas. There was one in her mind now, and I may as well impart it to the reader without delay. She was not quite so delighted with Rachel Torrance as she had been a month ago; it seemed to her that the young lady took up — socially speaking — too much room in the house; and she wondered how long she intended to remain, and whether it would be possible, without a direct request, to induce her to take her way back to Brooklyn. This last was the conception with which she was at present engaged; she was at moments much pressed by it, and she had thoughts of taking Florimond Daintry into her confidence. This, however, she determined not to do, lest he should regard it as a sign that she was jealous of her companion. I know not whether she was, but this I know, — that Mrs. Mesh was a woman of a high ideal, and would not for the world have appeared so. If she was jealous, this would imply that she thought Florimond was in love with Rachel; and she could only object to that on the ground of being in love with him herself. She was not in love with him, and had no intention of being; of this the reader, possibly alarmed, may definitely rest assured. Moreover, she did not think him in love with Rachel; as to her reason for this reserve, I need not, perhaps, be absolutely outspoken. She was not jealous, she would have said; she was only oppressed — she was a little over-ridden. Rachel pervaded her house, pervaded her life, pervaded Boston; every one thought it necessary to talk to her about Rachel, to rave about her in the Boston manner, which seemed to Mrs. Mesh, in spite of the Puritan tradition, very much more unbridled than that of Baltimore. They thought it would give her pleasure; but by this time she knew everything about Rachel. The girl had proved rather more of a figure than she expected; and though she could not be called pretentious, she had the air, in staying with Pauline Mesh, of conferring rather more of a favor than she received. This was absurd for a person who was, after all, though not in her first youth, only a girl, and who, as Mrs. Mesh was sure, from her biography, — for Rachel had related every item, — had never before had such unrestricted access to the fleshpots. The fleshpots were full, under Donald

Mesh's roof, and his wife could easily believe that the poor girl would not be in a hurry to return to her boarding-house in Brooklyn. For that matter there were lots of people in Boston who would be delighted that she should come to them. It was doubtless an inconsistency on Mrs. Mesh's part that if she was overdone with the praises of Rachel Torrance which fell from every lip, she should not herself have forborne to broach the topic. But I have sufficiently intimated 'that it had a perverse fascination for her; it is true she did not speak of Rachel only to praise her. Florimond, in truth, was a little weary of the young lady's name; he had plenty of topics of his own, and he had his own opinion about Rachel Torrance. He did not take up Mrs. Mesh's remark as to her being old enough.

"You must wait till she comes in. Please ring for tea," said Mrs. Mesh, after a pause. She had noticed that Florimond was comparing his watch with her clock; it occurred to her that he might be going.

"Oh, I always wait, you know; I like to see her when she has been anywhere. She tells one all about it, and describes everything so well."

Mrs. Mesh looked at him a moment. "She sees a great deal more in things than I am usually able to discover. She sees the most extraordinary things in Boston."

"Well, so do I," said Florimond, placidly.

"Well, I don't, I must say!" She asked him to

ring again; and then, with a slight irritation, accused
him of not ringing hard enough; but before he could
repeat the operation, she left her chair and went herself to the bell. After this she stood before the fire
a moment, gazing into it; then suggested to Florimond that he should put on a log.

"Is it necessary, —when your servant is coming
in a moment?" the young man asked, unexpectedly,
without moving. In an instant, however, he rose;
and then he explained that this was only his little
joke.

"Servants are too stupid," said Mrs. Mesh. "But
I spoil you. What would your mother say?" She
watched him while he placed the log. She was
plump, and she was not tall; but she was a very
pretty woman. She had round brown eyes, which
looked as if she had been crying a little, — she had
nothing in life to cry about; and dark, wavy hair,
which, here and there, in short, crisp tendrils, escaped
artfully from the form in which it was dressed.
When she smiled, she showed very pretty teeth; and
the combination of her touching eyes and her parted
lips was at such moments almost bewitching. She
was accustomed to express herself in humorous
superlatives, in pictorial circumlocutions; and had
acquired in Boston the rudiments of a social dialect
which, to be heard in perfection, should be heard
on the lips of a native. Mrs. Mesh had picked it
up; but it must be confessed that she used it without originality. It was an accident that on this

occasion she had not expressed her wish for her tea by saying that she should like a pint or two of that Chinese fluid.

"My mother believes I can't be spoiled," said Florimond, giving a little push with his toe to the stick that he had placed in the embers; after which he sank back into his chair, while Mrs. Mesh resumed possession of her own. "I am ever fresh,— ever pure."

"You are ever conceited. I don't see what you find so extraordinary in Boston," Mrs. Mesh added, reverting to his remark of a moment before.

"Oh, everything! the ways of the people, their ideas, their peculiar *cachet*. The very expression of their faces amuses me."

"Most of them have no expression at all."

"Oh, you are used to it," Florimond said. "You have become one of themselves; you have ceased to notice."

"I am more of a stranger than you; I was born beneath other skies. Is it possible that you don't know yet that I am a native of Baltimore? 'Maryland, my Maryland!'"

"Have they got so much expression in Maryland? No, I thank you; no tea. Is it possible!" Florimond went on, with the familiarity of pretended irritation, — "is it possible that you have n't noticed yet that I never take it? *Boisson fade, écœurante*, as Balzac calls it."

"Ah, well, if you don't take it on account of

Balzac!" said Mrs. Mesh. "I never saw a man who had such fantastic reasons. Where, by the way, is the volume of that depraved old author which you promised to bring me?"

"When do you think he flourished? You call everything old, in this country, that is n't in the morning paper. I have n't brought you the volume, because I don't want to bring you presents," Florimond said; "I want you to love me for myself, as they say in Paris."

"Don't quote what they say in Paris! Don't sully this innocent bower with those fearful words!" Mrs. Mesh rejoined, with a jocose intention. "Dear lady, your son is not everything we could wish!" she added in the same mock dramatic tone, as the curtain of the door was lifted, and Mrs. Daintry rather timidly advanced. Mrs. Daintry had come to satisfy a curiosity, after all quite legitimate; she could no longer resist the impulse to ascertain for herself, so far as she might, how Rachel Torrance and Florimond were getting on. She had had no definite expectation of finding Florimond at Mrs. Mesh's; but she supposed that at this hour of the afternoon, — it was already dark, and the ice, in many parts of Beacon Street, had a polish which gleamed through the dusk, — she should find Rachel. "Your son has lived too long in far-off lands; he has dwelt among outworn things," Mrs. Mesh went on, as she conducted her visitor to a chair. "Dear lady, you are not as Balzac was; do you start at the mention of his name ? — therefore you will have some tea in a little painted cup."

Mrs. Daintry was not bewildered, though it may occur to the reader that she might have been; she was only a little disappointed. She had hoped she might have occasion to talk about Florimond; but the young man's presence was a denial of this privilege. "I am afraid Rachel is not at home," she remarked. "I am afraid she will think I have not been very attentive."

"She will be in in a moment; we are waiting for her," Florimond said. "It 's impossible she should think any harm of you. I have told her too much good."

"Ah, Mrs. Daintry, don't build too much on what he has told her! He 's a false and faithless man!" Pauline Mesh interposed; while the good lady from Newbury Street, smiling at this adjuration, but looking a little grave, turned from one of her companions to the other. Florimond had relapsed into his chair by the fireplace; he sat contemplating the embers, and fingering the tip of his mustache. Mrs. Daintry imbibed her tea, and told how often she had slipped coming down the hill. These expedients helped her to wear a quiet face; but in reality she was nervous, and she felt rather foolish. It came over her that she was rather dishonest; she had presented herself at Mrs. Mesh's in the capacity of a spy. The reader already knows she was subject to sudden revulsions of feeling. There is an adage about repenting at leisure; but Mrs Daintry always repented in a hurry. There was something in the air — something impalpable, magnetic — that told her she had better not have come; and even while she conversed with Mrs. Mesh she wondered what this mystic element could be. Of course she had been greatly preoccupied, these last weeks; for it had seemed to her that her plan with regard to Rachel Torrance was succeeding only too well. Florimond had frankly accepted her in the spirit in which she had been offered, and it was very plain that she was helping him to pass his winter. He was constantly at the house, — Mrs. Daintry could not tell exactly how often; but she knew very well that in Boston, if one saw anything of a person, one saw a good deal. At first he used to speak of it; for two or three weeks, he had talked a good deal about Rachel Torrance. More lately, his allusions had become few; yet to the best of Mrs. Daintry's belief his step was often in Arlington Street. This aroused her suspicions, and at times it troubled her conscience; there were moments when she wondered whether, in arranging a genial winter for Florimond, she had also prepared a season of torment for herself. Was he in love with the girl, or had he already discovered that the girl was in love with him? The delicacy of either situation would account for his silence. Mrs. Daintry said to herself that it would be a grim joke if she should prove to have plotted only too well. It was her sister-in-law's warning in especial that haunted her imagination, and she scarcely knew, at times, whether more to hope that Florimond might have been smitten, or to pray that Rachel might remain indifferent. It was impossible for Mrs. Daintry to shake off the sense of responsibility; she could not shut her eyes to the fact that she had been the prime mover. It was all very well to say that the situation, as it stood, was of Lucretia's making; the thing never would have come into Lucretia's head if she had not laid it before her. Unfortunately, with the quiet life she led, she had very little chance to observe; she went out so little, that she was reduced to guessing what the manner of the two young persons might be to each other when they met in society, and she should have thought herself wanting in delicacy if she had sought to be intimate with Rachel Torrance. Now that her plan was in operation, she could make no attempt to foster it, to acknowledge it in the face of Heaven. Fortunately, Rachel had so many attentions, that there was no fear of her missing those of Newbury Street. She had dined there once, in the first days of her sojourn, without Pauline and Donald, who had declined, and with Joanna and Joanna's husband for all "company." Mrs. Daintry had noticed nothing particular then, save that Arthur Merriman talked rather more than usual, — though he was always a free talker, — and had bantered Rachel rather more familiarly than was perhaps necessary (considering that *he*, after all, was not her cousin) on her ignorance of Boston, and her thinking that Pauline Mesh could tell her anything about it. On this occasion Florimond talked very little; of course he could not say much when Arthur was in such extraordinary spirits. She knew by this time all that Florimond thought of his brother-in-law, and she herself had to confess that she liked Arthur better in his jaded hours, even though then he was a little cynical. Mrs. Daintry had been perhaps a little disappointed in Rachel, whom she saw for the first time in several years. The girl was less peculiar than she remembered her being, savored less of the old studio, the musical parties, the creditors waiting at the door. However, people in Boston found her unusual, and Mrs. Daintry reflected, with a twinge at her depravity, that perhaps she had expected something too dishevelled. At any rate, several weeks had elapsed since then, and there had been plenty of time for Miss Torrance to attach herself to Florimond. It was less than ever Mrs. Daintry's wish that he should (even in this case) ask her to be his wife. It seemed to her less than ever the way her son should marry,—because he had got entangled with a girl in consequence of his mother's rashness. It occurred to her, of course, that she might warn the young man; but when it came to the point she could not bring herself to speak. She had never discussed the question of love with him, and she did n't know what ideas he might have brought with him from Paris. It was too delicate; it might put notions into his head. He might say something strange and French, which she should n't

like; and then perhaps she should feel bound to warn
Rachel herself, — a complication from which she absolutely shrank.   It was part of her embarrassment
now, as she sat in Mrs. Mesh's drawing-room, that she
should probably spoil Florimond's entertainment for
this afternoon, and that such a crossing of his inclination would make him the more dangerous.   He had
told her that he was waiting for Rachel to come in;
and at the same time, in view of the lateness of the
hour and her being on foot, when she herself should
take her leave he would be bound in decency to ac-
company her.   As for remaining after Rachel should
come in, that was an indiscretion which scarcely
seemed to her possible.   Mrs. Daintry was an American mother, and she knew what the elder generation
owes to the younger.   If Florimond had come there
to call on a young lady, he did n't, as they used to
say, want any mothers round.   She glanced covertly
at her son, to try and find some comfort in his countenance; for her perplexity was heavy.   But she was
struck only with his looking very handsome, as he
lounged there in the firelight, and with his being
very much at home.   This did not lighten her burden, and she expressed all the weight of it — in the
midst of Mrs. Mesh's flights of comparison — in an
irrelevant little sigh.   At such a time her only comfort could be the thought that at all events she had
not betrayed herself to Lucretia.   She had scarcely
exchanged a word with Lucretia about Rachel since
that young lady's arrival; and she had observed in

silence that Miss Daintry now had a guest in the person of a young woman who had lately opened a kindergarten. This reticence might surely pass for natural.

Rachel came in before long, but even then Mrs. Daintry ventured to stay a little. The visitor from Brooklyn embraced Mrs. Mesh, who told her that, prodigal as she was, there was no fatted calf for her return; she must content herself with cold tea. Nothing could be more charming than her manner, which was full of native archness; and it seemed to Mrs. Daintry that she directed her pleasantries at Florimond with a grace that was intended to be irresistible. The relation between them was a relation of "chaff," and consisted, on one side and the other, in alternations of attack and defence. Mrs. Daintry reflected that she should not wish her son to have a wife who should be perpetually turning him into a joke; for it seemed to her, perhaps, that Rachel Torrance put in her thrusts rather faster than Florimond could parry them. She was evidently rather wanting in the faculty of reverence, and Florimond panted a little. They presently went into an adjoining room, where the lamplight was brighter; Rachel wished to show the young man an old painted fan, which she had brought back from the repairer's. They remained there ten minutes. Mrs. Daintry, as she sat with Mrs. Mesh, heard their voices much intermingled. She wished very much to confide herself a little to Pauline,—to ask her whether she thought

Rachel was in love with Florimond. But she had a foreboding that this would not be safe; Pauline was capable of repeating her question to the others, of calling out to Rachel to come back and answer it. She contented herself, therefore, with asking her hostess about the little Meshes, and regaling her with anecdotes of Joanna's progeny.

"Don't you ever have your little ones with you at this hour?" she inquired. "You know this is what Longfellow calls the children's hour."

Mrs. Mesh hesitated a moment. "Well, you know, one can't have everything at once. I have my social duties now; I have my guests. I have Miss Torrance,—you see she is not a person one can overlook."

"I suppose not," said poor Mrs. Daintry, remembering how little she herself had overlooked her.

"Have you done brandishing that superannuated relic?" Mrs. Mesh asked of Rachel and Florimond, as they returned to the fireside. "I should as soon think of fanning myself with the fire-shovel!"

"He has broken my heart," Rachel said. "He tells me it is not a Watteau."

"Do you believe everything he tells you, my dear? His word is the word of the betrayer."

"Well, I know Watteau did n't paint fans," Florimond remarked, "any more than Michael Angelo."

"I suppose you think he painted ceilings," said Rachel Torrance. "I have painted a great many myself."

"A great many ceilings? I should like to see that!" Florimond exclaimed.

Rachel Torrance, with her usual promptness, adopted this fantasy. "Yes, I have decorated half the churches in Brooklyn; you know how many there are."

"If you mean fans, I wish men carried them," the young man went on; "I should like to have one *de votre façon.*"

"You're cool enough as you are; I should be sorry to give you anything that would make you cooler!"

This retort, which may not strike the reader by its originality, was pregnant enough for Mrs. Daintry; it seemed to her to denote that the situation was critical; and she proposed to retire. Florimond walked home with her; but it was only as they reached their door that she ventured to say to him what had been on her tongue's end since they left Arlington Street.

"Florimond, I want to ask you something. I think it is important, and you must n't be surprised. Are you in love with Rachel Torrance?"

Florimond stared, in the light of the street-lamp. The collar of his overcoat was turned up; he stamped a little as he stood still; the breath of the February evening pervaded the empty vistas of the "new land." "In love with Rachel Torrance? *Jamais de la vie!* What put that into your head?"

"Seeing you with her, that way, this evening. You know you are very attentive."

"How do you mean, attentive?"

"You go there very often. Is n't it almost every day ?"

Florimond hesitated, and, in spite of the frigid dusk, his mother could see that there was irritation in his eye. "Where else can I go, in this precious place ? It's the pleasantest house here."

"Yes, I suppose it's very pleasant," Mrs. Daintry murmured. "But I would rather have you return to Paris than go there too often," she added, with sudden energy.

"How do you mean, too often ? *Qu'est-ce qui vous prend, ma mère ?*" said Florimond.

"Is Rachel — Rachel in love with *you ?*" she inquired solemnly. She felt that this question, though her heart beat as she uttered it, should not be mitigated by a circumlocution.

"Good heavens ! mother, fancy talking about love in this temperature !" Florimond exclaimed. "Let one at least get into the house."

Mrs. Daintry followed him reluctantly ; for she always had a feeling that if anything disagreeable were to be done, one should not make it less drastic by selecting agreeable conditions. In the drawing-room, before the fire, she returned to her inquiry. "My son, you have not answered me about Rachel."

"Is she in love with me ? Why, very possibly !"

"Are you serious, Florimond ?"

"Why should n't I be ? I have seen the way women go off."

Mrs. Daintry was silent a moment. "Florimond, is it true?" she said, presently.

"Is what true? I don't see where you want to come out?"

"Is it true that that girl has fixed her affections —" and Mrs. Daintry's voice dropped.

"Upon me, *ma mère?* I don't say it's true, but I say it's possible. You ask me, and I can only answer you. I am not swaggering, I am simply giving you decent satisfaction. You would n't have me think it impossible that a woman should fall in love with me? You know what women are, and how there is nothing, in that way, too queer for them to do."

Mrs. Daintry, in spite of the knowledge of her sex that she might be supposed to possess, was not prepared to rank herself on the side of this axiom. "I wished to warn you," she simply said; "do be very careful."

"Yes, I'll be careful; but I can't give up the house."

"There are other houses, Florimond."

"Yes, but there is a special charm there."

"I would rather you should return to Paris than do any harm."

"Oh, I sha' n't do any harm; don't worry, *ma mère*," said Florimond.

It was a relief to Mrs. Daintry to have spoken, and she endeavored not to worry. It was doubtless this effort that, for the rest of the winter, gave her

a somewhat rigid, anxious look. People who met
her in Beacon Street missed something from her
face. It was her usual confidence in the clearness
of human duty ; and some of her friends explained
the change by saying that she was disappointed
about Florimond, — she was afraid he was not
particularly liked.

VII.

By the first of March this young man had received
a good many optical impressions, and had noted in
water-colors several characteristic winter effects. He
had perambulated Boston in every direction, he had
even extended his researches to the suburbs ; and if
his eye had been curious, his eye was now almost
satisfied. He perceived that even amid the simple
civilization of New England there was material for
the naturalist; and in Washington Street of a winter's afternoon, it came home to him that it was a
fortunate thing the impressionist was not exclusively
preoccupied with the beautiful. He became familiar
with the slushy streets, crowded with thronging
pedestrians and obstructed horse-cars, bordered with
strange, promiscuous shops, which seemed at once
violent and indifferent, overhung with snowbanks
from the housetops; the avalanche that detached
itself at intervals, fell with an enormous thud amid
the dense processions of women, made for a moment

a clear space, splashed with whiter snow, on the
pavement, and contributed to the gayety of the Puritan capital. Supreme in the thoroughfare was the
rigid groove of the railway, where oblong receptacles,
of fabulous capacity, governed by familiar citizens,
jolted and jingled eternally, close on each other's
rear, absorbing and emitting innumerable specimens
of a single type. The road on either side, buried in
mounds of pulverized, mud-colored ice, was ploughed
across by laboring vehicles, and traversed periodi-
cally by the sisterhood of " shoppers," laden with
satchels and parcels, and protected by a round-backed
policeman. Florimond looked at the shops, saw the
women disgorged, surging, ebbing, dodged the aval-
anches, squeezed in and out of the horse-cars, made
himself, on their little platforms, where flatness was
enforced, as perpendicular as possible. The horses
steamed in the sunny air, the conductor punched the
tickets and poked the passengers, some of whom were
under and some above, and all alike stabled in
trampled straw. They were precipitated, collec-
tively, by stoppages and starts ; the tight, silent
interior stuffed itself more and more, and the whole
machine heaved and reeled in its interrupted course.
Florimond had forgotten the look of many things,
the details of American publicity ; in some cases, indeed, he only pretended to himself that he had forgotten them, because it helped to entertain him. The
houses — a bristling, jagged line of talls and shorts, a
particolored surface, expressively commercial — were

spotted with staring signs, with labels and pictures,
with advertisements familiar, colloquial, vulgar; the
air was traversed with the tangle of the telegraph,
with festoons of bunting, with banners not of war,
with inexplicable loops and ropes; the shops, many
of them enormous, had heterogeneous fronts, with
queer juxtapositions in the articles that peopled
them, an incompleteness of array, the stamp of the
latest modern ugliness. They had pendent stuffs in
the doorways, and flapping tickets outside. Every
fifty yards there was a "candy store;" in the intervals was the painted panel of a chiropodist, representing him in his professional attitude. Behind the
plates of glass, in the hot interiors, behind the coun-
ters, were pale, familiar, delicate, tired faces of
women, with polished hair and glazed complexions.
Florimond knew their voices; he knew how women
would speak when their hair was "treated," as they
said in the studios, like that. But the women that
passed through the streets were the main spectacle.
Florimond had forgotten their extraordinary numer-
osity, and the impression that they produced of a
deluge of petticoats. He could see that they were
perfectly at home on the road; they had an air of
possession, of perpetual equipment, a look, in the
eyes, of always meeting the gaze of crowds, always
seeing people pass, noting things in shop-windows,
and being on the watch at crossings; many of them
evidently passed most of their time in these conditions, and Florimond wondered what sort of *intér-*

ieurs they could have. He felt at moments that he was in a city of women, in a country of women. The same impression came to him *dans le monde,* as he used to say, for he made the most incongruous application of his little French phrases to Boston. The talk, the social life, were so completely in the hands of the ladies, the masculine note was so subordinate, that on certain occasions he could have believed himself (putting the brightness aside) in a country stricken by a war, where the men had all gone to the army, or in a seaport half depopulated by the absence of its vessels. This idea had intermissions; for instance, when he walked out to Cambridge. In this little excursion he often indulged; he used to go and see one of his college mates, who was now a tutor at Harvard. He stretched away across the long, mean bridge that spans the mouth of the Charles, — a mile of wooden piles, supporting a brick pavement, a roadway deep in mire, and a rough timber fence, over which the pedestrian enjoys a view of the frozen bay, the backs of many new houses, and a big brown marsh. The horse-cars bore him company, relieved here of the press of the streets, though not of their internal congestion, and constituting the principal feature of the wide, blank avenue, where the puddles lay large across the bounding rails. He followed their direction through a middle region, in which the small wooden houses had an air of tent-like impermanence, and the February mornings, splendid and indiscreet, stared into

bare windows and seemed to make civilization transparent.   Further, the suburb remained wooden, but
grew neat, and the painted houses looked out on
the car-track with an expression almost of superior-
ity.   At Harvard, the buildings were square and
fresh; they stood in a yard planted with slender
elms, which the winter had reduced to spindles;
the town stretched away from the horizontal pal-
ings of the collegiate precinct, low, flat, and immense,
with vague, featureless spaces and the air of a clean
encampment.   Florimond remembered that when the
summer came in, the whole place was transformed.
It was pervaded by verdure and dust, the slender
elms became profuse, arching over the unpaved
streets, the green shutters bowed themselves before
the windows, the flowers and creeping-plants bloomed
in the small gardens, and on the piazzas, in the gaps
of dropped awnings, light dresses arrested the eye.
At night, in the warm darkness, — for Cambridge is
not festooned with lamps,— the bosom of nature would
seem to palpitate, there would be a smell of earth
and vegetation,— a smell more primitive than the
odor of Europe, — and the air would vibrate with the
sound of insects.   All this was in reserve, if one
would have patience, especially from March to June;
but for the present the seat of the University struck
our poor little critical Florimond as rather hard and
bare.   As the winter went on, and the days grew
longer, he knew that Mrs. Daintry often believed
him to be in Arlington Street when he was walking

out to see his friend the tutor, who had once spent
a winter in Paris and who never tired of talking
about it. It is to be feared that he did not undeceive
her so punctually as he might; for, in the first place,
he was at Mrs. Mesh's very often; in the second, he
failed to understand how worried his mother was;
and in the third, the idea that he should be thought
to have the peace of mind of a brilliant girl in his
keeping was not disagreeable to him.

One day his Aunt Lucretia found him in Arlington
Street; it occurred to her about the middle of the winter that, considering she liked Rachel Torrance so
much, she had not been to see her very often. She had
little time for such indulgences; but she caught a moment in its flight, and was told at Mrs. Mesh's door
that this lady had not yet come in, but that her companion was accessible. Florimond was in his customary chair by the chimney corner (his aunt perhaps
did not know quite how customary it was), and
Rachel, at the piano, was regaling him with a composition of Schubert. Florimond, up to this time,
had not become very intimate with his aunt, who had
not, as it were, given him the key of her house, and
in whom he detected a certain want of interest in
his affairs. He had a limited sympathy with people
who were interested only in their own, and perceived
that Miss Daintry belonged to this preoccupied and
ungraceful class. It seemed to him that it would
have been more becoming in her to feign at least a
certain attention to the professional and social pros-

pects of the most promising of her nephews. If there was one thing that Florimond disliked more than another, it was an eager self-absorption; and he could not see that it was any better for people to impose their personality upon committees and charities than upon general society. He would have modified this judgment of his kinswoman, with whom he had dined but once, if he could have guessed with what anxiety she watched for the symptoms of that salutary change which she expected to see wrought in him by the fascinating independence of Rachel Torrance. If she had dared, she would have prompted the girl a little; she would have confided to her this secret desire. But the matter was delicate; and Miss Daintry was shrewd enough to see that everything must be spontaneous. When she paused at the threshold of Mrs. Mesh's drawing-room, looking from one of her young companions to the other, she felt a slight pang, for she feared they were getting on too well. Rachel was pouring sweet music into the young man's ears, and turning to look at him over her shoulder while she played; and he with his head tipped back and his eyes on the ceiling hummed an accompaniment which occasionally became an articulate remark. Harmonious intimacy was stamped upon the scene; and poor Miss Daintry was not struck with its being in any degree salutary. She was not reassured when, after ten minutes, Florimond took his departure; she could see that he was irritated by the presence of a third person; and this was a proof that Rachel had not yet begun to do her duty by him. It is possible that when the two ladies were left together, her disappointment would have led her to betray her views, had not Rachel almost immediately said to her: " My dear cousin, I am so glad you have come; I might not have seen you again. I go away in three days."

"Go away? Where do you go to?"

"Back to Brooklyn," said Rachel, smiling sweetly.

"Why on earth — I thought you had come here to stay for six months?"

"Oh, you know, six months would be a terrible visit for these good people; and of course no time was fixed. That would have been very absurd. I have been here an immense time already. It was to be as things should go."

"And have n't they gone well?"

"Oh yes, they have gone beautifully."

"Then why in the world do you leave?"

"Well, you know, I have duties at home. My mother coughs a good deal, and they write me dismal letters."

"They are ridiculous, selfish people. You are going home because your mother coughs? I don't believe a word of it!" Miss Daintry cried. "You have some other reason. Something has happened here; it has become disagreeable. Be so good as to tell me the whole story."

Rachel answered that there was not any story to tell, and that her reason consisted entirely of conscientious scruples as to absenting herself so long from her domestic circle. Miss Daintry esteemed conscientious scruples when they were well placed, but she thought poorly on the present occasion of those of Mrs. Mesh's visitor; they interfered so much with her own sense of fitness. "Has Florimond been making love to you ?" she suddenly inquired. "You must n't mind that — beyond boxing his ears."

Her question appeared to amuse Miss Torrance exceedingly ; and the girl, a little inarticulate with her mirth, answered very positively that the young man had done her no such honor.

"I am very sorry to hear it," said Lucretia ; "I was in hopes he would give you a chance to take him down. He needs it very much. He 's dreadfully puffed up."

"He 's an amusing little man !"

Miss Daintry put on her nippers. "Don't tell me it 's you that are in love !"

"Oh, dear no ! I like big, serious men, not small, Frenchified gentlemen, like Florimond. Excuse me if he 's your nephew, but you began it. Though I am fond of art," the girl added, "I don't think I am fond of artists."

"Do you call Florimond an artist ? "

Rachel Torrance hesitated a little, smiling. "Yes, when he poses for Pauline Mesh."

This rejoinder for a moment left Miss Daintry in visible perplexity ; then a sudden light seemed to come to her. She flushed a little ; what she found was more than she was looking for. She thought of many things quickly, and among others she thought that she had accomplished rather more than she intended. "Have you quarrelled with Pauline?" she said presently.

"No, but she is tired of me."

"Everything has not gone well, then, and you *have* another reason for going home than your mother's cough?"

"Yes, if you must know, Pauline wants me to go. I did n't feel free to tell you that; but since you guess it —" said Rachel, with her rancorless smile.

"Has she asked you to decamp?"

"Oh, dear no! for what do you take us? But she absents herself from the house; she stays away all day. I have to play to Florimond to console him."

"So you *have* been fighting about him?" Miss Daintry remarked, perversely.

"Ah, my dear cousin, what have you got in your head? Fighting about sixpence! if you knew how Florimond bores me! I play to him to keep him silent. I have heard everything he has to say, fifty times over!"

Miss Daintry sank back in her chair; she was completely out of her reckoning. "I think he might have made love to you a little!" she exclaimed, incoherently.

"So do I! but he did n't — not a crumb. He is afraid of me — thank Heaven!"

"It is n't for you he comes, then?" Miss Daintry appeared to cling to her theory.

"No, my dear cousin, it is n't!"

"Just now, as he sat there, one could easily have supposed it. He did n't at all like my interruption."

"That was because he was waiting for Pauline to come in. He will wait that way an hour. You may imagine whether he likes me for boring her so that, as I tell you, she can't stay in the house. I am out myself as much as possible. But there are days when I drop with fatigue; then I must rest. I can assure you that it 's fortunate that I go so soon."

"Is Pauline in love with him?" Miss Daintry asked, gravely.

"Not a grain. She is the best little woman in the world."

"Except for being a goose. Why, then, does she object to your company — after being so enchanted with you?"

"Because even the best little woman in the world must object to something. She has everything in life, and nothing to complain of. Her children sleep all day, and her cook is a jewel. Her husband adores her, and she is perfectly satisfied with Mr. Mesh. I act on her nerves, and I think she believes I regard her as rather silly to care so much for Florimond. Excuse me again!"

"You contradict yourself. She *does* care for him, then?"

"Oh, as she would care for a new *coupé!* She likes to have a young man of her own — fresh from Paris

— quite to herself. She has everything else — why
should n't she have that? She thinks your nephew
very original, and he thinks her what she is, — the
prettiest woman in Boston. They have an idea that
they are making a 'celebrated friendship,' — like
Horace Walpole and Madame du Deffand. They
sit there face to face — they are as innocent as the
shovel and tongs. But, all the same, I am in the
way, and Pauline is provoked that I am not
jealous."

Miss Daintry got up with energy. "She 's a vain,
hollow, silly little creature, and you are quite right
to go away; you are worthy of better company.
Only you will not go back to Brooklyn, in spite
of your mother's cough; you will come straight
to Mount Vernon Place."

Rachel hesitated to agree to this. She appeared
to think it was her duty to quit Boston altogether;
and she gave as a reason that she had already refused other invitations. But Miss Daintry had a
better reason than this, — a reason that glowed in
her indignant breast. It was she who had been the
cause of the girl's being drawn into this sorry adven-
ture; it was she who should charge herself with the
reparation. The conversation I have related took
place on a Tuesday; and it was settled that on the
Friday Miss Torrance should take up her abode for
the rest of the winter under her Cousin Lucretia's
roof. This lady left the house without having seen
Mrs. Mesh.

On Thursday she had a visit from her sister-in-law, the motive of which was not long in appearing. All winter Mrs. Daintry had managed to keep silent on the subject of her doubts and fears. Discretion and dignity recommended this course; and the topic was a painful one to discuss with Lucretia, for the bruises of their primary interview still occasionally throbbed. But at the first sign of alleviation the excellent woman overflowed, and she lost no time in announcing to Lucretia, as a Heaven-sent piece of news, that Rachel had been called away by the illness of poor Mrs. Torrance, and was to leave Boston from one day to the other. Florimond had given her this information the evening before; and it had made her so happy, that she could n't help coming to let Lucretia know that they were safe. Lucretia listened to her announcement in silence, fixing her eyes on her sister-in-law with an expression that the latter thought singular; but when Mrs. Daintry, expanding still further, went on to say that she had spent a winter of misery, that the harm the two together (she and Lucretia) might have done was never out of her mind, for Florimond's assiduity in Arlington Street had become notorious, and she had been told that the most cruel things were said, — when Mrs. Daintry, expressing herself to this effect, added that from the present moment she breathed, the danger was over, the sky was clear, and her conscience might take a holiday, — her hostess broke into the most prolonged, the most characteristic, and most bewildering fit of laughter in which she had ever known her to indulge. They were safe, Mrs. Daintry had said? For Lucretia this was true, now, of herself, at least; she was secure from the dangers of her irritation; her sense of the whole affair had turned to hilarious music. The contrast that rose before her between her visitor's anxieties and the real position of the parties, her quick vision of poor Susan's dismay in case *that* reality should meet her eyes, among the fragments of her squandered scruples, — these things smote the chords of mirth in Miss Daintry's spirit, and seemed to her in their high comicality to offer a sufficient reason for everything that had happened. The picture of her sister-in-law sitting all winter with her hands clasped and her eyes fixed on the wrong object was an image that would abide with her always; and it would render her an inestimable service, — it would cure her of the tendency to worry. As may be imagined, it was eminently open to Mrs. Daintry to ask her what on earth she was laughing at; and there was a color in the cheek of Florimond's mother that brought her back to propriety. She suddenly kissed this lady very tenderly — to the latter's great surprise, there having been no kissing since her visit in November — and told her that she would reveal to her some day, later, the cause of so much merriment. She added that Miss Torrance was leaving Arlington Street, yes; but only to go as far as Mount Vernon Place. She was engaged to spend three months in

that very house. Mrs. Daintry's countenance, at
this, fell several inches, and her joy appeared completely to desert her. She gave her sister-in-law a
glance of ineffable reproach, and in a moment she
exclaimed : "Then nothing is gained ! it will all go
on here !"

"Nothing will go on here. If you mean that
Florimond will pursue the young lady into this
mountain fastness, you may simply be quiet. He
is not fond enough of me to wear out my threshold."

"Are you very sure ?" Mrs. Daintry murmured,
dubiously.

"I know what I say. Has n't he told you he
hates me ?"

Mrs. Daintry colored again, and hesitated. "I don't
know how you think we talk," she said.

"Well, he does, and he will leave us alone."

Mrs. Daintry sprang up with an elasticity that
was comical. "That 's all I ask !" she exclaimed.

"I believe you hate me too !" Lucretia said, laughing ; but at any risk, she kissed her sister-in-law
again before they separated.

Three weeks later Mrs. Daintry paid her another
visit ; and this time she looked very serious. "It 's
very strange. I don't know what to think. But
perhaps you know it already ?" This was her *entrée
en matière*, as the French say. "Rachel's leaving
Arlington Street has made no difference. He goes
there as much as ever. I see no change at all. Lucretia, I have not the peace that I thought had

come," said poor Mrs. Daintry, whose voice had failed below her breath.

"Do you mean that he goes to see Pauline Mesh?"

"I'm afraid so, every day."

"Well, my dear, what's the harm?" Miss Daintry asked. "He can't hurt *her* by not marrying her."

Mrs. Daintry stared; she was amazed at her sister-in-law's tone. "But it makes one suppose that all winter, for so many weeks, it has been for *her* that he has gone!" and the image of the *tête-à-tête* in which she had found them immured that day, rose again before her; she could interpret it now.

"You wanted some one; why may not Pauline have served?"

Mrs. Daintry was silent, with the same expanded eyes. "Lucretia, it is not right!"

"My dear Susan, you are touching," Lucretia said.

Mrs. Daintry went on without heeding her. "It appears that people are talking about it; they have noticed it for ever so long. Joanna never hears anything, or she would have told me. The children are too much. I have been the last to know."

"I knew it a month ago," said Miss Daintry, smiling.

"And you never told me?"

"I knew that you wanted to detain him. Pauline will detain him a year."

Mrs. Daintry gathered herself together. "Not a

day, not an hour, that I can help! He shall go, if I have to take him."

"My dear Susan," murmured her sister-in-law on the threshold. Miss Daintry scarcely knew what to say; she was almost frightened at the rigidity of her face.

"My dear Lucretia, it is not right!" This ejaculation she solemnly repeated, and she took her departure as if she were decided upon action.

She had found so little sympathy in her sister-in-law, that she made no answer to a note Miss Daintry wrote her that evening, to remark that she was really unjust to Pauline, who was silly, vain, and flattered by the development of her ability to monopolize an impressionist, but a perfectly innocent little woman and incapable of a serious flirtation. Miss Daintry had been careful to add to these last words no comment that could possibly shock Florimond's mother. Mrs. Daintry announced, about the 10th of April, that she had made up her mind she needed a change, and had determined to go abroad for the summer; and she looked so tired that people could see there was reason in it. Her summer began early; she embarked on the 20th of the month, accompanied by Florimond. Miss Daintry, who had not been obliged to dismiss the young lady of the kindergarten to make room for Rachel Torrance, never knew what had passed between the mother and the son, and she was disappointed at Mrs. Mesh's coolness in the face of this catastrophe. She disapproved of her flirtation with Florimond, and yet she was vexed at Pauline's pert resignation; it proved her to be so superficial. She disposed of everything with her absurd little phrases, that were half slang and half quotation. Mrs. Daintry was a native of Salem, and this gave Pauline, as a Baltimorean and a descendant of the Cavaliers, an obvious opportunity. Rachel repeated her words to Miss Daintry, for she had spoken to Rachel of Florimond's departure, the day after he embarked. "Oh yes, he 's in the midst of the foam, the cruel, crawling foam ! I 'kind of' miss him, afternoons; he was so useful round the fire. It 's his mother that charmed him away; she 's a most uncanny old party. I don't care for Salem witches, anyway; she has worked on him with philters and spells !" Lucretia was obliged to recognize a grain of truth in this last assertion; she felt that her sister-in-law must indeed have worked upon Florimond, and she smiled to think that the conscientious Susan should have descended, in the last resort, to an artifice, to a pretext. She had probably persuaded him she was tired of Joanna's children.